Also by Andrew Taylor

About the Author

Andrew Taylor is the prizewinning and bestselling author of
crime novels that include the William Dougal series,
the Lydmouth series and the ground-breaking Roth Trilogy, as
well as historical crime novels *The American Boy* and
The Anatomy of Ghosts. Andrew lives with his wife in the Forest
of Dean, on the borders of England and Wales.

To find out more, visit Andrew's website,
www.andrew-taylor.co.uk and follow him on
Twitter, twitter.com/andrewjrtaylor.

ANDREW TAYLOR

The Sleeping Policeman

HODDER

First published in Great Britain in 1992 by Victor Gollancz Ltd

First published by Hodder & Stoughton in 2012
An Hachette UK company

1

A CIP catalogue record for this title is available
from the British Library.

Paperback ISBN 978 1 444 76570 0
Ebook ISBN 978 1 444 76571 7

Typeset in Plantin Light by Palimpsest Book Production Limited,
Falkirk, Stirlingshire

Printed and bound in the UK by Clays Ltd, St Ives plc

Hodder & Stoughton policy is to use papers that are natural,
renewable and recyclable products and made from wood grown
in sustainable forests. The logging and manufacturing processes
are expected to conform to the environmental regulations
of the country of origin.

Hodder & Stoughton Ltd
338 Euston Road
London NW1 3BH

www.hodder.co.uk

For Patricia

I

Tragedy is a word that has come to have several meanings. By most definitions, the Hanslope case had elements of tragedy. Afterwards, Dougal remembered that tragedy derives from two Greek words which can be translated as goat song.

And that was appropriate too, because in one sense of the word Graham Hanslope was undoubtedly a goat. Hanslope's goat song ended in discord on the southbound platform of the Bakerloo Line at Paddington Station. It ended with the arrival of a tube train at a few minutes after ten o'clock on the morning of Saturday 16 February. It ended, as tragedies so often end, with death and the destruction of hope.

It is always easy to say where tragedies end. It is much harder to say where they begin.

William Dougal met Graham Hanslope for the first time on Thursday 7 February. Hanslope had phoned the Private Investigations Division earlier in the week. The duty supervisor allocated him to Dougal and gave him an eleven o'clock appointment.

Hanslope was five minutes early. The guard at the desk phoned Dougal, who was sipping Kenya Peaberry and filling in his expenses sheet, an exercise in creative accounting. Eight minutes later Dougal strolled into reception. The foyer, a lofty place of imitation marble, wilting palms and smoked glass, was crowded with men in suits: the Company Security Division was in the throes of yet another sales conference. He went over to the desk to ask where Hanslope was.

The security guard was an elderly man with a red jolly

face and fluffy white hair: like Father Christmas minus the beard.

'Impatient sod,' he murmured, nodding towards a compactly built man of about thirty who sat on a green imitation-leather sofa in the corner. 'Thought he was going to walk out a moment ago.'

Hanslope was having trouble sitting still. His face was flushed and his hands and feet twitched. He had muddy-brown hair and his skull was roughly the size and shape of a football. As Dougal watched, Hanslope glanced first at his watch and then up at the black plaque on the wall. Here, emblazoned in golden letters, was the company's watchword:

CUSTODEMUS
24 hours a day, 7 days a week, 365 days a year.
Permanent peace of mind.

'Go on,' the guard said. 'Put him out of his misery.'

Hanslope looked up as Dougal approached. He was scowling.

'Mr Hanslope? I'm William Dougal. Sorry to keep you waiting.'

Hanslope stood up. They shook hands. Hanslope's skin felt hot and dry. His grip was unnecessarily firm. Dougal winced, and wondered what he was trying to prove.

'It's Dr Hanslope actually.' The voice was sharp, decisive and oddly aggrieved.

'In that case I'm not sorry.' Dougal massaged his right hand behind his back. 'It's usually the other way round.'

For the first time Hanslope looked properly at Dougal, who stared back. They were much the same height. Hanslope was a few years younger and a few stone heavier.

'I mean, doctors tend to keep me waiting. I take it you are a doctor of medicine?' Dougal smiled as he spoke, but it was no good: he realised that Hanslope thought he was being rude or at least making a rather tasteless joke. He added hastily, 'Come along to my office.'

He led the way through the swing doors and down the corridor to a small room overcrowded with furniture. A bird-dropping made a long diagonal streak down the frosted glass of the window. The place smelled of stale cigarette smoke and fresh coffee. Hanslope wrinkled his nose. Dougal took his visitor's coat, waved him to a chair and ambled behind his desk.

'I gather you just want an initial consultation at present? With the possibility of a full investigation?'

'Yes.' Hanslope wriggled. For an instant he looked much younger. He reminded Dougal of a child in a dentist's waiting room.

'I have to start by giving you these.'

Dougal opened a drawer and took out two sheets of paper, which he passed across the desk. Hanslope skimmed through them. Careful by nature, Dougal thought: the sort of person who never signs anything without reading it from top to bottom at least twice. The first sheet contained the credo of Custodemus's Private Investigations Division: what it considered lawful and ethical, and what it did not. The second was a schedule of charges. Hanslope raised his dark, strongly marked eyebrows at the fee for a consultation.

'It seems a bit steep.'

'Have you had a solicitor's bill lately? Or a plumber's? It's not unreasonable.'

'The woman I talked to on the phone should have warned me. Should have given me some indication.'

Dougal said nothing.

Hanslope shrugged. 'All right. Now I'm here, I suppose I might as well stay.'

'Cash, cheque or credit card will do nicely.'

'You mean you want me to pay you now?'

'It's company policy, I'm afraid.'

For a moment Dougal thought that Hanslope would jump up and leave. Company policy, in fact, left it to Dougal's discretion whether or not he insisted on payment before the initial consultation; it was a useful screening device for weeding out indigent or otherwise undesirable clients. Hanslope obviously had the money; but he was, equally obviously, the sort of customer who generally ends up awkward rather than satisfied.

'All right,' Hanslope said. 'I shall want a receipt.'

Breathing heavily, he took out a cheque book. He wrote in a rapid and barely legible scrawl. When Dougal examined the cheque he noticed that it was drawn on the account of Dr Graham Hanslope at the Paulstock branch of Lloyds Bank. Paulstock was a substantial market town in the West Country. Dougal wondered why Hanslope had come all the way to London to find a private investigator. He could have found one closer to home – in Bristol, certainly, or even in Paulstock itself. Perhaps he had felt that a London firm with an impressively large boxed advertisement in the *Yellow Pages* would not only minimise the risk of gossip but also offer a more professional service.

'It won't bounce, I promise you,' Hanslope said. His chin rose. The man was spoiling for a fight. Probably because he was scared.

'Good.' Dougal opened the top lefthand drawer. The rocker switch was mounted underneath the top of the desk. He flicked it on. That too was company policy. He picked up a shorthand pad and closed the drawer. 'Now, Dr Hanslope. How can we help you?'

'Can I be sure this will go no further?'

The usual question. Dougal said, 'You wouldn't last long in your job if you couldn't keep a professional confidence. The same applies to us.' He quoted from the Custodemus brochure. 'Our reputation is your guarantee.'

Three seconds slipped by. The clean, blunt fingers of Hanslope's right hand tapped the arm of his chair.

'I'm being blackmailed.'

Dougal nodded and stared out of the window.

'It's serious enough for me, I can tell you that,' Hanslope

4

said with a spurt of anger. 'A man in my position has to be very careful.'

'I realise that. Doctors are vulnerable people. What's it about?'

'I – ah – rather rashly started an affair with a patient. Or rather the patient started it.'

It took two to tango. Dougal began to make notes on the shorthand pad. He disliked the gloating expression that had flitted across Hanslope's face. It suggested that the man actually took a pride in his sordid little amours. Dougal said innocently, 'Am I right in assuming your lover is a woman? And above the age of consent?'

'Of course she bloody is. What do you think I am?'

It was not a question Dougal intended to answer. He smiled and said, 'We have to be sure of our facts. When did the black-mail start?'

'On Saturday. Someone phoned me and played back a tape.'

Hanslope paused. He had narrow eyes that were always on the move. The eyes were a strange, murky colour, difficult to identify. Dougal thought of a stagnant pond under a pale grey sky. Hanslope had not looked directly at him for more than a few seconds.

'That's last Saturday, I take it?' Dougal prompted him. 'The second of February?'

'Yes. Look here – how much do you need to know?'

'The more you tell me,' Dougal said, 'the more chance there is that I can help. So tell me everything. Just go back to the beginning.'

Going back to the beginning is always easier said than done. A tragedy which ends with a bang often begins with a series of whimpers. Hanslope, Dougal learned later, lied to him.

The tragedy ended on 16 February – at Paddington Station, on the southbound platform of the Bakerloo Line. It did not begin with Hanslope's visit to Custodemus House on Thursday 7 February or even with the blackmailer's phone call five days before. Afterwards, Dougal thought that, if one had to choose a beginning, he would have plumped for Sunday 27 January.

The incident with the sleeping policeman occurred on the evening of that day. Naturally Hanslope didn't mention it to Dougal, then or later. It did not reflect well on him.

2

On the evening of Sunday 27 January Graham Hanslope found himself a prisoner in his own house.

When he tried to leave, the back door wouldn't open. Once again, he twisted the knob and pulled. Once again, the door resisted him. Nothing was going right. The damp weather must have swollen the wood. He swore, and the loudness of his voice shocked him. The sound bounced like a ball through the darkened rooms.

He put down the carrier bag. The gin bottle clanked against the tonic. He tugged again at the brushed aluminium knob. It was cold and smooth: his fingers found it hard to get much purchase. He knew he could easily walk across the kitchen, down the hall and through the front door. But he wasn't going to give in. He was leaving by the back door and that was that.

The third time he tried, he wrapped both hands round the knob and jammed his right foot against the door frame. He grunted with strain. The door swung inwards. Graham staggered back, his arms flailing, and overbalanced.

The door slammed into the edge of the work surface on the right of the sink. The fall jarred his spine. Glass tinkled. One of the panes of glass in the upper half of the door had collided with the spout of the electric kettle. Damn it, damn her, damn everything. It was one of those evenings. Cold air, silvered with rain, surged into the house.

Graham fetched a dustpan and brush from the hall cupboard and a hammer, tacks and a rectangle of plywood from what would eventually be the sitting room. He swept up the glass on the floor and then picked out the jagged fragments that were still in the door. The cold and perhaps the gin made him clumsy. His fingers slipped on the wet glass and suddenly there was blood on the back of his hand and a stabbing pain that made him cry out loud.

Another delay. At least he wasn't in a hurry: no one was expecting him. Somehow the thought made him more miserable than ever and therefore angrier. He had tried to phone Rachel, to tell her that he would be arriving this evening instead of at lunchtime tomorrow, but she hadn't answered; she often visited her parents on Sunday evening. That was the trouble with women: they were never there when you wanted them.

He washed the cut under the tap, dabbed it with disinfectant and strapped a piece of Elastoplast over it. He decided to leave the rest of the glass in the door. He tacked the plywood hurriedly into place. The wind and the rain beat against his head, his neck and his hands. The plywood hung lopsidedly. A burglar would be able to lever it off with his little finger. Who cared? Graham had always believed in over-insuring his possessions.

He closed the door behind him and crunched across the gravelled yard to the VW Golf. The sky was black. He felt as though he were walking with his eyes shut. The silence, like the darkness, got on his nerves. Here at the back of the house Graham had nearly an acre of garden, and behind the garden were fields. It was very different at the front: from the upstairs windows you could see the yellow lights of the housing estates sweeping up the hill to the centre of Abbotsfield.

He found the car the hard way, by walking into it. The car keys were in a trouser pocket, which meant that he had to put down the carrier bag and unbutton his coat. It took him another long moment to find the right key and the keyhole. Too much gin, that was the trouble. He didn't even like gin.

All the while his anger swelled. The bloody cow: it was all her fault: the wasted evening at the house, the wind, the rain, the broken glass, the bleeding wound on his hand and the gnawing of unsatisfied desire.

Graham slid behind the steering wheel and dumped the

carrier bag beside the overnight bag on the back seat. The sooner he got going the better. He started the engine and let it run for a few seconds while he opened the glove compartment. Inside were two bars of Cadbury's Dairy Milk Chocolate. He opened one of them, divided it up into squares and laid them on the passenger seat.

The visibility was so bad that he had difficulty backing out of the yard and up the drive. He scraped the wing along the overgrown hawthorn hedge on the near side. In a spurt of irritation he accelerated out into the lane without looking where he was going. Luckily there was no other traffic.

The quickest way to reach the main road was to cut through the newest of the housing estates and then into the lane by the church. Beastly houses for beastly people. If he took that route he would pass the Burwells' seven-bedroomed monstrosity. It would be interesting to see if the lights were on. The bloody cow.

He braked too sharply for the turning into Meadow Way. The car skidded. Graham changed down into first and trod hard on the accelerator. The car leapt forward. He took one hand from the wheel. His fingers closed on a square of chocolate.

The car lurched. The bonnet lifted into the air. A dreamlike terror filled him: the car had transformed itself from a calm, subservient machine to a thing of power, uncontrollable and irresistible.

The front wheels of the Golf hit the ground. The impact triggered a memory that dispelled the dream: all entrances to the Meadow Way estate were barred by sleeping policemen.

The steering wheel spun out of his hand. The car slewed across the road. He glimpsed a dark shape through the windscreen, right in front of the bumpers. That was all it was in the rain and the darkness: a moving shadow with a white blur of a face.

Graham stamped at the brake. His foot caught the edge of the pedal and slipped on to the accelerator. The engine roared.

There was a thud. He stamped again and this time his foot hit the brake. The tyres squealed on wet tarmac. The car bucked, swung inwards and hit the kerb. The engine stalled.

Graham sat in the car. He watched the rain slanting through the beam of the headlights. Red dots blinked on the dashboard's display panel. Nothing else moved. On either side of him were wooden garden fences. There was a streetlamp, too, but it wasn't working.

He scrambled out. The plaster on the back of his hand snagged on the door handle; he barely noticed the pain. He walked round the car. The headlights blinded him. Then he saw a foot, or rather a woman's red-leather shoe – a lightweight affair that laced up to the ankle; a stupid thing to wear in weather like this.

'What the hell were you doing?' he said, his voice louder than usual and much higher in pitch.

He took a step forward. The girl was lying with her head and shoulders on the pavement and the rest of her on the road. He couldn't see her well – just the outline of her body; he assumed she was a girl because of her size and the femininity of the shoe.

Automatically, he bent towards her, his hand outstretched. Two things happened simultaneously. He heard an engine revving as it changed gear in the lane. And he remembered the gin.

Christ, he thought: that's all I need. He ran back to the car and flung himself into the driving seat. He groped for the keys. As the engine fired, the glare of headlights filled the rear mirror. The car in the lane was slowing. It was going to turn into the access road of the estate. Its driver was going to find him here with a dead girl in front of him.

The Golf was moving. The panic that possessed him left no room for conscious thought. A primitive guile remained, the residual cunning of the hunted. He turned right as soon as he could. He glanced in his rear mirror – no sign of the pursuing car; maybe the driver had stopped by the girl's body. He took the next left and then turned right again at the T-junction. He glimpsed the Burwells' house, well set back from the road. There were lights on both floors.

Graham drove at a sedate twenty-five mph between the rows of houses with double integral garages and curtained windows. He met no other cars and the pavements were empty. Thank Christ for this filthy January weather, thank Christ for the deadly dullness of a Sunday evening in Abbotsfield.

He rolled across the hump of another sleeping policeman. A moment later he reached the main road, which led through the centre of Abbotsfield; in ten miles he would reach Paulstock; and in two or three hours he would be in London.

It wasn't my fault, he thought. He took a square of chocolate.

Rachel lived in Shepherd's Bush, in a street of small, terraced houses that ran parallel to and just north of the Green. She had the upper floor of the house at the eastern end of the terrace.

Graham had no trouble parking there on a Sunday evening. Rachel's Fiat was missing from the Residents Only slot in front of her house. She was probably on her way home from her parents'.

It didn't matter. He still had a set of keys for the flat. She had never asked for them back and he had never bothered to return them. He glanced at the clock on the dashboard; it was after eleven. It occurred to him that she might be with someone else. He pushed the thought away. Rachel didn't want anyone but him.

Bag in hand, he ran across the glistening pavement and up the steps to the door. For an instant light gleamed in the bay window on the left. Rachel had told him on the phone that she had a new neighbour, a man. Graham unlocked the door and took the stairs two at a time.

He knew, because he was trained to know such things, that he was still in a state of shock. The nausea and the giddiness would pass. He followed the plan he had laid down for himself during the drive. It was important, perhaps vital, to be methodical. He went from room to room switching on lights. The place was a pigsty. Rachel lived permanently on the brink of domestic chaos.

He turned on the television and set the kettle to boil. In the kitchen he noticed that the cut on the back of his hand had reopened. The Elastoplast no longer covered the wound. A smear of dried blood ran down to his wrist.

He washed his hands carefully and found a fresh plaster in the bathroom cabinet. He poured himself a small whisky but did not drink it; he left the glass and the bottle on the floor beside the armchair nearest the television.

Before the kettle boiled he had unpacked his overnight bag and taken off his shoes. The *Observer*, neatly folded and obviously unread, was in the hall; he strewed the various sections on the sofa. He went into the kitchen, made himself a cup of decaffeinated coffee and emptied two-thirds of it down the sink. When he opened the refrigerator for the milk, he noticed that Rachel had bought smoked salmon. She knew he liked it. Dear Rachel. He returned to the living room and put the mug beside the whisky.

He looked around. He had done all he could. He was pleased with himself. He curled up in the armchair and used the remote control to change channels on the television. Pretty pictures of bright green hills beneath a blue sky with a lonely and invisible violin grating away like a chainsaw. Talking heads talking nonsense to each other. *Top breeders recommend only* . . . A rock band whose singer had protruding front teeth. The pictures flickered and nothing that was said or done made any sense. The noise made him wince. Besides, he wouldn't be able to hear Rachel's car arriving. Where was she? He was all ready for her. Why wouldn't she come?

He muted the sound and picked up part of the paper. The business news. He stared at it and the lines of print became fluid: they writhed and buckled; they twisted themselves together.

'No,' he said aloud. 'No. In any case, the girl may not be dead.' And in his heart of hearts he knew she was.

Graham hugged himself. He thought about Michael in an effort to cheer himself up. Tomorrow was Monday. Michael would be at school all day. Perhaps Graham would be allowed to take him out in the evening.

A key scratched in the lock. He forced himself to relax. Rachel came into the room. Her eyes widened when she saw him in front of the television. He watched her face. He saw disbelief there, followed by joy; and he was reassured.

'Graham—'

He forced himself out of the chair. His legs were shaky. Rachel plunged forward and swept him into her arms. It was like being embraced by a large, scented bear.

As she hugged him she emitted squeaks of pleasure. Graham buried his head in the angle between her neck and shoulder. He listened to the beating of his heart.

'Darling, why didn't you tell me you were coming tonight?'

'I tried,' he said. His voice came out as a whisper. He cleared his throat. 'I was going to do a couple of hours' work on the house. But I just couldn't wait to see you. So I phoned – it must have been about half-five. I guessed you'd gone to your parents'.'

He allowed his voice to rise at the end of the last sentence. Rachel rushed to answer the question he had not wanted to ask directly.

'You should have rung me there. I could have left earlier. My father wanted to show me the video he made at Christmas. It went on for hours.'

'I didn't want to mess up your evening. And I know how much they like seeing you. Besides . . .'

'What, darling? What is it?'

'Well, I thought my ringing might be a bit tactless. I don't think your parents like me.'

'That's their problem.' Rachel's arms tightened their grip. Graham gasped. 'You must have been here for ages.'

She raised her head and glanced round the room. He knew from past experience that love made her observant. It was a trait that had its inconvenient side.

'Two hours,' he said. 'Maybe three. It doesn't matter.' He swallowed. 'Not now you're here. Let me get you a drink.'

She released him reluctantly. As he poured her a whisky and ginger, she stripped off her raincoat and tossed it over the back of a chair. She wore black slacks and a heavy jersey. She had tied back her coarse, red hair with a black bow. Several tendrils had escaped. They trailed down her neck. In the subdued light her hair was the colour of the dried blood he had washed from the back of his hand.

'You're so beautiful,' he said quickly.

She looked at him, smiled and stretched her arms above her head, which had the effect of raising her breasts. Graham thought of her as pneumatically upholstered. You could reduce her body to a series of balloons of varying shapes and sizes. Usually he found her very sexy. Even her untidiness attracted him.

'What's wrong?' she said.

He gave her the glass and sat down. 'I'm just tired.'

'You're very pale. Are you eating properly?'

'Of course I am.'

'You need someone to look after you.'

'I'm all right, I tell you. It was a long drive. I've been on nights.'

She pushed the newspaper off the sofa and sank down beside him. She was heavier than he, so her weight made him swing towards her. He rested his head on her breast.

'I've got the next three days off work,' Rachel said in a careful, soothing voice. She worked as a receptionist for a dentist in Chiswick. 'We can spend the whole time in bed.'

'That would be wonderful.'

'You've cut yourself.'

'Just a nick. I broke some glass.'

'Would you like me to—'

'Don't fuss. Please. It's perfectly all right.'

She sniffed, debarred from an opportunity to mother him. 'Well, you should know, I suppose. Have you eaten?'

'I had a sandwich before I left Paulstock.'

'There's smoked salmon. Would you like me to—'

'No. I'm fine.'

'You need to go to bed. Come on, dearest. Let me help you.'

Graham let her help him up and guide him to the bedroom. She sat him on the bed and stooped to unlace his shoes.

'I'm sorry about this,' he said. 'I – I don't think I'll be much use for anything tonight.'

She looked at him. Her face blushed unbecomingly, right up to the roots of her hair.

'As if it mattered,' she said gruffly. 'As if it mattered.'

3

'Errowby wanted to see you,' Fintal said, and his face, brown and pitted like the shell of a walnut, cracked into a sly smile. 'About twenty minutes ago, it was.'

Detective Sergeant Oliver Rickford nodded. He tossed the file on the burglaries on to his desk. It landed with a slap on the imitation teak veneer, slid sideways, fell to the floor and disgorged its contents over the ash-coloured carpet.

'Rough night?' Fintal said.

Oliver shrugged. He stooped, which made his headache worse, and reassembled the file. Once he was safely in the corridor, out of Fintal's sight, he leaned against the wall and closed his eyes. Either his eyeballs had grown or his eyelids had shrunk. Fintal was a local man, and the Chief Inspector's spy. He would never make sergeant but in a sense he didn't need to. In the E Division mafia he wielded an authority wholly out of proportion to his rank. Oliver had already learned that the divisional headquarters at Paulstock was governed by a conspiracy of yokels.

The upper panel of Errowby's door was made of clear glass. The DCI was asleep at his desk, or at least his eyes were closed. Draped over the visitor's chair was a red tracksuit; Errowby had jogged to work again, and he wanted everyone to know it. Oliver tapped on the door. Errowby's eyes opened at once.

'Come!'

Oliver slipped inside.

Errowby sat up. He was a slim man, just above the regulation minimum height, with curly hair the colour of sand and a rosebud mouth.

'Good of you to turn up, Sergeant,' he said. 'Had a good night, have we?'

'I'm sorry, sir. I only got back at—'

'What I'd really like to know is why it took you so long to get to Willow Lodge.'

Oliver stared at Archbold's *Criminal Pleading, Evidence and Practice*, which lay on its side, spine outwards, on the desk. 'We got lost.'

'You – got – lost. Well, well. I appreciate you don't know the area.' Errowby paused, as if to emphasise that he had made a particularly damning point. 'But I didn't realise you had trouble map-reading. You did have a map, I take it?'

'Yes, sir.'

Neither Oliver nor the Detective Constable he had taken with him had been able to make the reality of the terrain last night conform with the Ordnance Survey map.

'You've been with us nearly a month, Rickford,' Errowby went on. 'Time enough to get to know the area. That should have been your first priority. Or maybe you big city boys wouldn't agree?'

Oliver let the silence drag on.

'Down in this part of the world,' Errowby said softly, 'we might even call it neglect of duty.'

Oliver looked up from Archbold and met Errowby's eyes, which bulged like a pair of blue marbles from his pink face. The DCI had crossed a watershed. Neglect of duty was punishable under Police Discipline Regulations. Not that he was serious; not yet – Oliver hadn't given him real grounds for complaint, and both of them knew it.

'Same one?' the Chief Inspector said.

The change of subject was so abrupt that Oliver floundered for a few seconds. He licked his lips. 'It looks like it, sir. The MO's the same: back door, no prints, just the easily portable valuables; mid to late evening, and the bloke was in and out like a dose of salts. The owner's a Londoner, hasn't been down since Christmas.'

'Neighbours?'

'The nearest house is a farm at the end of the road. The woman thinks she heard a car around ten thirty. And then about an hour later she was walking the dogs and saw the gate was open.'

'Walking the dogs? In the weather we had last night?'

'The rain had eased off by then.'

Errowby pursed his pink little lips. 'Get it in writing, Sergeant.'

'I did wonder if—'

'I'm not interested in your wondering. I want facts, Rickford, facts. If it's important, put it in the report. If it isn't, don't waste my time.' Once again, Errowby veered without warning to another subject. 'Now, do you think you can find your way to the hospital without getting lost?'

'Yes, sir.'

'I want you to get down there right away. There was a nasty little hit-and-run job last night, in Abbotsfield. You're going to talk to the victim and then organise a house-to-house. Fintal will give you the details. Think you can cope?'

'Surely the burglaries are—'

'You've read this force's policy statement. You've seen the statistics. The Chief Constable will not tolerate serious motoring offences.'

'No, sir.'

'You'll take a WDC – Sharon will do – and you're not going to ruffle any feathers, got it? None of your Metropolitan strong-armed tactics. The victim's a fifteen-year-old girl.'

Errowby paused. He stared at Oliver, who assumed this was a signal that the interview was over and turned to leave.

'Wait.'

'Sir?'

'You might find it useful to know the girl's name. Or hadn't that occurred to you? She's called Leonie Burwell.'

Sharon should have been another pariah at Paulstock because she not only came from Birmingham but had the misfortune to be a woman as well. However, she had survived over a year at E Division and was grudgingly tolerated by the yokels because she had a sharp tongue in her head.

'I thought this was your day off,' she said as she started the car.

'It was,' Oliver said.

'There's a whisper going round that Errowby won't be with us much longer.'

'Oh?'

'Canteen gossip. The head of B Division CID is retiring at Easter. They say that Errowby's putting in for the job.'

B Division included two of the larger towns in the county and its CID was commanded by a detective superintendent.

'I see.'

'I thought you might be interested.'

Oliver stared through the windscreen as they drove down the High Street. Sharon glanced at him.

'Leonie Burwell,' he said. 'Does the name mean anything to you?'

'They live in Abbotsfield,' Sharon said in a flat voice. 'The father's a builder. Quite well off.'

Oliver grunted. Abbotsfield was ten miles south of Paulstock; it was a small and shapeless town which thirty years earlier had been a village.

They drove the rest of the way in silence. The hospital was on the outskirts of town. Originally built in the 1920s, it had sprouted wings in the intervening decades. What was left of its once spacious garden was now a car park.

'You want the private ward,' the woman in reception said; and her lips tightened and turned down at the corners as though they had asked for the local brothel. 'Down the corridor and up the stairs.'

According to the ward sister, Leonie Burwell was suffering from concussion, three broken ribs and severe bruising. Her room was full of flowers and people – a man and two women. The colour television was on with the sound turned down. Oliver concentrated on the girl in the high bed.

She looked small for her age and her body was still childlike. She had a thin, pale face. Her blue eyes were fringed with sandy lashes. You couldn't see her hair because her head was covered with a bandage.

A burly man put down a cup and got up from the chair by the bed. 'I'm Kevin Burwell.'

He held out his hand. He had iron-grey hair and his collar was too tight for his fleshy neck.

'And this is my wife, Felicity.'

The woman sitting on the bed glanced without interest at Oliver and Sharon. Her eyes flicked back to her hands, which were coiled round the saucer beneath her coffee cup. She was a good ten years younger than her husband – in her late thirties, perhaps: a small blonde who spent time and money on her appearance.

Oliver introduced himself and Sharon.

'Would you like coffee?' a young nurse said. She had been examining the CID officers with the sort of interest usually accorded to wild and possibly dangerous animals.

Oliver shook his head. He turned to the ward sister, who was waiting in the doorway with the nurse beside her. 'Thank you, sister.' He shut the door behind them and turned back to the Burwells. 'First I'd like to say how sorry I am.'

He looked at the figure in the bed and tried the effect of a smile. Leonie stared back at him. He realised with a flash of panic that he had no idea what was going on in her mind. She was still a child, and children were mysterious.

'Obviously, I – we would like to catch the driver –' His tongue felt heavy in his mouth and he was finding it difficult to put the usual patter into words. 'Not just to punish him but to stop him doing it again, to someone else. So, if you feel well enough – and if your parents think it's OK – we'd like to ask you some questions.'

'Go ahead, Sergeant,' Burwell interrupted. 'There's no need to beat about the bush.'

'I gather it happened just after eight o'clock. It was raining hard. May I ask why you were out there?'

'I felt like a walk.'

Felicity Burwell's head jerked up. 'Is that the truth? Where did you go?'

Leonie ignored the first question. 'I just went as far as the lane. I turned back. I don't remember any more.'

'You must do,' Kevin Burwell said. 'Come on, think.'

'It's quite normal to forget in these circumstances, sir,' Oliver said. 'The memory may come back in time.'

Leonie didn't smile at him but her face lightened.

'Why were you really out there?' Felicity said. 'I want to know. The police want to know.'

'I'd been reading *Wuthering Heights*. I wanted to know what it felt like. The wuthering, I mean.'

'What?'

'It's a novel, Mother.' The thin voice trembled. 'By Emily Brontë.'

'I know it's a novel. Don't be—'

'Well, that seems perfectly reasonable to me,' Oliver said, raising his voice. 'In any case, it's not important. Now, can you remember meeting anyone?'

'No,' Leonie whispered.

'Any cars?'

'One or two, perhaps. I'm not really sure. I wasn't thinking about cars.'

'No, of course not,' Oliver said.

Leonie smiled at him.

'Can you remember your exact route?'

'The shortest way. From our house you cross the road, go on until the first right and then you take the first left. That brings you down to the lane.' Her voice began to tremble. 'That's where – that's where—'

'OK,' Oliver said. 'That's fine. You've been very helpful. Thank you.'

Kevin Burwell sat down heavily on the chair by the bed. 'I want the bastard who did this. I want his guts.'

'Yes, sir. And what were you doing?'

'Me?'

'Just for the record, sir. Helps us get a rounded picture.'

'My wife and I were having dinner. Our elder daughter was there. We were watching something on the box. But what's that got to do with it?'

'Did you know your daughter had gone out?'

'No.'

'Mrs Burwell?'

'It's a big house. I can't watch her every minute of the day.'

Oliver took a step closer to the bed. 'So you didn't want any dinner?' he said to Leonie.

'No.'

The door behind him opened.

'Oh – sorry,' a woman said.

Oliver swung round. The woman in the doorway smiled at him. He registered an intensely feminine combination of black, shoulder-length hair, blue eyes and creamy skin. He swallowed.

'I can come back later,' she said.

'My elder daughter, Joanna,' Burwell said.

'No – ah – we've just finished.' Oliver turned back to Burwell. 'For the time being, at least. We'll keep you informed, sir.'

'Oh yes,' Burwell said. 'I'm sure you will. As a matter of fact your Chief Inspector—'

Outside the room, the ward sister shouted. The words were indistinguishable but not the anger they expressed. Footsteps ran down the corridor. Joanna Burwell swung towards the disturbance. A woman cannoned into her, shouldering her out of the way.

Not a woman: a schoolgirl – a lumpish child with glasses, heavy legs and short, curly hair. She wore an unbuttoned duffel coat over a navy-blue cardigan and skirt. Her nose, which needed wiping, was red with cold. She ignored Joanna and stared past Oliver into the room.

'Get out,' Felicity screamed. 'Get out.'

The ward sister arrived, panting, with the nurse a pace behind her.

'Come along, young lady,' the sister said. She took the girl's arm.

The girl was looking at the stiff little figure in the bed. 'Leonie, are you all right?'

Sharon glanced at Oliver. He knew she was asking whether she should intervene. He didn't know the answer.

'I said, come along!' the sister snapped.

The girl raised her voice. 'Leonie, I—'

Felicity had stood up. Whether by accident or design, her body was between the two girls. She held out a shaking arm as if in accusation. 'Just get her out of here.'

Kevin, too, was on his feet. He said, not unkindly but with immense authority, 'Shouldn't you be at school, Tammy?'

The girl crumpled. Her head fell forward; her shoulders drooped. She allowed herself to be led away.

'Sorry about that,' Burwell said. 'A schoolfriend of Leonie's. Anyway, Sergeant: we'll be in touch.'

'We must be off ourselves,' Felicity said to no one in particular. 'Bye bye, darling. See you this afternoon. Is there anything we can bring you?'

Leonie was looking not at her mother but at Oliver, or perhaps at the doorway. She shook her head. Then: 'Oh yes. You can bring me *Wuthering Heights*. It's in my bedroom.'

Oliver and Sharon left first. As they were walking through the reception area, Sharon touched his arm.

'What do you reckon? Was she meeting a boyfriend?'

'Bit young, isn't she?'

'You'd be surprised. She's fifteen.'

'But young for her age, maybe.'

'Excuse me.' An elderly man in a flapping overcoat thrust his way between them; cycle clips fastened the cuffs of his baggy trousers, which increased his already striking resemblance to a scarecrow. 'Mr Burwell,' he called in a high, wheezing voice. 'Mr Burwell, could I have a word?'

Oliver glanced back. Kevin and Felicity Burwell were coming

23

through the swing doors that led to the private ward. Joanna must have stayed behind.

'Piss off,' Kevin Burwell said. He did not raise his voice but the words were clearly audible. 'Just piss off, will you?'

The old man sheered away. He began to pay unnatural attention to the contents of a noticeboard.

'Burwell's in a state, isn't he?' Sharon said. 'I suppose it's only natural.' She frowned as she spoke, as if she were not entirely convinced. 'Do you know why we're doing this? The CID for a relatively minor hit and run?'

'I think there's something we don't know.'

Oliver held the door open for her. They walked towards the car park. Tammy was sitting on a bench beside the path. She was crying. In her hands was a sodden paper handkerchief. She stood up as they approached.

'She's my friend, you see,' she said to Oliver. 'My best friend.'

'She'll be all right.' Oliver looked over his shoulder. The Burwells were still in the hospital. 'She'll probably be out in a few days.'

'Thank you,' Tammy said.

She looked from Oliver to Sharon. She opened her mouth to say something else. Then her eyes widened. Kevin and Felicity Burwell were walking briskly towards them. Tammy broke into a run.

4

'Four more houses.' Oliver stopped to wait for Sharon. 'Then we give up.'

He found it difficult not to take the job and the weather personally: it was surely no coincidence that Errowby had reserved this thankless task for the two outsiders under his command. He set off down the lane. 'Don't be so bloody paranoid,' he muttered.

'You what?' Sharon said.

'It doesn't matter.'

They spent half of the morning and, after half an hour for lunch, most of the afternoon trailing from house to house along the route Leonie Burwell had taken the previous night. The day was cloudy and dry, with a north-east wind that brought tears to the eyes. The light was already beginning to fade from the sky.

No one they met had admitted to knowing anything relevant to the enquiry. For the sake of completeness, and to pre-empt potential criticism from Errowby, Oliver had decided to visit the four houses that fronted on White Cross Lane. The lane zigzagged around the outskirts of Abbotsfield, forming the baseline of a triangle whose apex was in the centre by the church; it also marked the eastern boundary of the Meadow Way housing estate. All four houses were detached, but they had little else in common.

The one at the end, just beyond the telephone box, was as modern as Burwell's. A young woman with two red setters and two children below school age told them that she and her husband had gone to bed at seven o'clock last night and slept like the dead. Oliver gathered that she was proud of this achievement.

The second house they came to was a redbrick Victorian cottage with a rusting Bedford van in the garden and a satellite dish leaning at a drunken angle from the chimneystack.

'Police?' a woman said through the letterbox. 'What do you want?'

Oliver explained.

The door opened a few inches. A woman with dyed blonde hair stared at them. At the sight of Sharon she became a little less suspicious.

'Last night? We didn't hear a thing. We were watching telly most of the evening.'

'Thank you, Mrs . . .?'

'Perran.'

The door closed.

The third house in the lane was older than the others and set back further from the road – perhaps a small farmhouse which had lost its farm. No one answered their rings on the front-doorbell. Oliver and Sharon walked down the drive, which led to a yard at the back. They tapped on the door and peered through the window. Someone had tacked a piece of plywood across a pane of glass in the upper half of the door.

'Holiday cottage?' Sharon stared at the garden, whose formerly trim outlines were just discernible beneath the results of months of inattention.

'Who cares?' Oliver said.

'Wouldn't mind living here myself. A lot you could do with it.'

The fourth house was a small pre-war bungalow. There was in fact a fifth house beyond it, but this was still in the process of being built.

In the bungalow, bay windows bulged on either side of the front door. The woodwork had been freshly painted in red and blue; but both bays needed retiling and the brickwork was streaked with damp. A viburnum bush, at least five feet high and five feet broad, partially blocked the path near the door. But what really distinguished the place from every other house they had visited that day were the gnomes.

Sharon led the way up the path, which was made of crazy paving; time and weeds had increased its craziness. The small garden had been laid mainly to lawn, and the lawn had been covered with gnomes. There were gnomes on swings, on bicycles and on toadstools; there were sleeping gnomes, fishing gnomes and standing gnomes. It was difficult to estimate how many there were – anything from fifty to a hundred. They varied in height from six inches to two feet. Their owner had conferred a degree of uniformity on them by painting each of them red and blue to match the woodwork.

'Christ,' Sharon said.

The door opened before they reached it.

'Hello.'

Facing them was the old man who had tried to accost Kevin Burwell at the hospital. He was still wearing his overcoat and his cycle clips.

'Good afternoon, sir,' Oliver said. 'We're—'

The man flapped his arms. 'I know. My name's Nimp, Bert Nimp. I've been expecting you all afternoon.'

'Why's that, Mr Nimp?'

Nimp opened his mouth but for a moment said nothing. For some reason he was disconcerted. He ran the grimy nail of his forefinger along his upper lip, lifting the hairs that strag-gled down from his moustache. He smoothed his wispy beard.

'Mr Nimp?'

'Sorry. I'm getting a little hard of hearing. Just in the right ear.'

'Why were you expecting us?' Oliver shouted.

'Well, it's about the Burwell business, isn't it? That's why you've come. Poor Leonie. You've got to make enquiries. Of course you have.' He backed away from the door. 'But you won't mind if I ask to see your warrant cards, will you? Can't be too careful these days. It's sad, but there it is.'

Oliver and Sharon produced their cards. Nimp studied them.

'Come in, come in,' he said with an unexpected surge of hospitality. 'It's not the weather for doorsteps. Would you like some tea?'

He seemed disappointed when Oliver declined the offer. He ushered them into a sitting room. A small fire burned in the grate but it was very cold. On a table in the bay window stood a manual typewriter.

'Sit down, please.'

The three-piece suite was a little younger than Oliver and a little older than Sharon; it was upholstered in pink corduroy, now faded and stained.

'Now,' Nimp said before they had time to sit down, 'it happened just after eight o'clock – you know that, I expect. The poor child. I'd seen Leonie just a moment or two before.'

'You *saw* her?' Oliver glanced at Sharon, who was scribbling in her notebook. 'In the lane, you mean?'

'Yes, of course. I often see her. Though to be quite honest I didn't so much see her as hear her, if you know what I mean.'

'And where were you, sir?'

'In the garden. I – ah – I like a breath of fresh air before I settle down for the night.'

'But wasn't it raining rather hard?'

'Bless you, I don't mind a little rain, Sergeant. I was well wrapped up, and I had my umbrella. Anyway, it was dark by then, naturally, but the light was on in here, and the curtains weren't drawn, so I could see something of the lane. I was standing over there, near the door.' He waved in the direction of the viburnum. 'I doubt if they saw me.'

'They?'

'What?'

Oliver raised his voice. 'You mean Leonie wasn't alone?'

'Oh no. She was with Tammy Perran. You must have seen the Perrans' house? A terrible blot on our little landscape. I've been tempted to raise the matter with the council. I heard the girls say goodnight, see you tomorrow, that sort of thing. Then

I came inside. I usually have a hot drink about eight o'clock, you see, and—'

'So as far as you know, Leonie was alone when she turned off the lane?'

'That's what I've been saying.'

'How do you know Leonie?' Sharon said. 'Tammy's more or less a neighbour, but—'

'Oh, I know almost everyone in Abbotsfield.' Nimp glanced from Sharon to Oliver; and something in his eyes reminded Oliver of Fintal. A consciousness of knowing more than you did?

'So presumably you know Mr Burwell,' Oliver said. 'And he knows you. But why didn't he want to talk to you at the hospital this morning?'

'Oh. Yes, of course – I thought I'd seen you before.' Once again, the old man rescued his moustache from his mouth. 'Well, Kevin Burwell's a bit of a rough diamond at the best of times. And then I imagine he was in a state of shock, poor soul. Thirdly – and I must admit, quite candidly, that I bear some responsibility for this – he's not entirely at ease with the press.'

Nimp sighed. He was thin to the point of malnutrition yet his features had a rubbery quality – as if, suitably moulded, they would conform to any shape their owner required of them.

Oliver failed to keep the disbelief out of his voice. 'You're a journalist?'

'I'm the Abbotsfield correspondent for the *Paulstock Guardian.*' Nimp took a strand of his beard and coiled it round his fingers. 'For my sins. When you get to my age, you need some sort of an occupation. Especially since my wife passed away. Otherwise you just – well, run down. Like a clock.'

'I see. And why doesn't Mr Burwell like journalists?'

'There was a good deal of fuss when he built the Meadow Way estate.' Nimp stared through the bay window at the red roofs beyond. 'All that was farmland, you know, right up the hill. See the church tower at the top? That's where the old Abbotsfield is. People were very upset. You know how it is.'

Nimp's eyes were watering. 'Tempers run high. People say unkind things.'

'What sort of things?'

'What?'

'What sort of things?' Oliver roared.

'Oh, nothing worth repeating.'

Nimp retreated behind an increasingly opaque screen of coyness and deafness. He no longer wanted to talk to them, and Oliver had no reason to persist with this line of questioning. He rose to leave. Nimp came with them to the front door. He stared past them at his garden.

'The gnomes are very pretty, aren't they?' Sharon said.

Smiling, he looked up at her and nodded his head.

'The house next door – is it empty?'

Nimp's smiled vanished. 'It's not even built.'

'Not that one,' she said. 'The other way.'

'White Cross House? No one's living there at present. It's been bought by a doctor, actually. Young chap – he's redecorating it himself before he moves in.'

'I don't suppose he was around last night?' Oliver said.

'Not as far as I know.'

'I suppose we'd better have a word with him. What's his name?'

'Graham Hanslope. He lives in a flat in Paulstock, I believe, but he works here in Abbotsfield, up at the new Health Centre. But I wouldn't try to see him now.'

'Why not?'

'Because you'd have a wasted journey, Sergeant. I was up at the health centre myself this morning. The receptionist happened to mention that Dr Hanslope had gone to London for a few days.'

'Thank you, sir. You've been most helpful.'

At the gate, Oliver glanced back. Nimp was still standing in the doorway. He waved to them.

'By the way,' he called. 'Give my regards to Mr Fintal.'

Graham Hanslope was waiting by the school gates.

He was so excited that he barely noticed the cold. First they would go shopping – Kilburn High Road, perhaps, or Wembley; anywhere but here – and then they would find somewhere that sold kingsize burgers, milkshakes and ice cream.

Other adults, mainly women, were waiting by the gates. Most of them were West Indian or Irish. He felt jealous of their being able to do this every day. Not all of them were parents, he guessed: big sisters and grannies had been pressed into service.

He wished Michael would hurry. They didn't have much time. Perhaps – if the unthinkable happened and they connected Graham with the dead girl – this might be the last time he would see Michael for years. He bit his lips and tasted blood.

'Not later than six o'clock,' Graham's sister had said.

'Go on, Sue. Make it a bit later. Then we could see a film.'

'He'd get too excited. It's not as if it's the weekend. He's got school tomorrow.'

'Just this once, eh? Let me give him a bit of a treat?'

'No. You spoil him enough as it is. Anyway, he's getting a treat from you next month.'

'Please. He's my nephew.'

'You don't have to cope with him afterwards,' she shouted. '*I want this, I want that*. It's a bloody nightmare, Graham. So I want him back by six. You can give him his tea but don't buy him anything. Take it or leave it.'

And Sue had stared at him until he dropped his eyes in submission. She was three years older than he was and he still had not lost the habit of obedience to her. Besides, he didn't want to upset her, especially not today. She had agreed, with obvious reluctance, to allow Graham to take Michael out for the whole Saturday after Michael's birthday; they were going to Madame Tussaud's.

The doors opened. Children poured out. Black faces, brown faces and white faces; and none of them was Michael's. Their breath steamed in the cold, foggy air. They pushed one another and scrambled down the path. One boy's face was covered with blood.

As far as Graham could see, the school was wholly without

discipline. He wished with all his heart that he could take Michael somewhere else, to a school which would encourage the boy to make something of himself. Otherwise he would end up like his father: an unemployed brickie in a cockroach-infested council flat.

There at last was Michael. He wore muddy jeans, a t-shirt and trainers and he was carrying a brightly coloured quilted jacket under his arm. Didn't he feel the cold?

Michael was alone. He walked slowly down the path staring at the ground. The frame of his glasses was held together with Sellotape. A girl jostled him from behind. Michael stood aside, his head still bowed, to allow her to pass. Graham trembled – not with cold but with hatred of the girl.

'Michael,' he called. 'Over here.'

Frowning, the boy looked up. He saw Graham and broke into a run. Graham ruffled his hair. He would have liked to kiss him.

'Where's Mum?'

'At home. I'm taking you out for a meal.'

'Great.' Michael's expression was expectant and also anxious. Graham enjoyed everything about his nephew, even his greed. Everyone was greedy. Children had yet to learn how to conceal it.

'First I thought we might do a bit of shopping. Someone's got a birthday on the fourteenth.'

Michael nodded.

'Put your coat on. The car's down here.'

'Have you brought Rachel this time?'

'No.'

She had wanted to come but Graham wouldn't let her. She had come once before and spoiled it for Graham by monopolising Michael.

'Why? Would you have liked me to bring her?'

Michael shrugged. 'Where are we going?'

'You'll see. Oh, and Michael.' Graham laid a hand on the boy's shoulder. The bone felt delicate, as though the gentlest squeeze would snap it. 'If we do go shopping, it's between ourselves, OK? Your mum and dad mustn't know.'

'It's a secret, you mean?'

'That's it.'

'OK.' For the first time, Michael's sharp little face relaxed into a smile.

5

As far as Oliver could tell, Fintal hadn't moved at all in the seven hours since he had last seen him. He was still sitting at his desk with a pile of reports in front of him, an overflowing ashtray on his left and a half-full coffee cup on his right. The bastard was so warm he was in his shirtsleeves.

'Why didn't you tell me?' Oliver said.

His voice was ragged and too loud. Anger had crept up and taken him by surprise. There were at least a dozen people in the big office and he sensed that all of them were looking at him. For the moment he didn't care. It had been a bloody awful day and Oliver wanted to blame someone. Sharon muttered something about thawing her hands and getting a cup of coffee.

Fintal looked up and gave an exaggerated start. 'Sergeant Rickford. You gave me quite a shock. What can I do for you?'

'It's what you could have done that concerns me. You could have told me that Bert Nimp was one of your neighbourhood snoops.'

Fintal had the responsibility of collating the criminal information sheets amassed by the beat officers of Paulstock Division. Officers were encouraged to cultivate members of the public with a propensity for gossip. Everything was recorded – suspicions and rumours as well as facts; the majority of the subjects didn't even have criminal records. Fintal filed and indexed the material for possible use in the future. This mountain of information was his private kingdom, and he guarded it jealously. Such intelligence networks flourished all over the country – discreetly, because there was no statutory authority for the system, and the Home Office preferred to pretend it did not exist.

Fintal loosened his tie. 'Oh, you've met old Bert, have you? Quite a card, isn't he? Did he tell you?'

'No. He just dropped hints and was a little less forthcoming than he might have been.'

'Oh dear. He does need careful handling, there's no denying that.'

'Is he reliable as a witness?'

'I'd say so.' Fintal nodded slowly. 'That's to say he doesn't actually make things up, or not very often. Bit inclined to embroider, but aren't we all?'

'Mr Errowby's very keen to see this case cleared up.' Oliver waited for his meaning to sink in before adding: 'Got anything on the Burwell family?'

Fintal's eyes flickered. Oliver guessed he was weighing the certain pleasure of annoying an outsider against the possibility of arousing Errowby's anger.

'Kevin's a big wheel in the Masons, for what it's worth,' he said at last. 'You know he's a builder, I take it? Made a lot of money in the last ten or fifteen years.'

'Popular?'

'In Abbotsfield? Not so's you'd notice. He's trodden on too many toes.'

'How about his wife?'

'Felicity's his second wife – first one died; leukaemia, I think, something like that. She's local, though you wouldn't think it to hear her speak – her dad was a farmer. Inclined to stick her nose in the air by all accounts. Leonie's her daughter; the other one, Joanna, was by the first wife. You've probably seen Joanna around. She works in Paulstock – at that estate agent's opposite the Dragon.'

'She was at the hospital. Dark hair.'

'That's it. Quite a looker. As you no doubt noticed.'

'Does the name Perran ring any bells?'

'Jimmy Perran? Lives near Bert? He works for Burwell, or he used to. A chippy, I think. Bert doesn't like him but these days he keeps his nose clean.'

'He's got form?'

'Two years suspended for attempting GBH with a chainsaw.'

'Is that a joke?'

'Far from it. Happened one Christmas five or six years ago. Jimmy thought some bloke was making eyes at his missus. So he went for him with a chainsaw. Only thing was, Jimmy was drunk and the other bloke was an off-duty bouncer. That's why Jimmy's little finger on his left hand is a little bit shorter than it used to be.'

Oliver moved towards the door. He met Sharon coming the other way with two plastic cups of vending-machine coffee. 'Later,' he said to her. 'I've got to see Errowby.'

'Who said the other cup was for you?'

She slipped past him and headed for her desk.

'Anything else I can do for you?' Fintal asked; and he made the offer insulting.

Oliver turned back. 'What about Nimp's next-door neighbour?'

'Eh?'

'Hanslope. The new doctor.'

'Oh, him.' There was a curious undercurrent in Fintal's voice. Relief? Amusement? 'Comes from London. I heard he'd bought the house but I thought he hadn't moved in yet.'

'He hasn't as far as I know.'

'The only thing I know about him comes from the paper.' The walnut-shell face wrinkled. 'You should study your *Paulstock Guardian*, Sergeant, you really should. It's a mine of information. Dr Hanslope has just got engaged.' Fintal smiled up at Oliver. 'And the lucky lady is Joanna Burwell.'

Three thousand seven hundred pounds?

It wasn't possible. Felicity Burwell went through the credit card statements again. This time she used the calculator. She tapped in the totals. Half the purchases she didn't even remember making. And how had the interest reached such a ridiculous level?

The calculator disagreed with her total: it produced a figure that was a fraction over four thousand pounds. Felicity opened the centre drawer of the desk. The bank had sent her a letter about the overdraft. Something about settling up at her earliest convenience – as if it would ever be convenient to anyone but the bank. Underneath the letter she found another statement, this one from American Express. She had forgotten all about it. Her eyes filled with tears.

A sound disturbed her. She swung round. Darkness had fallen and the outside lights had switched themselves on. She was just in time to see the black BMW rolling towards the garage.

Kevin was home early. Her fingers gripped the back of the chair. She bundled together the statements, the letter and the calculator and thrust them into the drawer. By the time her husband came into the house, she was in the kitchen making a salad for dinner.

He kissed her on the cheek. She forced herself to kiss him back. Nowadays his coarse, bristly skin revolted her. She knew at once that he was angry or at least worked up about something. No point in mentioning the money. Not now. He was always difficult about money.

'Any news from the hospital?' he said.

'Nothing new. I rang half an hour ago. Joanna said she'd look in on her way home.'

Kevin put his briefcase down on the table. 'I see you found her book.'

Wuthering Heights was on the table. He picked it up and flicked through the pages. Felicity sensed that he was hesitating, which was unlike him.

'Who's Lara?' he said.

'What?'

'It says here' – he held up the book, open at the flyleaf – '*To Lara from Thomas.*'

'How do I know? Leonie probably got the book secondhand.'

37

He closed the book and dropped it on the table. His actions had an aimless quality that worried Felicity. Guilt sharpens the perceptions.

'What is it, Kevin?' she said. 'Is something wrong?'

'No, not really. It's just – well, I phoned Bernie Errowby from the car.'

'What did he say?'

'He's had people combing the neighbourhood all day but he hasn't come up with much.'

'Can't they do more?'

'Bernie's doing everything he can. He'd better.' He took off his overcoat and folded it over his arm; he was careful about his belongings. 'There were two small bits of news. Their forensic people came up with a bloodstain on Leonie's scarf. It's not her blood group. They're working on the assumption it's the driver's.'

'Not much use unless they find the driver.'

'That's confidential, by the way. The police want to keep it to themselves at present.'

'What was the other thing?' she said.

'They talked to Bert Nimp.'

'Horrible little man.'

'Yes. But according to him Leonie was talking to Tammy in the lane just before she was knocked down.'

'She lied to me.' Felicity hacked at the white cabbage. It was a relief to have a legitimate outlet for the tension. 'I knew it,' she went on. 'God, she's going to regret this.'

'I think she's been punished already.'

'You're too soft on her, Kevin.' Felicity hesitated. 'You know – this might even be a blessing in disguise.'

'A blessing?' Kevin yelled. 'Are you mad? Christ, if I ever get hold of the bastard who drove that car, I'll—'

'Darling, it's all right.' Felicity put her arms around him. She knew from experience that this quietened him down. She looked over his shoulder at the clock. If she were going to do jacket potatoes tonight, she should really have got the oven on by now.

'What do you mean?' His voice was muffled by her hair. 'A blessing?'

She eased herself away. 'That girl Tammy. The scene she made at the hospital – it was so embarrassing. But the one good thing about this business is that Leonie won't be able to see her for a week or two.'

Kevin said nothing.

'It's not exactly a suitable friendship, is it? Jimmy Perran's a convicted criminal, you told me yourself.'

'He's not a bad carpenter.'

'I think you should have a word with him, Kevin.'

'And say what, exactly?'

'There are lots of reasons. The girls have got their GCSEs in the summer and they need to spend their time working, not giggling in each other's bedrooms. And in the long run they'd both be happier with friends from their own backgrounds.'

'You're a snob.'

'I'm just trying to be realistic, darling. Someone has to be. You must admit that Leonie's at a very impressionable age. If only you'd see sense and send her away to school—'

'We've gone into all this. There's nothing wrong with the comprehensive. Anyway, we can't afford it.'

'What do you mean?'

'That surprised you, didn't it? In case you haven't heard, the building trade's in the middle of a recession. I'm stuck with twenty acres of land that I can't afford to develop. And if I sell, I'll make a loss – and that's assuming I can find a buyer in the first place. Meanwhile the interest on the bank loan goes up and up.'

'But surely it's only a temporary hitch? Anyway, when you sell off those Badger's Lane houses—'

'Don't you ever listen? I've been trying to sell them for the last twelve months. The market's dead. Meanwhile I've got to pay the sub-contractors and keep my own men busy. Oh, yes, and don't let's forget Joanna's wedding and all the trimmings she wants. So don't talk to me about the joys of private education, OK? Not now.'

'I – I didn't realise.'

'Because you weren't interested.' The anger slowly left his face. 'Don't worry. We'll survive.' He opened the door to the hall. 'I'm going to get a drink.'

'Kevin?'

'What is it?'

'Will you talk to Perran?'

He sucked in his heavy cheeks and stared at her. 'All right. If you insist. There's something else that Bernie said. I wasn't going to tell you but maybe you'd better know. You remember that sergeant of his we saw at the hospital?'

Felicity nodded. A tall, thin man with a permanent expression of disapproval and a long and slightly crooked nose.

'Rickford, that's the name. Apparently he came up with a theory. Just an idea, mind you. Maybe what happened to Leonie wasn't an accident. Maybe it was personal.'

'I don't understand.'

'It's not very difficult,' Kevin said. 'Maybe she was knocked down on purpose by someone with a grudge against me. Or even against you.'

'Alphonse,' Bert Nimp murmured. 'Billy. Claudia.' He patted their little heads and moved across the grass to the next group. The frost crunched beneath his feet. 'Donald, Edwin, Ferdie and George.'

At least it was dry tonight. He could see quite well. The red setters were barking up the lane: out for their last run in the garden; those dogs needed more exercise. A lorry rumbled along the main road.

'Henrietta, Ian, Jocasta and' – his hand fumbled for a moment before touching the fourth pointed hat – 'and Kenneth. Naughty Kenneth. Trying to get away from Daddy?'

The routine soothed him as it always did. Conversely, he disliked it when the ritual was interrupted. Last night, for example, Leonie and Tammy had forced him to stand beside Zenobia for several minutes in the pouring rain. He knew quite well that his behaviour might seem eccentric to an outsider and therefore took care to conceal it; but he had long before decided that it was harmless, and perhaps even beneficial.

Besides, the gnomes were not a responsibility he had created but one he had inherited. His wife, God rest her soul, had bought them one by one over the last nine years of her life. She began when they had to leave their old home, a cottage in the centre of Abbotsfield. It had been such a nice house with such a nice garden; so convenient for the shops and the church. Kevin Burwell had bought up the freeholds of the Nimps' house and four of the neighbouring properties. Burwell ejected the tenants, one by one; as the tenants left, he pulled down their houses; and finally he sold the land, with planning permission attached, to a supermarket chain in the early 1980s. For Muriel, perhaps, the gnomes had been a sort of compensation for losing Honeysuckle Cottage.

'Lawrence and Malcolm and Nigel . . .'

Nimp thought there might have been another reason why his wife started collecting them. Just before they had been forced to move to the bungalow, their only daughter and her family had left Bristol for Yorkshire. The house in Leeds wasn't really big enough for overnight visits, and their daughter always found good reasons for declining invitations to Abbotsfield. Nimp had never seen two of his grandchildren.

'Olive and Philip, Quentin and Russell. Where's Simon? *There* you are.'

Then his wife had her illness. Her mind wandered towards the end. She had little fancies. The gnomes worried her: what would happen to them when she was gone? She called them *my children*. Towards the end, she was convinced that someone was trying to steal them. Who on earth would want to steal a collection of garden gnomes? But there was no point in arguing with her. It was simpler to go round the garden and count them. One day, as she sat up in bed and looked through the bay window at the gnomes, she had decided that they should all have names.

'Thomas and Una . . .'

Labelling them had been easy enough, though they had needed a dictionary of Christian names to cope with certain letters of the alphabet like X,Y and Z; and some names – Xerxes and Xenophon, for example – had a distinctly pagan flavour. But memorising the sequence and fitting the names to individual gnomes had taken him months.

'Veronica, Waldo, Xanthippe – dear Xanthippe.' Nimp always patted her twice in memory of the dear departed. 'Yolande, Zacharias and Alfred, Berenice, Candia, Daniel and Eustace . . .'

'Look after my children when I'm gone,' Muriel had said on the day before she died; and Nimp had known that she was referring to her gnomes. He went out night after night, unless he was ill: 79 pats on 78 heads.

The gnomes were still in the positions Muriel had chosen for them. He had made only three changes to her arrangements. The original Queenie had disappeared – he suspected Jimmy Perran was to blame for that; the man was given to drunken pranks – and had to be replaced. He himself had accidentally beheaded Frederick, a secondhand gnome made of clay, and damaged him beyond repair: so another substitute had to be bought. And it had been Nimp's idea to paint them.

'Gordon, Harry, Imogen and John . . .'

Nothing complicated, he had decided: red hats, blue tops and red trousers or skirts. The uniformity was pleasing: it made them one family.

Finally he reached Xerxes, Yorick and Zenobia, who stood in a cluster near the front door. It was a pity that Leonie and Tammy had not come along earlier. A couple of minutes would have done it: he would have been outside; he would have heard the accident; he might have been the first to find Leonie as she lay bleeding – she must have been bleeding – by the sleeping policeman. Nimp sighed.

He went into the bungalow and made himself some Ovaltine. Humming quietly and still in his overcoat, he drew the sitting-room curtains and sat down at the table. He wound a fresh sheet of paper into the typewriter.

TRAGEDY AT ABBOTSFIELD

On Sunday night Abbotsfield was the scene of an almost-fatal accident. At 8 p.m. Leonie Burwell (15), younger daughter of prominent local developer Kevin Burwell, was knocked down and severely injured by a car at the junction of White Cross Lane and Meadow Way. She was returning home after visiting a friend. The driver failed to stop. Leonie is now recovering from her injuries in the private ward at Paulstock Hospital. Only her immediate family are being allowed to see her.

We understand that officers from Paulstock CID are investigating the incident. There are indications that this may not be a simple case of hit and run. Mr Burwell, whose reticence towards the press is well-known, declined to comment.

Nimp paused and sipped his drink, which was now lukewarm. He knew that when his contribution appeared in the *Paulstock Guardian* it would have been mutilated beyond recognition. Usually the prospect upset him; but not today.

The accident had cheered him up. The memory of it spread like a physical glow through his body. He hoped the girl would die.

6

On Thursday 31 January, Rachel got up early to make Graham's breakfast.

'Must you go back this morning?' she said as she refilled his coffee cup. 'Why don't you leave after lunch? I could always phone in and say I'm ill.'

'Sorry, love. I've got a stack of paperwork to get through before tomorrow.'

'When will you come back?'

'Soon.' He put his arm round her waist and squeezed the firm flesh. 'I promise.'

By nine o'clock Graham was travelling west against the rush hour. It was a relief to be alone again. Rachel's company had a smothering effect on him: after twenty-four hours he was gasping for air.

'Do you miss me?' she had said over and over again until he wanted to scream.

'Of course I do,' he would say; and in one sense at least the words were true. And she would look at him with that hungry look on her plump face, waiting for him to take the next and seemingly logical step: to say that he didn't want to miss her any more; to ask her to marry him.

Before Sunday evening, and on several occasions during the last three days, he had seriously considered ending their relationship. Rachel kept hinting about coming down to Paulstock, which would of course be fatal. And there was no doubt that she was making his life very complicated. On the other hand, her flat was very handy for when he wanted to see Michael and he would miss both her devotion and her acrobatic enthusiasm. Moreover, it might be wiser not to upset her until he could be sure that this business with the accident was not going to have repercussions. If the worst came to the worst Rachel could give him an alibi of sorts. Only one person had known he was due at White Cross House that night, and she wouldn't tell; she wouldn't dare.

The memory of the girl's red shoe had haunted him since the accident. In the toyshop with Michael on Monday, he had seen a girl in similar shoes. He had wanted to faint.

'Why are we leaving?' Michael had said, his voice high and aggrieved, as Graham towed him out of the shop.

'Because we're running out of time, and anyway I've got a better idea.' Graham opened his wallet and took out a ten-pound note and a five. 'Have this instead. It'll be easier to hide than a toy. Then you can get what you really want.'

If the business came out he would be finished. He imagined what prison would be like; he imagined being struck off; he imagined losing the future he had worked so hard to make possible. He had come a long way from the council flat in Dagenham and he didn't intend to go back.

He arrived in Paulstock a little before midday. He parked outside the flats in the residents' car park; but before going in he walked down the street to the newsagent's. He had timed it well: the *Paulstock Guardian*, which was a weekly newspaper, had just arrived. He also bought a pint of milk and two bars of milk chocolate.

Before he looked at the paper, he forced himself to go back to the car for his luggage; he walked at what felt like an exaggeratedly normal pace into the block and up to the flat. It was a curious feeling to be strolling along with one's destiny under one's arm. To his relief he saw no one he knew.

His flat was on the second floor. He unlocked the door and kicked aside the pile of letters on the mat. Once the door was shut, his calm deserted him. He dumped his bags on the little chest of drawers in the hall and tore open the newspaper.

He had half-expected a banner headline: GIRL MURDERED

BY ROADHOG. But there was nothing about an accident in Abbotsfield on the front page. He skimmed through the rest of the paper. Still nothing. He felt almost disappointed – cheated of knowledge that was his by right.

In the living room he sat down and worked his way more slowly through the newspaper. At last, on page seven, he found it tucked away among the gardening tips and the reports from Women's Institutes near the bottom of the page.

HIT-AND-RUN

A girl was seriously injured in a hit-and-run accident at Abbotsfield last Sunday. It happened around 8 p.m. at the junction of White Cross Lane and Meadow Way. Leonie Burwell (15), a pupil at Brush Hill Comprehensive School, is now recovering at Paulstock Hospital. Police have called for witnesses to come forward. Anyone with information should telephone Paulstock 85911 or contact their local police station.

Relief and shock made Graham feel lightheaded. He leaned forward and put his head in his hands. The girl was alive. That meant no one would be able to accuse him of manslaughter, come what may. And if the police were calling for witnesses, surely he could safely infer that they had no idea who the driver was?

But Leonie? He'd hit Leonie? His fiancée's sister? He began to laugh.

When, a few minutes later, he had sobered up, he realised that he should have guessed the girl in red shoes might be Leonie or Tammy Perran. Joanna had said with an air of disapproval that the two girls were always going to and fro between their houses. As far as he knew, Tammy was the only teenager who lived in White Cross Lane. He barely knew Leonie: he had talked to her for perhaps three minutes on the evening that he and Joanna had announced their engagement to the family. A small, shy girl; probably rather immature for her age.

He got up and walked up and down the living room: down

to the big window, back to the kitchen door. Did this change the situation? If Leonie had died, he and Joanna might have had to postpone the wedding. *Seriously injured* – what did that mean exactly? The real question was whether she could remember anything about the accident. Yes, there might be problems.

There were also advantages. As a doctor and a prospective brother-in-law, Graham should have every chance to monitor Leonie's condition; he should be able to find out if she remembered anything potentially damaging about the accident. He also thought it likely that the police would keep Kevin Burwell well-informed about their investigation – Burwell had boasted about his friendship with the local cops – and that he or Felicity would pass on any information they received. Burwell, Graham remembered with a shiver, was fond of his younger daughter.

'He tolerates me,' Joanna had told Graham. 'He loves Leonie.'

Leonie couldn't have seen him: even if she were conscious she must have been blinded by the headlights. It was just possible that she might have recognised his voice – but, if so, surely the police would have arrested him by now? His stomach lurched. They couldn't have arrested him. They didn't know where he was. He'd told Joanna he was going up to London to help a friend with some research but he hadn't told her where he was staying.

'I promised I'd do it months ago,' he had said. 'Before I'd even met you. And I owe Dave a favour or two as well. I'd feel terrible about letting him down at such short notice.'

'Of course you must go, darling,' Joanna said. 'After all, we've got the rest of our lives together.'

He had intended to phone Joanna while he was away but really, what with the competing demands of Rachel and Michael, he hadn't had a moment to himself. For all he knew the police had put a watch on the flat. The more he thought about it, the more likely it seemed: he had walked into a trap.

Graham's mouth was dry. He stood to the left of the window, pushed the curtain an inch away from the frame and peered down at the street below. There were dozens of parked cars. Nothing unusual in that. He was wasting his time: the police wouldn't use a marked patrol car.

At any moment there might be a knock on the door. He had to do something. His mind filled with pictures of himself: driving to Southampton and fleeing to France; opening his bag and selecting a lethal cocktail of pills; lying in a hot bath with the water changing from pink to red; putting his head between Rachel's breasts and crying 'Save me.'

In the event Graham did none of these things. He picked up the phone and dialled a number.

'Lees and Bright, estate agent's – can I help you?'

'May I speak to Joanna Burwell, please?'

'Who shall I say is calling?'

'Graham Hanslope.'

'Oh.' The receptionist's voice lost its boredom. 'Of course you can. Won't be a moment, dear.'

Good news, Graham told himself: Joanna's at work, so things must be near normal; and she isn't out on a job, so God must be on my side. Just as he was formulating a suspicion that the police might have calculated that Joanna would be the first person he would get in touch with, and therefore might have put a tap on the line, Joanna herself came to the phone.

'Graham,' she said. She added in a near-whisper that told him she was overheard, 'Darling, I—'

'Dearest, I'm so sorry,' he interrupted. 'I've just got back and heard the news. How's Leonie?'

'Much better. She'll be out of hospital by the weekend. The ribs will mend naturally – apparently they don't strap them up these days. She's still getting awful headaches, but the consultant says they'll probably wear off in a week or two.'

'Was she knocked unconscious, then?'

'Yes. She remembers nothing about it.'

'Graham let out his breath in a silent whistle.

'Graham? Are you still there?'

'Thank God she's all right.'

'Yes,' Joanna said, very seriously. 'Thank God. How was your research? Did you manage to do everything you wanted?'

'Fine. No problems. I'm sorry I didn't ring. I tried to, but you know how it is. Dave had booked a lab and we were working eighteen-hour days. It was horrendous.'

'It doesn't matter. Did you remember about this evening?'

'No. What?'

'It's Thursday,' she said with a hint of reproach. 'I said I'd help with the parish accounts. I can't get out of it.'

'Are you free for lunch?'

'I've got an appointment, I'm afraid. Will you be at the flat this afternoon?'

'Probably.'

'I'll try to drop in. I've got the wallpaper for the sitting room in the car. But I can't stay long.'

'I'm longing to see you,' Graham said.

'By the way, my parents wondered if you'd like to come to lunch on Saturday.'

'I'd rather have lunch by ourselves.'

'Of course, darling.' Once again, Joanna's voice was faintly reproachful. 'So should I. But we really need to talk to them about the wedding arrangements. The sooner the better. There's an awful lot to do.'

Graham agreed with all the enthusiasm he could muster. When he rang off he looked at his watch. He was hungry. But first he would wash and change. He always made it a rule to be scrupulous about such matters. A woman, like a dog, had a fine nose for the tell-tale smell of a rival.

On his way to the bedroom he picked up his bags and the pile of letters from the hall. As he turned towards the bedroom he caught sight of a white triangle on the carpet: a sheet of paper, most of which was underneath the chest of drawers. He picked it up. It was only a fly sheet advertising a dry-cleaning service. He was about to crumple it up when he realised that there was a line of letters hand-printed in blue felt-tip on the back.

Can't manage this evening. Sorry. Will phone.

God was still on his side. Everything was falling into place. Leonie wasn't in danger – and she was not a danger to him. And now this: it meant that there was nothing to connect him with White Cross House on Sunday night. The note must have come through the letterbox while he was out on Sunday afternoon and slid under the chest.

The phone rang while Graham was in the shower. He grabbed his towel and ran into the living room, leaving a trail of drips on the carpet.

'Hello?'

'You're back. How about this evening?'

At the sound of the voice, Graham's skin crawled with anticipation.

'Fine.'

'Usual place? Seven?'

'OK.'

He barely had time to get the word out before he was listening to the dialling tone. She was always very careful on the phone. He liked the brusqueness. It excited him.

As soon as he replaced the handset, the phone began to ring again. This time it was Rachel.

'Darling,' she said. 'You got home all right?'

He pictured her sitting at her desk in the dentist's surgery at Chiswick. Her body would be bursting out of the white coat. For an instant he wanted her very badly.

'I miss you,' he said.

Oliver Rickford had read in a magazine that women liked men with small bottoms. The article had a title like WHAT REALLY TURNS WOMEN ON. The ten masculine features they found most desirable had been listed in order of preference, and small bottoms had been near the top. Oliver remembered this because a small bottom was the only one of the qualities that he was absolutely sure he possessed.

On Thursday he dressed with care in a brand-new pair of

jeans, which certainly showed the bottom to best advantage even if they were uncomfortably tight around the waist. He wore his brown leather bomber jacket over a jersey he had bought in the Christmas sales and never worn before. Before he left his room he inspected himself in the full-length mirror on the wardrobe door. He suspected that he would never be able to make himself attractive to women; nature had endowed him with too many disadvantages. But at least he had done his best.

He had planned his day off with care. The Burwell case, such as it was, had prevented him from putting the plan into operation on Monday. He was going to find somewhere to live.

E Division was short of police accommodation; and Oliver had spent his first few weeks at Paulstock in a bed-and-breakfast run by the widow of a police officer. The house smelled of cats. Oliver knocked his head at least twice a day on the sloping ceiling of his attic bedroom. The dining room was dominated by an enlarged photograph of the landlady's late husband in his sergeant's uniform. Worst of all, the landlady considered herself an honorary member of the force and talked to Oliver about Paulstock policing, past and present, at every opportunity. It was almost as bad as living in the enclosed world of a section house.

There were six estate agents in Paulstock. Oliver left Lees and Bright until last. Twenty-five years ago, on the same principle, he had saved his most exciting-looking birthday present until the end. During the morning he covered the first five estate agents and made arrangements to view two flats in the afternoon. At lunchtime he had a bar snack in the Dragon. He sat by a window that overlooked the shopfront of Lees and Bright. While he waited he glanced through the flat details he had been given and read the *Paulstock Guardian*. At ten past two, Joanna Burwell returned from lunch. Oliver told himself that whatever happened he would be disappointed. At a quarter past two he left the pub, crossed the road and went into the estate agent's.

Joanna Burwell was at the back of the office. Her skin glowed: there was no other word for it. Oliver walked stiffly towards her. The tightness of his jeans made his legs feel like artificial limbs.

'Good afternoon.' Her skin was as smooth and perfect as double cream. 'What can I do for you?'

The speech he had rehearsed this morning vanished from his memory, erased by the force of her smile. He noticed the engagement ring.

Her forehead wrinkled. 'Haven't we met before?'

'Yes – on Monday at the hospital. My name's Oliver Rickford.'

Joanna glanced towards the other woman and then lowered her voice. 'Is everything all right? Is it about—'

'No, no – this is personal.' He watched the frown deepen and hurried on. 'That is, I'm interested in a flat.'

'To buy, you mean?'

'Not at this stage. I'm looking for a six-month lease with the option of renewing.'

Joanna opened a folder. 'Do sit down, Mr – Mr Rickford. I'll take your details.'

Suddenly everything became easy. He explained, as he had explained five times before, how his flat in Peckham was now on the market; once that was sold he would want to buy a small house in or around Paulstock; in the meantime he hoped to lease a flat, preferably in town.

Joanna came up with three possibilities: a basement in a Victorian house conversion; a three-bedroomed flat above a fish-and-chip shop; and Copeland Court.

'Copeland Court's a block of purpose-built flats in a cul-de-sac just beyond the library. We manage it for the freeholders. One of the studio apartments on the third floor is available for rent. The leaseholder's working abroad on a two-year contract and has asked us to let it for him.'

He listened less to her words than to the sound of her voice. She spoke quietly and precisely, giving each word its due weight. He was aware that she was making a sales pitch and that he should be listening to it critically. He gathered that the Copeland Court flat was smaller and more expensive than the others, but these were minor points beside the general desirability of the flat and its location. While she talked she kept her features unusually still. There was something delightfully old-fashioned, about her, he decided, a sort of decorum. If she were a flower, she would be a lily. He marvelled that a great ape like Kevin Burwell could have fathered her.

'If you'd like to see the flat,' Joanna was saying, 'I could take you there now.'

'That's very kind,' he said, knowing that whatever happened he would take this flat. 'If you're sure it's not too much trouble?'

It was an idiotic thing to say: she was doing her job, not doing him a favour.

'Not at all. In fact it will fit in rather well with another appointment I've got.'

He must have looked questioningly at her.

'With my fiancé, actually,' she said. 'He lives at Copeland Court.'

7

The Perrans had their main meal of the day in front of the television at six o'clock. On the evening of Thursday 31 January, they had beefburgers, oven chips and baked beans, followed by Black Forest gâteau and whipped cream. Suzette Perran and Tammy drank tea; Jimmy worked his way through a can of Carlsberg Special Brew.

They ate rapidly, each of them with an eye on the television. They were watching a video of a snooker match that Jimmy had missed on Sunday night. The coloured balls rolled silently across the green baize and collided with clicks that sounded unnaturally violent. The two men with narrowed eyes and black waistcoats circled the table. The commentator chattered away, his voice breathless with excitement. Tammy found it very restful.

When they had finished eating, her mother, still staring at the screen, lit a cigarette. She heaped the crockery, cutlery and trays into a pile with the tomato ketchup bottle, the vinegar and the salt balanced precariously on top.

'Wait,' Jimmy Perran said.

'I'll just put these in the dishwasher.'

The dishwasher had been a Christmas present from Tammy's father to her mother. It was still a novelty, and both Jimmy and Suzette enjoyed playing with it. If Tammy's father had a hobby, it was playing with gadgets: machines of all kinds flowed in and out of the house and in and out of the shed in the garden; they were usually secondhand and they came and went mysteriously.

'I said wait. You going deaf or something? I want to talk to you.'

Suzette rested the pile of trays on the back of the sofa. Tammy brushed crumbs from her jersey. On the screen, a white ball tapped the side of a red ball. The red ball slid into a pocket and disappeared. Tammy began to haul herself up.

'And you.'

She sank back in the chair. Her eyes were watering behind her glasses. Her father was a blur. She preferred him that way. She blinked and his outline cleared.

'Burwell had a word with me today.' Jimmy was looking intently at his lager can. 'He wants you to stop seeing that girl of his.'

Tammy sat bolt upright. She felt her cheeks burn. 'But – but we're in the same year. We go to school on the same bus. How can I stop seeing her?'

'That's not what he means.'

'He's got a cheek,' Suzette said. 'You should have told him where to get off.'

'I could have done. But I didn't. Because I happen to think he's right.'

'Why?' Tammy shouted.

Jimmy leant across the gap between their chairs and hit her with the back of his left hand. He sat back and lit a cigarette. Tammy could guess the answer. They had already had a wave of redundancies at Burwell's; and according to Leonie there would be more before Easter. Her father's job was on the line. And probably Kevin Burwell had sweetened what he had said with the promise of a tenner or two.

'I don't want her coming here, all right?' Jimmy said. 'And I don't want you running round to their house any more. Not unless you want me to beat the shit out of you.'

'It's her that put him up to it.' The ash from Suzette's cigarette trembled; it fell on to the pile of plates. 'That bitch.'

'Besides,' Jimmy said, 'you've both got your exams this summer. You should be working. Not mucking about.'

Tammy suspected he was quoting Burwell. It was the first time her father had shown any interest whatsoever in her academic career.

'She was round here on Sunday night, wasn't she?' Jimmy went on. 'Bert Nimp saw the pair of you nattering in the lane.'

'Nosy old bastard,' Suzette said mechanically.

'So if it weren't for you, she wouldn't be in hospital.'

Tammy squeezed her hands together in her lap. It would be fatal to shout at him again. Nothing she could say would make any difference.

'It's all your fault.' Her father upended the can over his mouth. A few drops dribbled into his mouth. He crumpled the can in his right hand. 'And you'll start now.'

'Doing what?'

'Working for your exams. Go and do your homework.'

Tammy stumbled out of the room and up the stairs. Her bedroom was dark and cold. She did not turn on the light. She sat on the bed and listened. A burst of applause from the television. The clatter of crockery. The thump of her mother closing the dishwasher.

Before Christmas, Tammy and Leonie had melted four candles and made crude wax images of their parents. Each image had something belonging to the parent it represented: a nail clipping from Mrs Burwell; two strands of hair from Suzette's hairbrush; a scummy line of stubble from a discarded razor blade of Mr Burwell's; and a hardened ball of catarrh from the underside of Jimmy Perran's armchair.

They had stuck pins in the images. There was no discernible effect. In the New Year, they slipped into the Burwells' drawing room, where there was an open fire, and dropped the four figures on a glowing bed of coal. 'If that won't do it,' Leonie had said, 'nothing will.' The wax sizzled and flared into flame. Their parents remained obstinately healthy.

'I'm going up the Boar,' her father shouted from the living room. 'If you're not ready in two minutes I'm going without you.'

'What have you done with my handbag?' her mother called back from the kitchen. 'Have you been at my purse again?'

Why, Tammy wondered, did her parents always shout at each

other? Leonie said that it was better than what her parents did, which was whisper in corners; at least you had a better chance of knowing what was going on.

Ten minutes later she heard them in the hall. Her mother shouted goodbye. Tammy didn't answer. The front door banged. Tammy heard the slam of the Cortina's doors. After what seemed like an age, the engine fired and the headlights came on. Their beams filled the bedroom with a flickering half-light. Tammy looked at her hands. They were pale, like a ghost's.

When the sound of the car had died away, she switched on the lights and ran downstairs. The phone was on a wall-mount in the kitchen. Tonight there was no need to use the callbox in the lane.

She dialled the hospital and asked for the private ward. When the nurse or whoever it was answered the extension, Tammy put on her posh voice and asked to speak to Leonie.

'Who shall I say is speaking?' the nurse said.

'Joanna Burwell,' Tammy said haughtily. 'Her sister.'

At a quarter to seven, Graham Hanslope reached Abbotsfield. He passed the health centre and drove through the town and out the other side. He had set himself a test.

This, in reverse, was the route he had taken on Sunday night. It was important: a way of proving that he was capable of rising above an unpleasant memory.

He turned into the Meadow Way estate and rolled over the first sleeping policeman. There were lights in some windows of the Burwells' house. He threaded his way through the little roads to Meadow Way itself. The junction with White Cross Lane was only yards away. The pavements were empty. They had mended the streetlamp. He slowed. The Golf bumped gently across the second sleeping policeman. Nothing to it.

He parked in the yard at the back and carried the rolls of wallpaper through the kitchen and into the hall. The house was warm – in this weather it paid to leave the central-heating on. He didn't bother to turn on the light; the kitchen door was open and he didn't want to advertise his presence. He nudged open the sitting-room door and stopped abruptly.

A face was pressed against the window.

No: he'd imagined it. As he moved, it was no longer there. Just a visual illusion. He ducked back and tried in vain to recapture it. Probably an impurity in the glass had reflected back a gleam of light from the kitchen. One tended to read meaning into the meaningless; he had made a face from a pale grey blur just above the sill.

Still, there was no harm in being careful. He unlocked the front door and stepped outside. Nothing was moving. The only sound was the barking of the dogs down the lane.

Graham went back inside and relocked the front door. As he was stooping to draw the bottom bolt, he heard a noise from the kitchen. The click of a closing door? But it was only ten to seven. He began to sweat, which was foolish. The hammer was where he had left it on Sunday – just inside the sitting room. He picked it up. In the corner of his eye he caught a flicker of movement in the kitchen doorway.

'Hello, Graham,' Felicity said. She slipped her key to the back door into a pocket.

'You're early.'

'Aren't you pleased?'

She came into the hall and kissed him hard on the mouth. He kissed her vigorously to show how pleased he was.

'You're hurting me.' She pulled away. 'What are you doing with that hammer? Planning to mug me or something?'

'I was going to make the back door more secure. I broke a pane of glass when I was leaving on—' He had nearly said it: *on Sunday*. In a rush he went on, 'You know, after last time.'

'How could I forget?' Felicity said.

She was wearing what she called her dog-walking disguise – a long Barbour jacket with its collar turned up and a woollen hat that concealed her hair. She could have been old or young, male or female. The dog itself, an elderly and intensely lazy black labrador, would be tied up in the garage. Almost certainly it was already asleep.

'Do you want a drink?'

Sometimes she liked a stiff gin-and-tonic beforehand. He remembered he had left the new bottle of gin in the boot of the car.

'Later, perhaps,' she said. 'Let's go upstairs.'

She was usually businesslike but tonight he had expected her to want to talk – about the accident and Leonie; he had imagined himself having to reassure her, to coax her into the bedroom. He hung back.

'Where's Kevin?'

'In Paulstock. Some masonic committee.'

'What if he tries to phone you?'

'I said I might nip out and see Margaret.'

Margaret was a friend who ran an ailing teashop near Abbotsfield church.

'Does she know about me?'

'Of course not, darling. No names, no packdrill. I've done the same for her.'

She took his hand and pulled him towards her. Her urgency infected him. Giggling like children, they ran hand in hand up the stairs.

Afterwards Graham brought them drinks. They were in the big bedroom at the back of the house. It was the only room he had finished redecorating. The heavy, claret-red curtains made an efficient black-out.

Felicity was naked under the duvet. Her small body was hard and lithe like an adolescent boy's. Now it was over, he wished she would get dressed and go.

'I'm sorry about Sunday,' Felicity said. 'Kevin suddenly decided he didn't want to visit his mother after all.'

'That's OK. I got your note in time.'

As a matter of politeness, Graham joined her on the bed; he would have been more comfortable in the armchair. She sat up, and her nakedness made his clothes seem a little ridiculous. They clinked their glasses together. He had only tonic in his glass, though he didn't tell Felicity that. He drank very little alcohol except when he was angry or depressed.

'How's Leonie?'

'Coming out on Saturday. You and Joanna are coming to lunch, aren't you? She should be home by then. I gather we're all going to have a nice chat about the wedding. Have you seen Joanna yet?'

'Briefly. This afternoon.'

Felicity smiled. 'This is all her fault, isn't it?'

'How do you mean?'

She punched him lightly on the shoulder. 'You know quite well.'

'She believes in waiting till we're married, 'Graham said stiffly. 'I have to respect that.'

'For your sake I hope it's worth waiting for.'

He wondered, not for the first time, whether the greater part of his attraction for Felicity was the fact that he was engaged to her stepdaughter.

Felicity lay back on the pillows. 'I think you're enjoying this. You know – having Joanna and screwing me at the same time. Good for the little male ego, eh? I wouldn't be surprised if you've got someone up in London, too. What's going to happen after you're married? I warn you: Joanna's the possessive type.'

Graham sipped his drink. He wanted Joanna very badly and she had made it clear that the only way he would get her was through marriage. In the circumstances he didn't mind that: a GP needed a wife and by all accounts Kevin Burwell was a rich man. Besides, he thought he might be in love with her.

'Don't worry,' Felicity went on. 'I shan't make waves.' She stroked his arm with her fingertips. 'I'll be here if you want me or the perfect mother-in-law if you don't.'

He moved his arm away. He stared at the carpet with post-coital self-pity. He wondered what she wanted. Women were all the same – Felicity, Joanna and Rachel: they wanted things he couldn't or didn't want to give them. The nice thing about Michael was that it was so easy to satisfy his desires.

Graham's eyes focused on a piece of mud near the armchair in the corner. What was it doing there? He had hoovered this room on Sunday evening – early on, before he had realised that Felicity wasn't coming. Too many questions. For example, why was Felicity being so bloody obliging?

'Graham? Knock, knock. Are you still there?'

'Of course I'll still want you. The question is, whether—'

'I said, don't worry. I understand.' Without warning her face crumpled. She leaned closer, and irritated him still further by spilling her drink on the duvet. 'Graham, I've got a problem. Can I talk to you about it? If Kevin finds out, he's going to murder me.'

8

Kevin Burwell sat in the BMW and nursed his anger. He hated to be kept waiting at the best of times, and these were not the best of times.

At last the silver-grey Rover approached from the south along White Cross Lane. He checked the clock on the dashboard. Errowby was nearly ten minutes late and Burwell was doing him a favour by being here at all.

The Rover was running behind the ragged hedgerow, the old field boundary dividing the building site from the public highway. The car signalled right and, rocking over the ruts, crawled up the track; its tyres sprayed the gleaming wings with mud. It stopped a few yards behind the BMW. Errowby was in the passenger seat and a young man was driving him: so presumably he was technically on duty. Burwell had the contempt of the self-employed for those who ran their private lives at the taxpayers' expense; and no doubt these so-called public servants were paid double-time for turning out on Saturday.

The nearside door swung open. Burwell got out of his own car and buttoned his overcoat. Errowby, his butter-yellow curls glinting in the thin winter sunlight, skipped up the track with a rolled-up architectural drawing under his arm. Bernie Errowby ran everywhere. The man was offensively and enviably healthy. Burwell noticed with pleasure that he wasn't wearing Wellingtons, and that the neat brown brogues were already spattered with dirt.

'Kevin, glad you could make it.'

'I haven't got much time. It's Saturday, you know. We've got people coming for lunch.'

'This shouldn't take long. Looking good, isn't it?' Errowby waved the drawing at the roofless walls, the scaffolding, a rusting cement-mixer and a stack of concrete blocks. 'I had an idea about the tropical fish. What about a whole wall of glass in the lounge? The effect would be stunning.'

'Maybe.'

'It was the wife's idea, in fact. I—'

'Any news?' Burwell interrupted.

Errowby pursed his tight little mouth and adopted an expression suitable for a pallbearer. 'I'm sorry, Kevin: I really am. We've pulled out all the stops on this one.'

'So you haven't got any leads?'

'As I told you, we've got the bloodstain. Once we get a suspect, it'll be easy. If his genetic fingerprint matches the bloodstain's, that's it.' Errowby slapped his right fist on the palm of his left hand. 'Wham, bam, we've got him. No court in the land would argue with that.'

'But you haven't got a suspect.'

'These things take time. I won't pretend it'll be easy. We may be unlucky. But it won't be for want of trying, I can promise you that.'

As he talked, Errowby was eyeing his dream house. Over the months the dream had grown. At first, Burwell had encouraged this: the more the project mushroomed, the greater the profit would be. In its latest guise the house was going to have five bedrooms, two en-suite bathrooms and a jacuzzi. Downstairs there would be parquet flooring throughout, except in the kitchen, which would have marble. A firm of landscape architects had submitted a series of proposals for the one-and-half-acre garden; these now included a heated swimming pool and a small artificial lake with a pump-driven waterfall.

'What have you actually done this week?' Errowby asked. 'I thought you were hoping to get the roof on.'

'And I thought I was going to get the second payment on account,' Burwell said. 'By the thirtieth of November, wasn't it?'

'Kevin, I've explained about that. As soon as my mother-in-law's house is sold—'

'It's been on the market for nearly twelve months. Why don't you get a bank loan on the strength of it? Or take out a second mortgage on your own house?'

'I'm looking into both those options very seriously.'

'I've given you two months' leeway, Bernie. I'm sorry, but I just can't afford to give you any more. Times are hard.'

Errowby seemed not to have heard. 'And I've had a bit of good news this week. Keep it under your hat, but B Division is in the bag.'

'That means promotion?'

'Detective Superintendent. And salary to match. About time too. All being well, I'll start at Easter.'

'Are you sure?'

'As much as you ever can be. The present bloke's let things slide, and they're easing him out – early retirement due to ill-health. I gather they're looking for a man with a bit of drive, with the right experience, with local knowledge; and a man who's physically and mentally fit.' Errowby preened himself. 'I play squash with the Assistant Chief Constable who handles personnel. He's the one who'll be pulling the strings at the promotion board. Strictly between ourselves, he's given me the nod.'

'Well, that's great,' Burwell said, riding his anger like a great wave. 'I'm delighted for you. I shall get down on my knees right now and thank almighty God for his wisdom and benevolence. And in the meantime you're too incompetent to find the bugger who nearly killed my daughter and you can't be bothered to pay your debts.'

'Look, Kevin, I've tried to—'

'You think that makes it all right? The fact you've tried? The point is, you *failed*. You—'

'Hush,' Errowby said.

It was not the policeman's voice but his face that stopped Burwell in mid-flow. He was staring intently to the right. His mouth was open. The teeth looked at though they were poised to bite someone.

'Did you hear it?'

Burwell shook his head.

'Someone's there. I heard footsteps.'

Beside the track ran a crumbling stone wall, four feet high, surmounted by a much younger, wooden fence, which brought the overall height up to seven feet; it formed the northern boundary of Errowby's land. The vertical planks had weathered badly: some hung askew, and others were cracked; as the wood had expanded and shrunk it had squeezed out the knots and left peepholes behind. Errowby was already peering through one of the holes.

Burwell stepped across a puddle and put his eye to another hole. He stared through the leafless branches of an overgrown japonica bush at dozens of red-and-blue gnomes disporting themselves on a lawn stained with moss.

He was just in time to see Bert Nimp slipping round the corner of his bungalow.

'Yes, a policeman,' Graham Hanslope said, wiping his feet on the mat. 'With a female accomplice, actually.'

Felicity shut the door. 'But what did they want?'

'They just called on the off-chance to see if I'd been at the cottage last Sunday. And I said, no, I hadn't been down since Friday.'

No doubt he was finding this amusing. He was enough of a bastard for that. Kevin had spent that Friday evening at one of those interminable masonic functions in Paulstock. Felicity and Graham had bounced around in the big bed for nearly two hours. The gin had given her a hangover next morning.

'Anyway,' he went on, 'that's why I'm a bit late. I must say the police are being very thorough. And so they should be, of course. Is Leonie out of hospital?'

'She's upstairs in bed – the journey took it out of her.'

'Darling!'

Joanna bounded down the stairs in a manner that revealed her long and beautifully shaped legs without, of course, any hint of indecency. Felicity had not seen them together since they got engaged. She expected Joanna to throw herself into Graham's arms. Instead she slowed as she reached the hall, perhaps to give Graham more time to admire her attractions. When she reached him she offered him her cheek. Graham threw his arms around her and kissed her on the lips.

'I've missed you so much,' he murmured.

'Why don't you take Graham into the drawing room and get him a drink?' Felicity said. 'I'm sure you two have got lots you want to talk about.'

'Where's Daddy?' Joanna asked.

'He had to go out unexpectedly – a business meeting. He'll be back at any moment.'

Felicity reached the kitchen with her dignity intact. Once the door was safely closed, she began to tremble. She hadn't realised it would be so difficult. In a couple of years, she told herself, he'll start running to fat; that sort of compact, hard-muscled body always does. And Joanna will never be able to keep him satisfied. It'll probably end in divorce.

She picked up the big cut-glass bowl she had planned to use for the green salad. She had never liked it – it had been a wedding present from one of Kevin's dreadful friends. Her eyes closed: she squeezed them shut to hold in the tears.

Suddenly she lurched forward and pushed the bowl away from her. It sailed across the table and shattered on the floor.

'What was the policeman like, darling?'

Graham shrugged. 'About my age. Not a pretty picture – he had one of those long, thin noses with a kink in the end.'

'We've met him,' Kevin said; he had sat in silence for the last ten minutes, his whisky untouched on the table beside him. 'Tall bloke. Rickford's his name. He's a detective sergeant.'

'You'll never guess,' Joanna went on. 'He's going to be a

neighbour of yours. He's leasing one of the studio flats at Copeland Court. He should be moving in next week.'

'Just as well I shall be moving out.' Graham grinned at her. 'They say policemen lower the tone of a neighbourhood.'

'In that case you might be unlucky,' Kevin said. 'You could have Bernie Errowby living two doors down from you in White Cross Lane.'

Graham raised his eyebrows. 'Errowby? Should I know him?'

At the same time Felicity said, 'What do you mean by "could have"?'

'I mean that unless he finds some money he's not going to have a house to move to. I told him straight: if I have to, I'll sue him.'

'Is that wise, Kevin?'

Her husband scowled. 'He's the one who's being stupid.'

'Errowby's the head of Paulstock CID,' Joanna explained to Graham.

'How *is* the decorating coming on?' Felicity asked him. 'You've been at it for ages. You must be doing a very painstaking job.'

'Slow but sure, Mrs Burwell. It's the wrong time of year, of course. And finding the time is the big problem.'

'You must call Kevin and me by our Christian names. No need to be so formal.'

He smiled his thanks, and ignored this barb as he had ignored the preceding one.

'It'll have to be done by Easter,' Joanna said. 'We've got to have somewhere to live. The flat's too small.'

'It will be, darling. I've already finished the bedroom.'

'I'm going to start helping you.'

'I'd love that.'

He looked at her as if he meant it, and Joanna looked back with adoration in her silly-cow eyes. Felicity felt sick.

'Shall we move into the dining room?' she said. 'Lunch should be ready.'

★   ★   ★

During lunch Felicity realised that there was no need to plan the wedding. Joanna had already done it. It only remained for the others to receive her instructions and foot the bills.

It was to be a white wedding, of course, in St Thomas's. Joanna wanted four bridesmaids, one of whom would be Leonie. The men would wear morning dress – all of them; not just the leading players in the ceremony. The reception was to be at Hampton Hall, a country-house hotel between Abbotsfield and Paulstock. Joanna thought they would have two to three hundred guests.

'Don't you think that's a little bit lavish?' Felicity suggested. 'They charge the earth at Hampton Hall.'

Joanna shook her head. 'I want it to be *nice*,' she said.

'Oh well,' Kevin said. 'If it's what you want.'

After lunch they had coffee in the drawing room. Joanna distributed lists; she had been busy with the word-processor and the photocopier at Lees and Bright. Each of them received an order of service, a guest list, an array of menus and quotations from Hampton Hall, and four pages of suggested wedding presents.

'It's all provisional, of course.' Joanna patted Graham's hand; they were sitting side by side on the sofa. 'I did most of it while you were in London. If you want any changes, just say.'

Graham, Felicity thought, looked bemused. He would have to be a brave man to suggest alterations of any significance, and a fool to believe that Joanna would accept them. He took another After Eight from the box beside him.

'You've been working amazingly hard,' he said, not committing himself either way.

Joanna blushed with pleasure. 'You'll have to give me a list of the people you want to invite.'

'Not many. About twenty people, perhaps.'

'I was wondering if you'd like your little nephew to be a page boy.'

'I don't think he'd like it.'

'Are you sure? I think having a page boy could be rather sweet.'

'No,' Graham said. 'Not Michael.'

'Have you asked Leonie about being a bridesmaid?' Felicity said. 'She might not want to either.'

'I'm sure she will,' Joanna said. 'Every girl of her age wants to be a bridesmaid.'

'She's going through a difficult patch at present.'

'Because of the accident?' Joanna smiled sweetly at her stepmother. 'Or because of Tammy Perran?'

'Both.'

'What's the problem with Tammy Perran?' Graham said.

'Have you met her? She's a friend of Leonie's. Rather unsuitable, I'm afraid, and in more ways than one.' Felicity suddenly saw a chance of enlisting medical support. 'Kevin and I feel that they're – well, unhealthily close, if you know what I mean. We're trying to prise them apart. What would be your advice? Professionally, as it were.'

'I'm not a psychologist so I can't advise you professionally,' Graham said. 'But Leonie's just a child, isn't she, when all's said and done. I expect she'll grow out of it in a month or two.'

'But there's no harm in our helping the process along, is there?'

'I suppose not. As long as it's done tactfully.'

'There,' Felicity said to Kevin. 'You see? Graham agrees.'

Kevin grunted. '"Tactfully"?'

'We're getting away from the point,' Joanna said. 'We're supposed to be talking about our wedding.' She switched her attention back to Graham. 'I've got some cousins on my mother's side who'll do for the other bridesmaids – a family of three girls; a bit younger than Leonie but that won't matter.'

'I don't want to be a bridesmaid.'

Everyone looked round. Leonie was standing in the doorway. She wore a faded blue dressing gown over her pyjamas. Her feet were bare.

'What do you think you're doing, young lady?' Kevin said.

'I was bored.'

'Come along.' Felicity stood up. 'Let's get you back to bed. Graham, I wonder if—'

He followed her to the door. After all, Leonie was one of his practice's patients so it was natural enough for her to ask and difficult for him to refuse. Felicity knew that she was unlikely to get another chance.

The examination didn't take long. They left Leonie watching a black-and-white costume drama on television. Felicity stopped on the stairs, forcing Graham to stop too.

'Have you had a chance to think about it yet?' she murmured.

'I'm sorry. The answer has to be no.'

'Look, even a small loan, a few hundred, would—'

'No. It's just not possible. What with the house and everything I'm fully stretched.'

'You don't have to look so bloody pleased about it.'

'There's another thing,' he went on. 'I've been thinking. You heard what Joanna said about helping me with the house. I think we should call it a day. Too risky. You'd better give me back the key I gave you.'

'You little *shit*.'

He waited in the hall while she fetched the key. She threw it at him. He caught it neatly.

'It's just for the time being,' he said. 'Who knows what will happen later?'

'I know one thing that won't be happening. You disgust me.'

When Graham said goodbye, Joanna allowed him to touch her breasts, albeit through several layers of clothing. They were alone in the conservatory. He thought that talking about their wedding had excited her.

'Graham,' she said, removing his burrowing hand. 'Everything will be all right, won't it?'

'Of course it will, darling,' he said, persevering with the other hand. He added absently, 'Anyway, what do you mean?'

'Our wedding. Moving into White Cross House. I couldn't bear it if something went wrong.'

He was so surprised by her vehemence that he stopped fondling her. Usually she was so controlled; that was part of her charm for him. The control wasn't due merely to her superstitious attachment to Christian morality – it went deeper than that.

'Darling, I feel just the same. You know how much I—'

'You don't know what it's like living here,' she interrupted.

He wished she would change the subject. 'But surely, darling, this is your home. Your father—'

'I told you. Daddy just tolerates me. I'm a sort of leftover from his past. Felicity can't wait to get rid of me. I think she's jealous – I think she fancies you.'

'Rubbish,' Graham said.

'As for Leonie – as far as she's concerned, I hardly exist.'

Joanna's eyes brimmed with tears. Graham took her hands and kissed them.

'Don't worry,' he murmured. 'I'll take care of you. Just you wait till we're—'

The door opened with such force that it slammed into the back of a wicker armchair.

'Oh,' Felicity said. 'Sorry. Am I interrupting something? I thought you'd left, Graham.'

'He's just going,' Joanna said. 'Aren't you, darling?'

Graham drove back to Paulstock in a good mood. The phone was ringing as he let himself into his flat. The caller gave up just before he reached it. It was a minor annoyance – not enough to dent his good humour. He had done everything he had intended to do at the Burwells'. He was proud of managing to give Felicity the push. She was becoming boring – quite simply not worth the risk. And this was especially true now that Joanna was showing definite signs of weakening.

The phone rang again as he was heating soup for his supper. He turned down the gas and went to answer it. Joanna, perhaps, or Rachel.

'Yes?'

'Is that Dr Hanslope?' The voice was no more than a whisper, ageless and sexless.

'Speaking. Who is this?'

'Listen to this.'

There was a click at the other end of the line; and at once he heard tinny voices, sometimes barely audible above the occasional creaking noise and a continuous background hiss.

'Have you seen Joanna yet?'

'Briefly. This afternoon.'

'This is all her fault, isn't it?'

'How do you mean?'

'You know quite well.'

'She believes in waiting till we're married. I have to respect that.'

'For your sake I hope it's worth waiting for. I think you're enjoying this. You know – having Joanna and screwing me at the same time. Good for the little male ego, eh? I wouldn't be surprised if you've got someone up in London, too. What's going to happen after you're married? I warn you: Joanna's the possessive type.'

9

'Please, God,' Oliver murmured. 'Be a sport.'

After a dry weekend, the weather had changed: it had become much milder and it rained almost without ceasing for forty-eight hours. Soon after dawn on the morning of Wednesday 6 February the rain at last decided it had had enough. Oliver stared through the window of the CID office at the grey roofs of Paulstock and prayed for a dry day and, more urgently, that the Chief Inspector would for once be late.

But the night shift still had quarter of an hour to run when Errowby arrived. He jogged in his red tracksuit through the double doors, nodded to Oliver and pranced across the room to the noticeboard. He began to flick through the night's entries in the grid crime and duty books.

'You're moving today, aren't you, Rickford?'

'Yes, sir.'

Oliver waited for the pronouncement that would wreck his plans. But the Chief Inspector turned back to the grid crime book, perhaps because he felt that the pleasure of ruining a subordinate's day was worth savouring. A minute passed.

Sharon came into the office. She grimaced at Errowby's back and grinned at Oliver. She was wearing very tight jeans, which – he couldn't help noticing – showed her figure to advantage, and she had done something different to her hair.

'Morning, sir,' she said to Errowby.

He did not reply. She sat down at her desk and began to write up her diary. On Wednesdays the Chief Inspector went through everyone's diary looking for trouble.

'I hope it stays dry for you,' Errowby said without turning round. 'Oh, and by the way. The Burwell case.'

'It's going nowhere, I'm afraid.'

Errowby grunted, a curious noise that made Oliver think of pigs scrambling round a trough at feeding time. The Chief Inspector's grunts were often used to express disapproval; this one, however, sounded almost benign.

'Why are you wasting time on it, then? I want to see some progress on those housebreakings. Did you see the *Guardian* last week?'

'The editorial?'

'Right. They're starting to snipe at us. Next time they'll be making hints about police inefficiency. And the time after that it'll be something worse. So let's see some results, eh?'

He swept out of the office to shower and change. Oliver looked at Sharon and found that she was already looking at him.

'Is it his birthday?' she said.

'Someone said he was playing squash last night.'

'With his mate the ACC? Our loss is B Division's gain, eh? The poor buggers.'

Oliver began to clear his desk. He was never comfortable with women who swore. He knew it was irrational, a relic of his Chapel upbringing. But he couldn't imagine Joanna Burwell swearing.

'All set for the move, then?'

He nodded.

'Have you got much to do?'

'Enough. Most of my stuff is in store so I'll need to buy a few things.'

The conversation foundered. A moment later Sharon said, 'Not much fun living out of suitcases.'

'No.'

'I did it for six weeks when I first came down here. Makes you feel like a nomad with a landlady. You get the worst of both worlds.'

'That's right.' Oliver, disagreeably aware he should be making a reciprocal effort, went on, 'But you've fixed yourself up now?'

'It's a flat over the newsagent's at the end of Park Street. Bit tatty, but it's home.' She hesitated. 'Look, you're not going to have much time for cooking tonight. If you want to come over, I'll do you my famous Spanish omelette.'

'No,' Oliver said. 'Thank you all the same, but I've already got something on this evening.'

She bent her head over her diary. 'That's all right, then.'

He wondered why he'd lied. He glanced at her. His eyes lingered. He was going to say that perhaps he could postpone whatever it was he planned to do and take her up on the famous Spanish omelette; but as he opened his mouth the internal phone on his desk began to ring.

'CID.'

'The Black Mask strikes again.' Wilson, the uniformed sergeant on the desk downstairs, could be relied on to be drearily facetious at any time of the day or night. 'Another case for our intrepid detectives.'

Oliver pulled a pad towards him. 'OK.'

'Reported break-in, eighty-nine Poolway Road. Nosy old lady just phoned in: widow, name of Fish, lives next door at ninety-one. House has been empty since the owner died last week. Want me to go on?'

'No,' Oliver said. As Wilson had been talking, Fintal had come in; and Oliver had waved him over. He covered the mouthpiece of the phone and passed the handset to Fintal. 'It's for you.'

If you stood on the highest part of the rockery and craned your head to the left, you could see across Dr Hanslope's garden and into the Perrans'; you could get quite a good view of the shed leaning against the high back wall.

Nimp could remember when the shed was just an open store; the Perrans' predecessors had used it to house an ancient Austin Seven and a pile of logs. Jimmy Perran, however, had added a front wall of concrete blocks, with a door in the centre flanked by large and obviously secondhand iron-framed windows. The door was secured by a padlock and curtains were always drawn across the windows.

As the rain had stopped, Nimp went out after breakfast to have a look at the shed. No doubt the alterations had been done without the benefit of planning permission. He wondered if the council ought to know. But the Perrans would almost certainly guess who had drawn attention to the matter. Perhaps it would be wiser to live and let live.

Winter or summer, Jimmy spent a lot of time in there. He had run a power line down from the house. Sometimes he backed his car or his van right up to the door.

'Lost your ball, have you?'

Nimp jumped. His foot slipped on the wet stone. Had he not had a firm grip on the wall he would have fallen. He turned round.

'You startled me, Jimmy.'

Perran was standing at the bottom of the flight of steps that wound up through the rockery. He wore jeans with a hole in the right knee and a black leather jacket.

'I – I thought you'd be at work.'

Perran bent down and picked up a stone about the size and shape of a cricket ball. 'I'm off sick.'

'I'm sorry to hear that, Jimmy.' Nimp rested his back against the wall. 'Nothing serious, I hope.'

'I'll survive.'

Perran smiled. He raised his arm and skipped, leaning backwards, like a fielder throwing the ball at the wicket.

'No, Jimmy, no—'

Perran threw the stone. Nimp covered his face with his hands. He tried to crouch but his body refused to obey him. The stone smashed into the wall a yard to his left. It fell into the branches of a cotoneaster. A few grains of mortar trickled down the wall.

Nimp folded his arms across the front of his overcoat to

stop them shaking. 'Jimmy,' he said with an attempt at dignity, 'I hope you don't think I—'

'You could have come a cropper on that stone,' Perran said. 'So I thought I'd better tidy it away.' He put his foot on the lowest step. 'Slippery, isn't it, after all this rain. And all those weeds would make it easy to trip.'

Nimp nodded, no longer trusting himself to speak.

'Mind you take care on your way down. You could have a nasty fall, an old man like you. Very nasty.'

'What do you want?'

'Old bones break easy, they say. Or there again you might hit your head on a rock.'

'I shouldn't want to do that.'

'I'll tell you the best way to avoid it. Don't go up there in the first place. There you are. Simple.'

'That's a very good idea, Jimmy. Very thoughtful of you.'

'That's what neighbours are for. Suzette's run out of sugar. She wondered if you could lend us a cupful.'

'Of course. Only too glad.'

Perran waited, still smiling, while Nimp crept down the steps. His legs shook. He noticed that Perran wasn't carrying a cup. Nimp hurried through the gnomes, almost tripping over Eustace, to the back door. Perran followed him into the kitchen.

'Must be lonely here by yourself,' Perran said, glancing around. 'Just you and the gnomes, eh? Does it worry you sometimes?'

'I manage, thank you.' Nimp opened the door of the walk-in larder and looked for the sugar. In his haste he knocked over the flour. Two apples thudded, one by one, on to the tiled floor.

'I mean, what if you had an accident? You could lie here for days and no one would know.'

'Here. Take this. No need to return it – I've got plenty.'

Nimp thrust a full packet of caster sugar at Perran, who weighed it in his hand as he had weighed the stone. His hands, Nimp noticed, were out of proportion to the rest of his body:

rough-skinned and muscular, they should have belonged to a giant. The tip was missing from the little finger of the left hand.

'Thanks,' Perran said. 'You won't forget now, will you?'

'I'm sorry?'

'To take care of yourself. Remember, you're not as young as you were. But don't worry, Bert. Me and Suzette will keep an eye on you. That's what neighbours are for.'

'Leonie's fine,' Joanna said on Wednesday evening. 'But Daddy says the police have given up trying to find the driver.'

'That's terrible.' Graham put down his glass of mineral water, stretched his arm along the back of the sofa and leant a little closer to her. This was the first time she had come uninvited to the flat; he interpreted it as a good omen. 'But I assume there's nothing they can do.'

'Did you know they have a clue? That's what makes it so frustrating for Daddy. They're not making it public, but they've found a bloodstain on Leonie's scarf. It was a new scarf. So they think the blood may belong to the man who knocked her down.'

'The man?'

'It's usually a man, isn't it? Women drivers are much more sensible. Anyway, I suppose they know his blood group if nothing else.'

Graham made a rapid recovery while she was talking. The news was unsettling but not fatal. True, it was foul luck – that the cut on his hand had still been bleeding and that the rain had failed to wash away a drop of blood; and a bloodstain was the sort of hard evidence that would never go away. However, looking at it sensibly, he could see no need to panic. The police had found out nothing damaging in the last eleven days, and now it seemed they weren't even trying.

'If the police have found a bloodstain,' he said, 'they can tell a lot more about him than his blood group. It means that they could probably make a positive or negative identification if they found a suspect.' He turned as he spoke, allowing his hand to drop as if by accident on Joanna's shoulder. 'Nowadays you can separate the DNA from a blood sample and track down the hypervariable regions. They're almost as unique as a fingerprint.'

'It sounds awfully technical, darling.' Joanna inched away from him. 'Talking of Leonie, she's agreed to be a bridesmaid.'

'How on earth did you manage it? You're a marvel.' Graham's experience had led him to believe that flattery, the less subtle the better, was one of the most efficient erotic crowbars at man's disposal.

'Oh, the poor dear was feeling off-colour on Sunday. She's really quite sensible.' Joanna stared complacently at her legs; she was wearing black tights today and, in Graham's view, the complacency was fully justified. 'Especially if you approach her in the right way.'

'Which I'm sure you did. You've got a talent for handling people. It was one of the first things I noticed about you.'

Joanna rewarded him with a smile that made him feel quite ill with lust. She drained her orange juice.

'Have another drink.'

'No, I really must get home.'

'Please stay.' His hand fell to her breast. He squeezed what felt like an armour-plated bra. 'We could go out to dinner. Or I'll cook you something here.'

He tried to kiss her but she turned her head away.

'Don't spoil it, Graham.' She disengaged herself and stood up. 'You know what we agreed.'

'I know what you said.' His voice sounded sulky even to himself.

She smoothed down her skirt and avoided his eyes. 'Not until we're married. It's for your sake as much as mine. You wouldn't thank me for it. Not in the long run.'

'For God's sake—'

'Please, Graham.'

He almost said it: *Stop hiding behind your God, you brainless bitch.*

'Sorry,' he muttered.

Suddenly it occurred to him that perhaps God had nothing to do with it. Perhaps she believed that if she gave way to his advances he would no longer need to make her Mrs Graham Hanslope. At least it showed how much she loved him. Or did it? Perhaps it merely showed how badly she wanted to escape from her family or how badly she wanted a home of her own. *The selfish bitch.* Self-pity flooded over him. Women were all the same.

Joanna flashed a forgiving smile at him. 'Haven't you got tomorrow off? You can take me out to lunch if you want.'

'I'm going up to London,' he said curtly.

'Again?'

She waited for him to expand. Instead he fetched her coat from the hall.

'Well then,' she said, turning her back to him as he helped her into it, 'I probably won't see you again until Saturday afternoon.'

'Probably not,' he agreed.

'Shall we meet at White Cross House after lunch?'

'As you like.'

'I haven't done any decorating for years.'

He said nothing. She buttoned up the coat. In silence he escorted her down to the car. In the communal hall they met Oliver Rickford coming in with his head bowed over a box of groceries.

'Good evening,' he said; he glanced at Joanna with startled eyes and began to sidle past them.

'Did you move in all right?' Joanna said.

'Fine, thanks.'

'I'm so glad. You know my fiancé, I think? Graham Hanslope – Oliver Rickford.'

'We have met. If you'll excuse me . . .'

Rickford broke away and headed for the waiting lift. Graham and Joanna walked out to the car park.

'That copper fancies you,' he said as he opened the door of her car. For all he knew it was true.

'Oh, don't be ridiculous.' Her voice was breathless. 'He's just a bit shy. A lot of men are. You'd be surprised.'

Graham laughed. 'He may be shy but he still fancies you. And what do you think of him?'

'I wish you'd stop this. You bring everything down to this – this *animal* level. It's horrible.' Joanna climbed into the car without offering him her cheek. She was trembling. She started the engine and made an effort to speak normally: 'Well, goodbye, darling. See you on Saturday.'

Graham slammed the door.

10

Graham was early. At 10.25 a.m. on Thursday 7 February, he emerged from the Underground at Charing Cross and walked down to the Embankment. It was too early in the year for there to be many tourists. The other pedestrians hurried along, dour-faced, their heads bent to ward off the wind.

In the Embankment Gardens, scruffy pigeons pecked the paths and gulls wheeled overhead. Graham made a detour to avoid a derelict person of indeterminate age and sex huddling on a bench. Vagrants made him uneasy; they offered a glimpse of the pit into which poverty might tip you. This one was flanked by a protective screen of plastic bags. He, she or it raised their head to watch Graham pass.

'Snuff air.' The voice was male and raised to a hoarse shout that blended with the roar of engines. 'Snuff air.'

Graham hurried on. Later, as he stared at the river, a sense of foreboding crept over him. He blamed it on the weather, the scenery and the sight of that disgusting old tramp; there ought to be a law to keep the homeless off the streets. He hated these grey London days when the Thames smelled like a great serpent slithering in its own slime through the city. Shivering, Graham left the Embankment and walked north towards the Strand. The smell of the river rose above the traffic fumes and pursued him across roads and around corners. He was still shivering when he turned into Sussex Court at ten to eleven. Perhaps he was fighting a virus.

'It's not fair,' he muttered to himself.

The address he wanted was near the end of the alley. Custodemus House resembled a police station – one of those miniature fortalices in concrete built just after the war with no window less than ten feet above the pavement. As Graham climbed the steps to the front entrance a security camera examined him. For an instant he hesitated. Was this visit really wise? Events had forced him into a corner. Somehow he had to find a way out. But coming here might make matters even worse.

Clearly he did not look like the vanguard of a rioting mob for the great doors swung inwards before he reached them. Inside he glimpsed a foyer crowded with palm trees in tubs and men wearing lapel badges. Immediately to the right of the doors was a reception desk. A uniformed guard was looking at him. He had white hair, a red face and a blue uniform.

The doors that opened of their own volition and the guard who stared at him: between them they prevented Graham from turning tail. He had left it too late to change his mind without looking foolish.

'Good morning, sir,' the guard said. 'And how can I help you?'

'My name's Hanslope. I have an appointment at eleven with Mr Dougal.'

'If you ask me,' Mrs Fish said, 'he should have gone into a home long ago. Getting senile, he was. And the son in Bristol never bothered to come down. It's not right, is it? Not fair on the neighbours, either.'

'Let me get this straight,' Oliver said, expertly separating the wheat from the chaff. 'He died last week on Monday. The son came down, and there was an announcement of the death in last week's *Guardian*. The funeral was last Friday. And since then the house has been empty?'

Mrs Fish nodded. She was a small, plump woman in her sixties and everything about her was sensible: her short grey permed hair and her steel-rimmed glasses; the absence of make-up apart from a light dusting of face powder; the mud-coloured cardigan, the thick tweed skirt and the sturdy brown lace-up shoes. Her face wore what seemed to be a permanent expression of disapproval, as if she had never come to terms with the fact that the rest of world was not as sensible as she.

'What made you think the house had been burgled?' Sharon asked.

'I'll show you,' Mrs Fish said to Oliver; she had ignored Sharon since their arrival. 'Come into the kitchen.'

The kitchen window was at the side of the house. If you were standing at the sink you could see over the fence to the top of the matching window in the side wall of the house next door.

'Yesterday morning, the top flap of that window was a little bit open,' Mrs Fish said. 'Oh aye, I said to myself: looks like trouble. If I told the old fool once, I must have told him a hundred times. You need window locks these days, I said. At least they waited till he was dead.'

'They?' Oliver said without much hope.

'Half the world seems to have got light fingers. I blame the welfare state myself, and the comprehensives, of course. These kids grow up with no sense of right or wrong. The ones that are too stupid to get jobs start stealing. And your lot don't do much to stop them.'

'We try.'

'Anyway, why are you here? I thought they'd finished yesterday.'

'Just checking on things.'

'More like bolting the stable door after the horse has gone. You won't get the stuff back. You won't get the men who did it.'

'Did you hear anything on Tuesday night? A car starting up in the early hours, for instance?'

'No. I was asleep, like all decent folk should be. I said all this yesterday. Couldn't your friend read his notes or something?'

'We understand you have a spare key. May we borrow it?'

'You're gluttons for punishment, aren't you? The place still smells, you know. It was me that found the old fellow.'

'We'll cope.'

She pursed her lips, opened a drawer and gave them a key. 'It's the back door. And make sure you lock up carefully.'

Keeping well clear as though they were carrying an infectious disease, Mrs Fish ushered them down the hall and out of her house.

Oliver unlatched the gate of 89 Poolway Road. 'What's up with her, do you think?'

'According to Fintal she was done for shoplifting about twenty years ago,' Sharon said. 'Pleaded not guilty and got six months' suspended.'

Graham had not anticipated the immense and immediate relief that confession brings: telling someone – *anyone* – made this horrible affair easier to bear. A trouble shared is a trouble halved. The relief was swiftly followed by irritation. Dougal took it all so casually.

Graham gave him an edited version of his affair with Felicity Burwell, one that suggested he was more sinned against than sinning. While he talked he watched Dougal. He was a slim man with badly cut brown hair; in his late thirties, Graham guessed, and on the scruffy side. On his desk was a photograph of a woman and a baby. Both blondes. The woman might be quite good-looking. It was hard to tell because the photograph was angled in such a way that Graham could not look closely at it without making his interest obvious.

Suddenly Dougal started asking about the blackmailer's phone call. 'This tape recording. You're sure it was you?'

Graham felt himself flush. 'Yes, our conversation was taped.' An old legal description of adultery, 'criminal conversation', floated into his mind. 'It wasn't just – ah – *noises,* you understand. Names were mentioned, I'm afraid. It was quite obvious who we were.'

'Man or woman?'

'I don't know. The voice was a whisper.'

'And what exactly did the blackmailer want?'

'Five hundred pounds in used notes, small denominations.'

'It sounds a disturbingly modest demand.'

'What do you mean by that?'

'There are two ways to blackmail someone. Either you go for the jackpot right away or you think of it as a longterm relationship. If it's the latter, there's a lot to be said for starting off with a relatively small demand. Did you pay up?'

Graham nodded.

'That was foolish, of course. And now you're afraid that he or she may come back for more?'

'There were reasons why it seemed wiser to pay.'

'Such as?'

'To get a breathing space. Time to work out what to do for the best.'

'What were the arrangements?'

'I was to leave the money in a plastic carrier bag on a building site near my house. There's a hedge at the back with a footpath along the other side. I was told I'd find a small yellow drum – builders' rubbish; it used to contain concrete. I had to leave the money there by Tuesday evening.'

'And the tape?'

'Would be posted back to me. So far I haven't had it.'

'Were you at home on Tuesday evening? Weren't you tempted to try to find out who the blackmailer was?'

'It wasn't as simple as that.' Graham explained that he was not living in the house at present, and that in any case he had been on call that evening. 'Besides, it was dark and there's nowhere to hide.'

'What's beyond the footpath?'

'Open fields.'

'If you want us to take this further, perhaps you'd draw me a map. Now, how did the blackmailer make the tape? A tape recorder in the bedroom?'

'Presumably.'

'So either he knew when you'd be there or he had a voice-activated tape recorder. Any sign of a break-in?'

'It wouldn't have been difficult. I noticed a bit of mud on the carpet, which was odd because I'd hoovered the previous Sunday evening. I hadn't been there since then.'

'How would he have got in?'

'A pane of glass in the back door got broken. I covered the hole with a bit of plywood. You could probably prise it off quite easily. There's a Yale but there's something wrong with it – you can't deadlock it.'

Dougal scribbled a few words on the pad in front of him. 'All this suggests that it's someone who lives locally, someone who knows you, doesn't it? Have you made any enemies? Is there anyone who has a reputation for poking his nose into other people's business?'

'There's an old man who lives in the house between mine and the building site. Mildly eccentric and certainly nosy.'

'Sounds a possibility. Though you'd think he wouldn't arrange for the drop to be on his doorstep.' Dougal tapped the point of his biro on the pad. 'Look, Dr Hanslope, blackmail is a serious crime. Why didn't you get in touch with the police?'

Graham had hoped that Dougal would be sufficiently tactful or self-serving to avoid this question. 'I told you,' he said. 'In my position—'

'That's nonsense. They'd be discreet.'

'I can't be sure of that. The head of the local CID is a close friend of the woman's husband.'

'He'd still be unlikely to gossip. He'll have his career to think about.'

Graham shook his head. 'It's a risk I just can't take.'

'Well, you should. My advice is go to the police.'

A flurry of rain smacked against the window. Graham stared at the schedule of charges on his lap. His hands had been sweating and the shiny paper was smudged with damp.

'Can't you do something?' he blurted out.

'You've given me very little to go on. You must see that.'

'But if there *is* another blackmail demand, would you come down and find out what you can?'

'I could try. But I'd need a lot more information and I can't promise results. And whatever happens it wouldn't be cheap. As I said, your best bet is the police.'

'If I knew who it was, you see, I could cope with it.'

'You'd fight fire with fire, you mean?'

'That's one way of putting it.'

'The trouble with playing with fire,' Dougal said, 'is that you tend to get burned. You said you had reasons for paying up. In the plural. What were the others?'

'Did I? I don't remember.'

'At the beginning I asked you to tell me everything – everything that might conceivably be relevant. If I'm going to help I need to know what you know.'

'I've told you what I know.'

The slight emphasis on the last word betrayed him. Dougal pounced. 'But not what you suspect.'

'As it happens, the – ah – woman in question is in a bit of a financial hole. In fact she tried to borrow money from me. Also I lent her a key to the house – we meet there, you see. Or rather met. I've got the key back now, but she could have got in when I wasn't there. On Saturday I told her I thought it would be better if we – ah – terminated our relationship.'

'I see. In other words, just before the blackmailer phoned, you'd refused her a loan and given her the push?'

'You could put it like that.'

'Money and revenge: two birds with one stone? But if it came out, she could end up in prison with a ruined marriage behind her. Would you say she's that desperate?'

'How should I know?' Graham said.

'If she were jealous as well . . . Am I right in thinking that there's someone else in the picture?'

'You might as well know. I suppose you'll have to if you're going to help. I'm engaged to be married to her stepdaughter.'

Oliver and Sharon walked down the side of 89 Poolway Road. Next door, Mrs Fish watched them through her kitchen window.

Poolway Road was on the outskirts of Paulstock, a residential development built in the 1960s. The houses were small, modern and detached.

'The bloke wouldn't have parked at the front,' Oliver said. 'He's not a fool.'

He passed the back door and followed the concrete path that bisected the length of the garden – a rectangular strip of grass protected by lines of evergreens on either side; it was drab, damp and green. The path led down to a bolted gate. He opened it and stared at the playing fields beyond.

Sharon pointed at a new, single-storey building a hundred yards to their left. 'That's a football and cricket pavilion,' she said. 'Burwell's firm built it, in fact. He made a great song and dance about only wanting to cover his costs. So there was a picture of the great philanthropist on the front page of the *Paulstock Guardian.*'

The building was much too small to have a resident caretaker. 'Nothing to stop our friend parking there,' Oliver said. 'He'd be out of sight under the trees. There's even a path, so he wouldn't have got his feet wet. Easy enough to climb over the gate.'

They went back through the garden and into the house, which – despite Mrs Fish's dark hints – smelled of nothing worse than old age and stale air. Yesterday, the Scene of the Crime Officers had been through the place. They had established that the intruder had worn gloves and that he had forced the window catch with a flat-bladed tool, probably a one-inch chisel. The last burglary, the Willow Lodge job on Sunday 27 January, had been done by someone with a chisel.

Oliver and Sharon went from room to room. No one had tidied up. Drawers lay upside down on top of their contents. Cupboard doors hung open. The mattresses had been tossed off the beds; it was surprising how many people still entrusted their portable assets to the oldest of hiding places.

As always the chaos depressed Oliver. The scene of a burglary was a taste of anarchy; and the flavour turned his stomach. At least in this case the real victim was already dead.

'Even if he had a rucksack or something, he can't have carried off anything very bulky,' Sharon said as they went back to the kitchen. 'Not without a car handy. Must have really pissed him off. All that Victorian mahogany downstairs would fetch a bob or two.'

One problem was that they did not know exactly what was missing. No one had had time to make an inventory of the dead man's possessions since his death and before the burglary. According to Fintal, the son hadn't been down to Paulstock for eighteen months; he was a tyre salesman with too many commitments; he earned a large income and didn't have time to spend it. His visits to Paulstock last week had been as brief as possible, and he hadn't even made a start on clearing out the house. He had told Fintal that his father might have had a few bits and bobs of his mother's jewellery; that there used to be an old engraving, an eighteenth-century map of Somerset, in the living room; and that his father had thought that banks were immoral.

Oliver paused, his hand already on the back-door knob. 'That's odd.'

'What is?'

He crouched, opened the cupboards under the work surface and glanced at their contents, which the thief had hardly disturbed. He pushed aside the teapot and examined the pair of electric sockets behind it. 'What did the old man use to heat his water in?'

'No kettle? What about a saucepan?'

'It'd be somewhere obvious.' Oliver pointed to a ring of grime around one of the sockets. 'He had something plugged in there more or less permanently.'

They checked with Mrs Fish when they returned the key. The old man had bought a jug kettle a few months before he died; she remembered him complaining that it wasn't as efficient as his old one.

Afterwards they went back to the car. Sharon slid into the driving seat. She was about to start the engine when Oliver told her to wait.

'What do you think?' he said. 'Same bloke?'

'I wouldn't bet on it.'

Oliver pulled an Ordnance Survey map out of the pocket in the passenger door. 'Why not?'

'For starters this is in a town, and whoever did it had to walk back to his car. Also, all the other jobs were miles away.'

'Eight since October. This would be number nine.' He bent over the map. He had already made eight crosses in red felt-tip; he added the ninth in Paulstock. 'OK. See a pattern?'

Sharon leaned over the map. He smelled her perfume and had to force himself not to edge away from her. What made it worse was that part of him would have liked to move closer.

'They're all over the shop,' she said. 'I think we could be dealing with two or three separate operators.'

'Imagine the crosses are enclosed in a circle. Where would the centre be?'

She frowned. A strand of her hair touched Oliver's cheek.

'The nearest town or village, you mean? I suppose it would be somewhere like Abbotsfield.'

The interview at Custodemus had disturbed Graham more than he liked to admit. Thanks to his job, he was used to dealing with most people he met from a position of strength. In his surgery a doctor is omnipotent; and even in ordinary life he is often accorded the sort of respect that used to belong to the clergy. The only problem was that Graham was vulnerable when the roles were reversed. When the senior partner in the practice disagreed with a diagnosis, for example, or when Sue treated him as her baby brother, he tended to react with either anger or confusion. In these situations, which were familiar, he had learned to some extent how to cope; he now knew how to conceal what he was feeling. But when he found himself unexpectedly on the defensive, as had happened this morning, the old difficulty recurred.

'Of course I wasn't at my best,' he reassured himself over lunch in Covent Garden. 'It's this bloody flu.'

In the afternoon he decided to cosset himself. He went to

Hamley's and spent a little over fifty pounds on Legoland models for Michael; it was as if he were twenty years younger and buying them for himself. Michael's birthday was exactly a week away, on the fourteenth of February. Sue could not reasonably object to Graham's giving his nephew a few presents.

Later he had tea in Fortnum and Mason's; the food and the company of well-groomed women helped him to regain his serenity. He took the Underground to Chiswick. He reached the dentist's surgery in Belmont Road ten minutes before it closed.

Rachel was delighted to see him. Graham watched her lighting up with an interior glow like a Hallowe'en pumpkin. She drove him back to her flat. On their way in, they met Rachel's new neighbour in the flat downstairs. He was a tall, bony young man and he obviously wanted to chat. They pushed past him, rushed upstairs and made love on the living-room carpet.

Afterwards Rachel asked him how long he could stay. He told her that he had to catch a train leaving Paddington in an hour and a half; in fact he was in no particular hurry. He saw the glow fade and die. He felt himself again. He felt safe.

'I've missed you so much,' she said. 'Why can't I come and see you?'

'I've told you: it's a tiny flat and I'm working all the hours God brings. I don't want to spend my spare time there too.' He nuzzled her breast. 'I want to come and find you here.'

'It sounds as though you miss London as much as you miss me.'

'Don't be stupid.'

'Have you got someone else down there?'

This was getting boring. Graham cupped her face in his hands and kissed her. 'If you could see the women they have down there, you wouldn't ask that question. I'd sooner shag sheep.'

She giggled.

'Anyway, what about you? I bet your neighbour's aching to slip between your sheets.'

'Jack? He's just a boy.'

His pretended jealousy soothed her, as he had known it would. For a few minutes he let her stroke him. If only, he thought, I could combine Joanna with Rachel: life would be perfect. Then he remembered why he was in London, why nothing could be perfect until that difficulty was sorted out. He pushed Rachel's hand away.

'I have to go soon. Do you mind if I have a shower?'

11

Simba was responsible for Felicity's decision to go to White Cross Lane. For the first time in her life, the labrador served a useful purpose.

Kevin had bought Simba as a puppy when Leonie was a toddler. 'It's good for kids to have a dog around,' he'd said to Felicity. 'Anyroad, it'll be company for you during the day.'

If Simba counted as company, Felicity would have preferred to be left alone. She needed walking and feeding; she had to be forcibly ejected from the house several times a day; in her old age she rediscovered the incontinence of youth; she required to be ferried with expensive frequency to the vet's; like a moulting, semi-detached shadow she followed Felicity round the house and pined when they were parted for any length of time; she barked at innocent strangers and once – a point in her favour – she had bitten Bernie Errowby when he made a pass at her mistress. For that was the worst of it: Simba loved Felicity, and a love you cannot return makes you feel guilty.

Usually Kevin took Simba for her walk on Saturday mornings. Today, however, he had claimed that he had to go to Paulstock to play golf and talk business; and he said that he wouldn't be back until teatime. Felicity replied that it was a typical male excuse: he was going out to enjoy himself; he was evading his responsibilities by pretending to be working.

By ten o'clock she could not decently postpone the walk for any longer. Simba had been whining for the last half an hour. Felicity was unable to delegate the job because Leonie had gone out to the library, and Joanna was still in her bedroom, titivating herself, no doubt, for her afternoon rendezvous with Graham.

Felicity slipped the collar over Simba's head and took her outside.

Simba was responsible for what happened next because she made Felicity angry. Had Felicity not lost her temper, both of them would have been more than satisfied by the routine five-minute walk (or, in Simba's case, waddle) round the block. But once outside, the labrador decided not to co-operate. Felicity had to drag her down the drive. Finally she lost her temper and, sheltered by the shrubbery from prying neighbours, gave Simba a thrashing with the lead.

'Right, you fat bitch,' Felicity said, panting. 'Today you're going to get a proper walk.'

She tugged Simba across the road and took her down to White Cross Lane, beyond which was a field where Simba in the far-off days of her youth had chased rabbits. It was a bright, clear morning; the air was cold and hard at the back of Felicity's throat and her cheeks tingled; by the time she reached the sleeping policeman, the place where Leonie had nearly died, she was almost enjoying herself.

'Good morning, Mrs Burwell.' Bert Nimp came round the corner, a shopping basket on wheels rattling behind him. He touched his hat. 'A fine day.'

She muttered a reply. Unlike Kevin, she didn't hate Mr Nimp, but he gave her the creeps. When she was a teenager, he had been one of the churchwardens at St Thomas's; and there had been a rumour that he liked to fondle young girls in the vestry.

'Do you happen to know if Dr Hanslope is coming over this morning?'

She stopped, not bothering to conceal her irritation. 'No, why should I?' she said, more sharply than she had intended. Simba collapsed on the pavement and rested her head on her paws.

'I thought perhaps – ah – Joanna might have mentioned something. It's nothing important. Just that the guttering behind his garage is leaking, and I wondered if he knew.'

The sun was in Felicity's eyes: she couldn't see Nimp's face. He was waiting for her to reply, his left hand cupped behind his ear. She might have imagined the malice in his voice. He couldn't possibly know about her and Graham. They had been too careful.

'I'll ask Joanna to mention it,' she said coldly. 'I think she's seeing him this afternoon.'

'Don't think I'm interfering but a leak like that can cause a lot of damage in the long run.'

'I'm sure you're right.' Felicity yanked Simba to her feet. 'Well, I must be going.'

Nimp touched his hat again. 'So glad to see Leonie up and about again. She looks as fit as a fiddle this morning.'

'Yes, it is a relief. Goodbye.'

She had reached the junction before the implication dawned on her. Nimp had seen Leonie this morning: yet the library was in the opposite direction from White Cross Lane.

Simultaneously, Simba barked and pulled on the lead – not to the left, where the entrance to the field lay beyond Bernie Errowby's building site, but to the right. Suzette Perran was hanging out washing in the front garden of her house. Leonie and Tammy Perran were fifty yards away, walking down the lane.

'Leonie!' Felicity shouted.

Her daughter turned.

'Come here.'

Leonie walked slowly towards her mother. The bag of library books was slung over her shoulder. Her face was pale and calm. Tammy stayed where she was, by the phone box, following Leonie with her eyes and shifting her weight from foot to foot. Suzette, a peg between her teeth, stared at them over the washing line.

'You've started lying to me now, have you?' Felicity said when Leonie was too close for them to be overheard.

'I said I was going to the library. I am.'

'Not with Tammy you aren't.'

Leonie shrugged.

'I want you to go home. You can take Simba with you.'

'Aren't you coming?'

'In a moment.'

Leonie's eyes flickered. She trailed away with Simba trotting after her. Felicity crossed the road. Tammy was still standing in the middle of the lane but Felicity ignored her. She leant over the low wall of the Perrans' front garden.

'I want a word with you.'

Suzette removed the peg from her mouth. 'Oh, aye?'

'I thought my husband had had a chat with yours.'

'Daresay he has. They work together, don't they?'

Felicity examined Suzette: the unwashed hair; the spotty cheeks; the remains of yesterday's make-up on the face; the pink, fluffy high-heeled slippers on the feet. The contrast with her own trim appearance reinforced her sense of righteousness.

'A little chat about Leonie seeing too much of Tammy. I thought he'd explained that Leonie just can't afford the time this year, what with exams and everything. It's nothing personal, but there it is.'

'I can't help it if they bump into each other. It's a free country, isn't it?'

'I hope Leonie isn't still coming to your house.'

'How do I know? I'm out most of the day.'

Suzette turned away as if ending the conversation. She hung up a peach-coloured nylon nightdress that was presumably her own; it was not much larger than a string vest and would conceal roughly as much of her body.

Felicity smiled. 'You work part-time at the Cattery, don't you?' The Cattery was the ailing tea shop near the church.

'What's that to you?'

'Margaret Telford's a good friend of mine. She's always saying how easy it is to get waitresses. All these young girls – practically falling over themselves to earn a bit of pocket money.'

Suzette picked up her laundry basket, which was still full of wet washing. 'I've got to go now.'

'Still, I imagine it's a great consolation to you both.'

'You what?'

Felicity widened her eyes in mock surprise. 'Having two incomes, of course. One can't be too careful these days, can one? Especially now the building trade's in a recession. It must be such a worry for you.'

'I don't know what you're talking about.' Suzette's voice lost its defiance. 'Look, it's nothing to do with me. If our Tammy isn't—'

'I mustn't keep you any longer, Mrs Perran. Do tell Jimmy I was asking after him.'

Felicity crossed the road. Tammy was standing in the same position as before, examining her hands. The girl was slow to the point of backwardness, Felicity thought – perhaps her parents were related to each other; inbreeding used to be a common problem in Abbotsfield, and pockets of it still existed.

She walked briskly into Meadow Way, buoyed up by the consciousness of a job well done, of a duty enjoyed. You had to handle these people firmly; it was the only sort of language they understood. Jimmy Perran roared past her in his blue Cortina. Felicity did not wave.

When she got home, Simba was waiting in the hall. Felicity scratched the dog's head. It looked as if Joanna was still upstairs; her letters lay untouched on the hall table. Music – the rhythmic disco drivel that Leonie liked so much – filled the house. Leonie was playing it far too loudly in her bedroom, no doubt as a form of protest.

Felicity didn't bother to take off her Barbour jacket but straightaway marched up the stairs. Today, for once in her life, she was standing no nonsense from anyone. She charged into Leonie's bedroom. Leonie was lolling on the bed. When she saw her mother, she turned her head to the wall. Felicity ripped the plug of the sound system from its socket.

The sound of retching filled the silence.

'What on earth—'

She wheeled round and went back to the landing. The

bathroom door was opposite Leonie's, and it was a few inches ajar. Felicity pushed it open. Joanna, still in her dressing gown, was kneeling on the floor with her arms wrapped round the bowl of the lavatory.

'What's wrong?'

Joanna retched again for an answer. The room smelled sour.

'Tummy bug,' Felicity said. 'You'd better get back to bed as soon as you can. Take a bowl with you, just in case.'

Joanna raised her head. She looked, and no doubt was, drained. 'I feel awful,' she croaked.

'Well, get into bed.'

'I can't. I'm meeting Graham this afternoon.'

'Don't be ridiculous. You're not meeting anyone. I'll bring you up a hot-water bottle, and I suppose we'd better take your temperature.'

Moving like an old woman, Joanna hauled herself up by the wash basin. She splashed water on her face and hands.

'Could you phone him for me?' she whispered. 'I don't think I could face talking to anyone.' As if to reinforce the request, she moaned and knelt once more by the lavatory.

'All right. Is he at the Health Centre this morning?'

'He should be at the flat. The number's in my diary.'

Felicity, who knew the number by heart, rummaged through Joanna's extraordinarily tidy handbag; she found the diary and took it downstairs. She didn't want to ring Graham. But there was some consolation in being the bearer of what she assumed would be bad news, and even more in the spectacle of Miss Bossy-Boots laid low. She decided to phone from the kitchen while she was waiting for the kettle to boil for the hot-water bottle. Simba was lying in front of her.

'Piss off, Fatso,' Felicity said, and strode towards the phone. It began to ring just before she picked it up.

By the time Kevin Burwell returned to the bar, Harold Quarme had bought the first round and staked their claim to the table in the bay window. It was only just after midday but the room was already filling up. For many members, golf in February was not really an outdoor pastime.

'Sorry to be so long,' Burwell said. 'I promised to phone my mother before lunch. She's difficult to stop in mid-flow.'

Quarme, who was thin and anxious and had looked prematurely middle-aged since his early teens, smiled and took a tiny sip of his very weak whisky.

'I thought we'd lunch here,' Burwell went on. 'If that's all right with you?'

Quarme nodded.

Burwell repressed a sigh. Harold Quarme had never uttered an unnecessary syllable in the thirty-five years that Burwell had known him. 'Cheers, then.' He finished his whisky. 'Can I get you another one of those?'

'No, thank you.'

'The reason I wanted to—'

'You blind or something?'

The shouted words silenced the room. Everyone looked towards the bar. Chief Inspector Errowby was standing on tiptoe and pulsating with anger. The object of his rage was a tall man with a hangdog expression on his face; Burwell knew him slightly – he was one of the partners in Lees and Bright. June Errowby was hanging on to her husband's arm and trying to pull him away.

'You did that on purpose, didn't you? My wife's dress is *soaked.*'

'It's only a few drops on the sleeve, dear.'

Errowby brushed her hand away. 'Well?'

The estate agent apologised in a high, piping voice and tried to buy Errowby a drink to replace the one that had been spilled. The barman offered Mrs Errowby a cloth.

The membership secretary appeared, wringing his long, limp hands. 'It was an accident, Bernie. You must see that. Could have happened to anyone.'

'An accident?' Errowby snarled. 'There've been too many bloody accidents lately. Come on, June. We're going somewhere more civilised.'

The Chief Inspector towed his wife out of the room; her face telegraphed her own apologies from the doorway; then they were gone. After two more seconds of silence, a buzz of conversation broke out – more muted than before, in case the Errowbys were still in earshot.

'What's up with him?' Burwell said.

Quarme was studying the contours of the golf course. 'Been on a short fuse these last few days,' he murmured.

'Oh aye?'

'Heard he got into a slanging match with a solicitor on Thursday. Outside the Magistrates' Court. My reporter got it down verbatim. Can't use it. Shame.'

Harold Quarme was editor and part-proprietor of the *Paulstock Guardian* and its three sister newspapers.

'He's getting promotion, you know.' Burwell believed that people shouldn't make confidences they didn't want broken. 'You'd have thought he'd be on top of the world.'

'Not confirmed.'

'Have you heard something, Harry? Was Bernie being a bit premature?'

'Don't know. But it would fit.'

'Wouldn't surprise me. I don't think he's much good at his job. You know what he told me last weekend? They've given up on trying to find out who ran down Leonie. Makes you sick, doesn't it?'

'No leads?'

Burwell told him about the bloodstain. 'And the only other idea they had was that someone might have done it on purpose. Trying to get at me or Felicity.'

'Nasty.'

'Just a theory. I've made a few enemies in my time, I know that. You can't earn a few bob without upsetting people, and that's the truth of it.' Burwell hesitated. An opening had appeared. He might as well be direct. 'Oddly enough, that's one reason why I wanted to have a chat with you today. Over the years I've had a lot of trouble with Bert Nimp. I don't suppose there's any chance of you putting him out to grass?'

The buzzer on his door took Graham by surprise. He had been watching the car park of Copeland Court from the living-room window but no visitors had driven in during the last ten minutes. He opened the door. Felicity pushed past him into the flat.

'You shouldn't have come here,' he said.

Felicity removed her driving gloves and tossed them on the sofa. 'It's your own fault. I couldn't talk on the phone. Don't you understand, this is an emergency?'

'Where did you leave your car?'

'Don't worry. In the car park behind the Co-op.'

'Is this something to do with Joanna being ill?'

She shook her head and sat down suddenly. 'I had a phone call this morning. I was just about to phone you – for Joanna, I mean. Graham, someone's trying to blackmail us.'

'Blackmail *us*?'

'Me – us: in this case it's the same thing.'

She took a paper handkerchief from her bag and rolled it between her hands. For a moment Graham was afraid that she was going to cry. He sat down not on the sofa but at a safe distance on the chair opposite it. The story emerged in fits and starts while Felicity's fingers shredded the tissue. Like the rest of her, her hands were small and seemingly delicate. As she talked, he had a vision of her falling from his second-storey window and shattering like a porcelain figurine on the tarmac of the car park.

The details of the phone call were familiar: the whispering voice; the section of tape; the amount of money required; and the place where it was to be left.

'The money has to be there by six o'clock on Tuesday evening. But I haven't got any money. As you know.'

He tried to change the subject: 'Who do you think's behind it?'

'God knows. It has to be someone local, I suppose. Bert

Nimp? Jimmy Perran? Neither of them likes me. And I had a row with Perran's wife this morning. For all I know it's Bernie Errowby himself. He and Kevin have quarrelled. And he's always been a bit funny with me ever since I wouldn't let him feel me up at a party.'

'It could be almost anyone. In a way we're both public people.'

She took the point at once. 'Yes. Lots of people know who we are, and we wouldn't know them from Adam. Like Tom Fool.'

Graham said, keeping his voice as neutral as he could: 'You've thought about going to the police?'

'With Bernie in charge? Be your age, Graham. It would all come out and then Kevin would divorce me, unless he hit me over the head with a hammer instead. And think what it would do to Leonie. Anyway, what would I live on?' Her face twisted. 'Come on, let's be honest. It's not as if you're going to make an honest woman of me.'

Felicity squeezed the scraps of tissue together and made a ball. She tossed it on the coffee table between them. Graham huddled into his chair. He wished she would stop looking at him.

'You'll have to help me,' she said.

'Surely you can raise five hundred?' Graham nodded at her. 'That necklace is gold, isn't it? And you must have other jewellery.'

'There isn't time. Besides—'

'Take it into Bristol, to a pawnbroker's.'

She shook her head. 'Kevin would notice. Besides, you're being stupid: this is your problem as much as mine. That phone call could have come to you just as easily as to me. Maybe you're next on the list.'

'I don't see why I should be the one to pay.'

'Nothing's free, my love,' she said with the muted triumph of a chess-player saying, 'Check-mate, I think.' 'Screw now, pay later. Imagine what Joanna would say.'

'It's not easy,' he said. 'You see—'

'Come off it. You quacks are rolling in it.'

'I'm not a full partner yet. I've got nearly three years to go. That means I only get a reduced share of the profits.'

'If this comes out you won't get another penny. You'd be a liability. They'd squeeze you out of the practice, wouldn't they? And then what? Do you think you'd find it easy to get another job? What do they do these days? Do you get struck off the list for adultery?'

Graham opened his mouth but found he had nothing to say, or at least nothing he could put into words.

'Cat got your tongue?' Felicity asked. 'You've got five minutes to make up your mind. If you won't put up the money, you'll just have to take the consequences.'

'What would you do?'

She smiled, and Graham saw two rows of white and perfectly regular teeth.

'Tell Kevin, of course. What else is left?'

12

'Days like this,' Sharon shouted, 'make me wonder if Sainsbury's have got any vacancies for check-out girls.'

Oliver managed to catch the words before the wind snatched them away. She had emerged from the shelter of the bicycle shed just as he was locking the door of his car. The timing struck him as suspicious: perhaps he was imagining it but she seemed always to be popping up when he wasn't expecting her. As it was, they spent much of their working lives together. It was almost as if someone had told her to keep an eye on him. Articulating the suspicion to himself made him realise how absurd it was: Paulstock was making him paranoid.

'It is a bit fresh,' he said.

He reeled as he moved away from the car and the full force of the wind hit him. He struck out for the side entrance into divisional headquarters. Sharon fell into step beside him.

'A bit fresh? I'd call that a bit of an understatement. I suppose you're looking forward to another day strolling through the wide open spaces of Abbotsfield.'

Oliver shrugged and held open the door for her. They had spent most of yesterday, Monday, in Abbotsfield at the mercy of the weather and the vagaries of human nature. Sharon had made it quite clear that she held him personally responsible for such an unpleasant and, as it turned out, fruitless way of passing the time.

Errowby had at first sneered at Oliver's idea that the burglar lived in or near Abbotsfield.

'It's just sticking pins in a map,' he'd said – in front of Fintal, which had made it worse. 'Dear God, is that the best you can come up with? Next thing we'll know, you'll want a consultation with Madame Fifi and her crystal ball.' He grunted with delight at his own wit and Fintal sniggered in the background.

On Monday morning, however, the Chief Inspector had arrived freshly converted to the principle, or at least to the working hypothesis, that this villain did not foul his own nest. Indeed, the force of his revelation had had the curious side-effect of blotting out his memory of Oliver's advancing the same idea the preceding Thursday. Errowby was behaving erratically. Oliver had thought that perhaps he was reading too much into it: perhaps the Chief Inspector was always like that. But Sharon said he was becoming even less predictable than before, and even Fintal had been overheard in the canteen muttering darkly about the male menopause.

The computer and Fintal's card index had produced a list of forty-nine names and addresses. All but one were male. All of them lived in Abbotsfield or within a radius of five miles. A handful had past convictions for house-breaking; others had form for other crimes; but most of them were in the frame simply because someone – an officer from the local section station, a social security snooper, or Bert Nimp – had at some point in their lives noted down a suspicion about them.

Yesterday, Oliver and Sharon had concentrated on A to H. Out of sixteen names they had traced fourteen men: not a bad score. Many of the people they sought lived their lives in the shadowy depths of society where statisticians rarely penetrate. They saw the police as their natural enemies, as offensive weapons in the hands of the faceless authorities. You could not interview such men: you had to interrogate them. If you wanted to get anywhere, you had to reciprocate their hostility. Yesterday had been one of those days when Oliver wondered if he were not merely in the wrong division but in the wrong job.

One man, being dead, was completely in the clear. Three had definitely moved out of the area, though they might conceivably have come back. The others were for a variety of reasons, ranging from lack of transport and acute alcoholism to religious mania and a jealous wife, unlikely to have been developing a promising career as a house-breaker.

Oliver and Sharon walked along the corridor to the main reception area. Sergeant Wilson was on the desk.

'Mr Errowby's been looking for you,' he said to Oliver. 'Mislaid a fingerprint, have you? Broken your magnifying glass?'

They went upstairs to the CID office. Errowby was standing by Oliver's desk and rifling through his in-tray.

'So there you are, Rickford.' The Chief Inspector shut the file he had been reading. 'You finally decided to honour us with your presence today. Come into my room.'

Oliver followed him down the corridor. He was quite prepared to be told that the villain they wanted had turned out to be an old age pensioner from the Isle of Dogs.

Errowby picked up a transparent plastic folder from his desk. 'Take a look at that. Came in this morning's post.' Inside the folder was a photocopy of a single sheet of paper and an envelope addressed to Errowby. The message, like the address, was printed in neat block capitals: *LEONIE BURWELL. BLUE Y REG CORTINA.*

'Forensic's checking out the originals,' Errowby said. 'Doubt if the lazy buggers'll find anything. Anyway, it's the sort of cheap stationery that Woolworths sell by the ton.'

Oliver peered at the photocopy. The envelope had a first-class stamp. 'I can't read the postmark.'

'Abbotsfield. Posted yesterday in time for the midday collection.'

'Jimmy Perran drives an old blue Cortina. Could be Y-reg.'

'Fintal's getting on to Swansea: he'll give you a list of the others.'

'You mean you're taking this seriously?'

'Dangerous driving? Smashing up a child? In my book that doesn't count as comic relief.'

'Yes, sir,' Oliver said. 'I meant the letter.'

'Are you questioning my decision, Sergeant? You want to get that down in black and white?'

'No, sir. Of course not. I just—'

'There may not be anything in it, laddy. But I want to know for sure. See if you can get this one right, OK?'

'And you want me to carry on with the other business?'

Errowby cast his eyes up to the ceiling. 'What do you think, Rickford? Use your head. Same location, isn't it? And I don't suppose you'll need all day to check out every blue Y-reg Cortina in Abbotsfield.'

'So you're limiting the frame to Abbotsfield?'

'For the moment, yes. I won't go into all the reasons.' Errowby pursed his lips, pouted and then gave way to temptation. 'Like the limited quantity of manpower at my disposal. Like the pathetically inadequate quality of what little manpower I've got.'

'Yes, sir.'

'Well, what are you waiting for?' Errowby answered the question himself. 'Oh, and while you're at it, see if you can squeeze a blood sample out of Jimmy Perran.'

Graham was late. He hated unpunctuality in others; in himself, however justified, it made him uncomfortable. The house calls after surgery had taken him longer than usual. At present he could not afford to skimp the time he spent on patients. Grateful patients might make the difference between survival and ruin.

If Kevin Burwell learned what his wife had been up to and made a formal complaint to the General Medical Council, it would almost certainly mean the end of Graham's career as a doctor: he would be struck off. In his worst moments he saw himself sinking into destitution, into the bottomless quagmire that must surely have claimed his father when he had run away from home and family. Graham had been five at the time. He had grown up among whispers and hints and veiled warnings. He shared his father's shame and shouldered, as the one remaining male in the family, some of the guilt. His mother, his aunts, the children in the playground all taught him the same lesson: he himself could become one of the nameless people whose lives are bounded by carrier bags and cardboard boxes; anyone could, but he was more likely than most because his father's tainted blood ran in his veins. As the derelict on the Embankment had said, it wasn't fair. But it happened. And Kevin Burwell could make it happen.

Very occasionally, however, the GMC had been known to temper justice with mercy. Graham had heard of one case where an adulterous GP had been presented as the hapless victim of a predatory woman; and his patients had queued up with testimonials to his sterling character and professional abilities. The man's reputation must have been scarred for life but at least he had survived; he had been lucky.

Since Felicity's ultimatum on Saturday, Graham had tried to be the perfect GP: obliging to his colleagues, and painstaking and courteous with his patients. It was extraordinarily time-consuming. After three days of strenuous perfection he felt exhausted and irritable. Nevertheless, he dared not hurry his house calls. It was well after one o'clock by the time he reached Paulstock, and he had to be back in Abbotsfield for a clinic at two. It would have been easy to arrange the meeting for Abbotsfield, but Graham had wanted to be discreet.

At this time of day the car park at Copeland Court was almost empty. Graham spotted Dougal immediately. He was sitting in a blue Sierra reading a newspaper. Graham reversed the Golf into the slot beside him. To his annoyance Dougal merely rolled down his window and waited.

Graham got out of his car. 'You'd better come up to the flat.' He decided against apologising for being late; after all, he was paying Dougal for reading the newspaper. 'Have you had lunch?'

'Not yet.'

'I'm in a hurry so I'm afraid I can't offer you any.'

Dougal sneezed. Graham led the way up to his flat. The place was a mess. He had been so busy since the weekend that he hadn't had time to tidy up. He went into the kitchen.

'I dropped off the money last night,' he said over his shoulder.

Dougal blew his nose. 'There's still time to change your mind.'

'It's out of the question. Do you mind not standing so close – I don't want to catch your cold. Besides, the – ah – other party wouldn't agree.'

'If you're right about her being the blackmailer, that's hardly surprising.'

Graham rummaged through the refrigerator and the cupboards above it. He hadn't even time for a cup of coffee. He stuffed an apple and a hunk of elderly Cheddar into the pockets of his raincoat. Dougal waited in the doorway. His silence got on Graham's nerves.

'I've been thinking about the best way to approach this,' Graham said. 'If you come—'

The doorbell rang.

'Damn. Stay in the kitchen, will you?' Graham pushed past Dougal and into the hall. He opened the door. The world swayed as though someone had nudged it.

'Saw your car outside,' said Kevin Burwell. 'Thought I'd pop in for a moment.'

Despite his size Burwell was light on his feet. Before Graham could stop him, he was inside the flat and standing by the open door of the kitchen. He looked expectantly at Dougal.

'Didn't realise you had a visitor, Graham.'

'Ah – this is William Dougal. Kevin Burwell.' Graham added, 'William's an old friend. From London.'

'Pleased to meet you.' Burwell squeezed Dougal's hand. 'Another quack, eh?'

'Not exactly.'

'I'm in a bit of a hurry,' Graham said. 'I've got to get back for a clinic.'

'I won't keep you.' Burwell stepped into the living room. He was looking more cheerful than Graham had seen him for weeks – since Leonie's accident, to be precise. The smell of his aftershave seemed to fill the entire flat. Graham wanted to gag.

'Had a bit of good news this morning,' Burwell said.

'Oh yes?'

Graham's voice rose to a squawk on the last syllable: as he followed Burwell into the room he caught sight of Felicity's driving gloves. They were partly covered by a cushion on the sofa; she must have left them behind on Saturday. Burwell could hardly mistake them – they were small and made of an eye-catching combination of beige cotton and lilac leather. Graham slid past Burwell and sat down heavily on top of the gloves.

'The police have finally come up with something. An anonymous tip-off, I gather. Bernie Errowby's very hopeful.'

'Wonderful.' Graham retied his shoelace in case either of his visitors was wondering why he had sat down. Suddenly he realised what Burwell had said. He sat up and said in a rush, 'Is it a name, or what?'

'Bernie wouldn't say, not over the phone.' Burwell glanced at Dougal, who was standing beside him. 'Maybe Graham hasn't mentioned it to you. My younger daughter was knocked down a couple of weeks ago. Hit-and-run. We're trying to trace the driver.'

Dougal glanced at Graham. 'How terrible.'

'If only I'd been at the house that evening instead of in London,' Graham said; the more a lie was repeated, the more it was accepted as truth. 'I might have seen something. At least I'd have been on the spot to help.'

'Well unfortunately you weren't,' Burwell said.

'Was your daughter badly hurt?' Dougal asked.

'She's recovering. Still gets headaches.'

Graham heard what they were saying but the words barely registered. Someone must have seen the car, someone who didn't want to get involved. Surely, though, if the someone had named him as the driver, the police would have been here or at the Health Centre by now? On the other hand they might have missed him while he was out on his house calls. Perhaps Errowby had in fact told Burwell what the tip-off said, and

Burwell had come to the flat for a preliminary gloat; or perhaps only the presence of Dougal was restraining him from violence.

'Of course I realise there may be nothing in it,' Burwell was saying. 'It's a crazy world – this could just be someone's idea of fun.'

'You never know,' Dougal said. 'You may strike lucky.' His face hardened, and he added with sudden vehemence, 'I hope you do.'

Graham frowned and glanced at his watch. He had fifteen minutes before the clinic began. Burwell took the hint.

'I'll be off, then. I'll see you this evening, Graham. Bernie and June are coming, as a matter of fact.'

'I thought—'

Burwell grinned. 'You thought me and Bernie weren't on speaking terms at present? So did I until he phoned me this morning. Maybe I was a little hasty the other day. One good turn deserves another, eh?'

Graham nodded, his mind filling with the unwelcome prospect of an evening with the Burwells and Errowbys. 'I hope I can make it. Did Joanna tell you I'm on call this evening?'

'That's all right. You're almost one of the family. You can come and go as you please.' Burwell swung the force of his personality towards Dougal. 'What about you? Are you staying overnight down here?'

Dougal smiled and tilted his head in a way that might have been either a nod or a shake.

'Tell you what, why don't you come to dinner as well?'

Graham swallowed. 'I really couldn't—'

'Don't be stupid. Felicity would be delighted. Any friend of yours is a friend of ours.'

'That's very kind of you,' Dougal said. 'If you're sure I wouldn't be in the way.'

'Of course you wouldn't. So I'll see you both this evening. Maybe we'll have some good news by then.'

'I do hope so,' Dougal said.

'Don't get up. I'll see myself out.'

With a wave of a gold-ringed hand, Burwell was gone. The flat door slammed behind him. Only the smell of his aftershave remained. Graham lay back on the sofa. His shirt was damp with sweat.

'Shit.'

'What's the problem?' Dougal asked.

For one mad instant Graham considered telling him the whole truth. 'Why the hell did you accept?'

'His invitation? Excuse me.' Dougal blew his nose once more. 'If I've got this right, Felicity must be your mistress – and quite possibly your blackmailer, too. You'll want me to assess her, to keep an eye on her this evening. It's too good a chance to miss.'

'As it happens, I've got other plans for you.'

'Well, in that case you can make my excuses to the Burwells.' Dougal smiled. 'You're the boss, Dr Hanslope.'

13

Leonie and Tammy sat together near the back of the school bus. The bus normally dropped them outside the house where the red setters lived on the corner of White Cross Lane. On Tuesday afternoon, however, the two girls got off in the centre of Abbotsfield and took refuge in the library.

They were meant to be doing a coursework project on the effects of the Agrarian Revolution on the lives of ordinary people in Somerset. It would serve as an excuse if they were seen together.

'They can hardly blame us for working,' Leonie said. 'It's what they keep telling us we should be doing.'

If working meant sitting side by side at the same table with the same book open in front of them, what else could Leonie and Tammy do? It wasn't their fault that the library had only one copy of the book they both needed to use; with her usual attention to detail Leonie had checked the catalogue to make quite sure that there was not another copy.

They talked quietly until five, when the library closed. As they came down the steps, which were well-lit by a light above the double doors, a car went past.

'Oh Christ,' Tammy said. 'That was Dad.'

'Wouldn't he have stopped if he'd seen us?'

'Depends. You know what he's like.' Tammy, already tense, felt her muscles tightening still further. Please God he hadn't seen her. Not tonight. It wasn't much to ask. 'I'll just have to be extra specially careful.'

They walked back home together. By now it was almost dark. Habit made them skilful: they avoided streetlamps and lighted windows; they followed a roundabout route that lessened the chance of meeting anyone they knew. Despite the risk, Tammy insisted on taking Leonie almost as far as the Burwells' drive. Since that terrible evening in January she hated the thought of Leonie's being out alone, especially after dark. Leonie was so small, so delicate and so defenceless.

'You'll be all right by yourself?' Leonie said, suddenly reversing their roles.

'Don't worry.'

'I could come with you.'

'No. I won't do anything stupid, I promise. I remember what you said.'

'Good luck. Try and phone me.'

'If I can.'

'Use the office number. They've got people coming to dinner. About half past eight would be the safest time.'

Tammy bit her lip. 'I can't bear all this.'

'It won't be for much longer.'

They said goodbye. Tammy went on alone. In White Cross Lane a strange car, a two-year-old Escort, was parked behind the Cortina outside her parents' house. This pleased her. God must have been listening. If her parents had visitors they wouldn't have time to interfere with her.

The lane was darker and much quieter than the Meadow Way estate behind her. Apart from her parents' house, the only light came from the crack between the curtains of Mr Nimp's sitting room.

She took her time, deferring for as long as possible the moment of meeting her father. Ten minutes later, she opened the gate and walked down the side of the house towards the back door. She heard voices in front of her, which made her pause, all senses alert. Her father was walking towards the house from the shed with a tall man looming over him.

'It's just a workshop,' she heard her father say, his voice sullen. 'I hardly use it in winter. You can ask anyone.'

The two men reached the wedge of light that spilled through

the kitchen window. Tammy recognised the stranger at once: it was the policeman she had met at Paulstock Hospital, the ugly one who had witnessed her disgrace in Leonie's room and later been kind to her; he had told her that Leonie was going to be all right.

They stopped before they reached the back door. The corner of the house was between them and Tammy, but she could still hear them.

'Did you use your workshop when you changed the front wings of your car?' the policeman asked.

'Who told you that?'

'I had a look at the car, Mr Perran. When did you change them?'

'I don't know. Must have been weeks ago.'

'Two weeks?'

'More than that.'

'Why did you change them?'

'Usual reason. They were more rust than metal.'

'Still got them, have you?'

'Of course I bloody haven't.'

'What did you do with them?'

'Dumped them in a skip. In Bristol, I think it was. I just happened to be passing.'

'You don't mind if we borrow your car, do you? Just for twenty-four hours.'

'You can't do that. Not unless you—'

'Perhaps,' said the policeman, so softly that Tammy could barely hear him, 'you're worried about how you'd get to work without your car. No problem, Jimmy. I'll have a word with your boss, explain the circumstances. It's Mr Burwell, isn't it? I'm sure he won't mind if you're a bit late. Maybe he'll offer you a lift himself.'

'I can use my van to get to work. There's no need to talk to Burwell.'

'So you don't mind if we borrow your car?'

'You can take it if you want. Not that you'll find anything.'

'The offside rear tyre is worn below the legal minimum. That'll do for starters. And while we're at it, we'd like a blood sample from you. You can call in at—'

The closing of the door cut off the rest of the conversation. It was growing even colder. Tammy hugged herself in an attempt to keep warm. After a moment she went back to the front of the house. The living-room window was not double-glazed. She heard voices inside but she could not distinguish what they were saying. There was no point in getting colder so she let herself into the house by the front door. The living-room door was ajar. The policeman was saying something about a kettle.

'Hello,' she called. 'I'm home.'

The voices stopped. Tammy dumped her duffel coat in the hall. Her mother, cigarette in hand, appeared in the doorway of the living room. She looked flustered.

'Go and do your homework upstairs,' she said. 'I'll give you a shout when your tea's ready.'

'You got visitors?'

'Your dad's talking business with someone.'

Tammy took her bag upstairs. Her mother had told her another lie; grown-ups lied all the time. The voices began again. Without turning on the light, she went to the window and stared up the hill at Abbotsfield. She imagined how it would look if a bomb landed on it: how the walls would fly apart, how the roofs would lift into the air; how cars would become balls of fire and how the lights would go out, one by one; and how, if she opened the window, she would be able to hear the screaming, diminished by the distance into the squeaking of mice.

There was a flash of light on her right. Not in the front garden of White Cross House but beyond it. Tammy rested her cheek on the cold glass. Bert Nimp had opened his front door. For a moment he stood on the step with his overcoat flapping around him. He shut the door and stole down the path to his gate.

He did not go into the lane. He stood by the gate among

his gnomes. Waiting? Watching? Listening? Maybe all three. Tammy wondered what he was thinking. It was difficult to imagine how someone so old and solitary could have any thoughts at all.

Nimp was not alone. He had Gordon, Harry, Imogen and John to keep him company. His mind still felt numb. The phone call this afternoon had left him literally breathless.

Not even Quarme himself, but an underling: some double-barrelled cub reporterette with a cut-glass voice and endless vowels.

'It's nothing personal, Bert,' she'd said – the use of his Christian name grated; he was certain they had never met. 'Mr Quarme wanted me to stress that. It's a policy decision, you see. And, as I say, it won't take effect until the end of March.'

He had tried to fend off the inevitable: 'If it's a question of money, perhaps—'

'No, it's nothing like that. We're overhauling the whole system of local correspondents, which is part of a much wider exercise – we're doing a complete strategic overhaul. It's a question of looking to the future, to the *Guardian* Group in the next century. Mr Quarme feels that we're not doing enough to attract younger readers.'

'Young people don't buy the *Paulstock Guardian*,' Mr Nimp pointed out. 'Their parents do.'

'We aim to change that. To be honest, Bert, we have to. At present our demographic readership profile is heavily weighted towards the elderly. It's a diminishing market by definition – I'm sure you see that. We just can't afford to sit back with all the competition from the free press and local radio. Wider in-depth coverage: that's the key. It'll bring in the readers of all age groups *and* the advertising that goes with them.'

'I still don't understand why—'

'I'm so glad we've been able to have this little talk. Mr Quarme was most insistent about explaining things properly. He'll be writing, of course. And, Bert, may I say on a more personal note how much I've enjoyed reading your work? It's been both a pleasure and privilege.'

Nimp had put down the phone. 'You bitch,' he'd said to the darkening room around him. 'You bitch, you bitch, you bitch.'

And now, as he waited by the gate to the lane with his hand resting lightly on Gordon's pointed hat, Nimp wondered whom they would get to replace him. Maybe that other bitch, Margaret Telford, the one who ran the Cattery; it would make sense – she was a friend of Felicity Burwell's. He had lived in this area long enough to know how it worked. He should have seen the writing on the wall last autumn when Kevin Burwell doubled his regular advertising space in the *Guardian* and he and Harry Quarme started inviting each other to dinner.

What now? He remembered what he had said to Sergeant Rickford: 'When you get to my age, you need some sort of an occupation . . . Otherwise you just – well, run down. Like a clock.'

The Perrans' door opened. Nimp caught a glimpse of Jimmy Perran, his big hands clenched against his legs. Rickford and the policewoman came out but Perran stayed in the house. Instead of getting into their car the police officers went over to the Perrans' Cortina, which was parked on the lane. After a moment, the woman got in and drove off. How interesting: so that was the way the wind was blowing. Rickford stood watching her until the Cortina's tail-lights had vanished. He shrugged and walked towards the Escort.

'Sergeant Rickford?' Nimp called.

'What is it?' The policeman passed the Escort and walked along the frontage of White Cross House. 'Mr Nimp?'

'That's right.'

'What can I do for you?'

'It may be the other way round.' Nimp waited until Rickford was only a few feet away; he turned his good ear toward the policeman. 'There's someone behaving suspiciously.'

'Where?'

'White Cross House. I saw him sneaking round the back.

He must have been in there for an hour. Before that he drove down here without stopping, and later he was wandering round Abbotsfield – I kept seeing him while I was shopping. Perhaps I should have phoned you earlier. But he wasn't acting like a burglar.'

'Do you recognise him?'

'A complete stranger. Drives a blue Ford Sierra. It's funny, though. He's left the car up in town, outside the Boar.' Nimp pushed a scrap of paper towards Rickford. 'I phoned them and got the registration number.'

'It does sound a bit odd – though as you say it doesn't sound like a burglar. But I'll check it out.'

'Shall I come with you?'

'Better not, sir. You go back inside. I'll let you know what happens. By the way – have you noticed Mr Perran using that shed in his garden recently? Moving stuff in and out, for example?'

Nimp was sorely tempted to tell Rickford what little he knew. But the memory of that unpleasant chat with Perran was too fresh in his mind: it would be wiser not to rush into anything, to give himself time to think about the implications.

'I wouldn't know, I'm afraid. My house doesn't overlook their garden. There's White Cross House between us.'

'Doesn't matter. Just a thought. Anyway, you go inside and I'll radio in to tell someone what I'm doing. And thank you for your help.'

What a polite policeman, Nimp thought as he pottered up his path. He wished they were all like that.

'Tammy! Come here.'

The muscles in her stomach contracted. Tammy knew by the tone of her father's voice that a bad time lay ahead. She had learned from experience that the way he handled humili- ation was to pass it on either to her mother or to herself.

Quickly she marked her place in *Wuthering Heights*, left the book on her pillow and ran downstairs. Her father was standing with a can of lager in his hand by the fire in the living room. Her mother was sitting on the sofa, smoking furiously and staring at the television. She did not look up as Tammy came in. She seemed wholly absorbed in what the man on the screen was saying: something about interest rates.

'Here. No, closer than that.'

Jimmy made her stand inches away from him on the hearthrug. His eyes had narrowed, which had the effect of emphasising the blank, black pupils. 'I saw you coming out of the library,' he said. 'With Leonie Burwell. I couldn't believe my eyes.'

Tammy muttered their excuse about the shared coursework. On the bus and in the library it had sounded perfectly reasonable. It *was* perfectly reasonable. But she should have remembered that her father was not a reasonable man.

He leaned forward so she could smell the alcohol on his breath. 'I warned you. Didn't I warn you?'

'You're not being fair.'

He seized a lock of her hair with his free hand. He chose a spot where the skin is sensitive, just in front of the ear. He pulled. Her glasses fell off. She squealed, and tried in vain to pull away. Her eyes filled with tears. He forced her down to her knees.

'Jimmy . . .' her mother said.

'You shouldn't have said that, Tammy.' For once he spoke softly, almost caressingly. 'You really shouldn't. In a moment you'll tell me how sorry you are.'

Tammy knew that he was right. Also she knew that there was no point in trying to short-circuit the process by saying sorry now because her father liked to take his time; and she knew that he wouldn't mark her body because he was too clever for that.

'Next time I see you with her,' he said, 'there'll be more of the same. And that won't be all. I'm getting sick of this. Sick and bloody tired. I'll pack you off to your gran in Bristol. Permanently.'

'Wait a minute,' Suzette said, frowning. 'You never—'

'Shut up, you stupid cow.' He turned back to Tammy and lowered his voice again: 'Your gran knows how to deal with stupid girls.'

'Please, Dad. I want to stay here.'

She saw the delight in his face and realised what a fool she had been. She had given him a present: the location of a weak spot.

Still holding her hair, he put the lager can carefully on the mantelpiece behind him. Then the huge hand came towards her. Slowly. Jimmy Perran liked to take his time.

From the lane White Cross House looked deserted. All the windows at the front were in darkness.

Oliver walked as quietly as possible down the drive to the yard at the back of the house. The drive funnelled the wind towards him and tugged at his hair and his coat. He felt as though he were swimming in air, swimming against the current and in danger of drowning.

The lights were on in the kitchen. Oliver peeped through the nearest window, which was uncurtained. A man about his own age was sitting at the table with a mug beside him. He wore a tan raincoat and a scarf. He was smoking a hand-rolled cigarette and reading a book.

It looked innocent enough. But why had the man left his car up at the Boar, nearly a mile away? Oliver knew as well as anyone that this was not the weather for walking.

He tapped on the door, noticing that Hanslope hadn't got round to mending the broken pane of glass; but there was no sign of a forced entry. Not that there would be if the square of plywood had been replaced.

The man at the table glanced up, his finger marking his place in the book. He walked without haste towards the door. His thin face showed no sign of panic. I'm wasting my time, Oliver thought: the story of my life.

'Hello. Can I help you?'

Oliver flashed his warrant card and asked what the man was doing. He spoke bluntly, almost rudely, because he felt a fool.

The man sneezed, apologised and said, 'I'm staying here for a night or two. I'm a friend of Graham Hanslope's.'

'Your name, sir?'

'William Dougal.'

'On holiday, are you?' It was a funny time and place for a solitary holiday.

'Sort of.' Dougal showed Oliver the book, which had the words 'Bound Proof' on the cover. 'I do freelance work for publishers – I came here for some peace and quiet.'

'I understand you left your car in the town centre.'

Dougal nodded. If this line of questioning surprised him he showed no sign of it. 'At the Boar. I had a late lunch there, you see, and a couple of drinks. There was just a chance I was over the limit, so I thought I'd walk. Better safe than sorry.'

'You won't mind if I check with Dr Hanslope, sir? Nothing personal – we've had a spate of burglaries in the area.'

'Of course not. There's a phone in the hall. He should be at the Health Centre – he's got an evening surgery.'

Dougal could not have been more helpful. He showed Oliver where the phone was, gave him the number of the Health Centre and retreated tactfully to the kitchen. The receptionist at the surgery was less obliging; Oliver quietly lost his temper and hit the woman with the majesty of the law. She buckled under the onslaught and put through his call.

'Hanslope.'

'This is Detective Sergeant Rickford, sir.'

'Yes? Well, what is it?'

'Can you confirm that a Mr William Dougal is staying with your permission at White Cross House?'

'Of course I can. Is that all you want?'

'Yes, sir.'

Hanslope slammed down the phone without saying goodbye.

Oliver stood for a moment in the hall with the phone bleating in his hand. After Easter this house would be Joanna Burwell's home. She would adorn it like a lily in a vase. She would walk up those stairs, hold this phone, cook meals for her bastard of a husband in the kitchen. Oliver knew he'd been a fool to come here. White Cross House made him sick with sorrow and envy; sick with love.

Behind him, William Dougal cleared his throat.

Oliver swung round. He wanted to snarl at someone. Anyone.

Douglas was standing in the kitchen doorway. For the first time he smiled, which transformed his face. 'There's tea in the pot. Would you like a cup?'

14

'I'm afraid the money's gone,' Dougal said. 'Your friend must have come early.'

Graham kicked the door shut. He pushed aside Dougal's book and put down his bag on the kitchen table. 'Was it there this afternoon? I assume you bothered to look.'

Dougal bent down to pick up the book, which had fallen on the floor. 'Yes. That was at half past three. No one else was around, not even workmen on the building site.'

'Bloody hell. Did that policeman make you late?'

'No – he came afterwards. I was in position with the camera just before six. Just as you told me. Nothing was moving so I thought I'd check.' He sneezed. 'The money had gone. I did warn you this might happen.'

'I thought they'd wait till the deadline. Wait till it was completely dark. Were there any signs of them? Footprints, that sort of thing?'

'None that I could see. I'll have a proper look in the morning.'

Graham wondered if Dougal had taken the money himself. It was unlikely, he conceded reluctantly; Custodemus was a reputable company. But Dougal must be relieved not to have to spend an unknown period of time lurking outside on a night like this. This added to Graham's sense of grievance.

'That's a great help. What the hell am I paying you for?'

Dougal leaned back in his chair. 'I'll tell you if you really want to know.'

'You'll do what?'

'We get a number of clients like you.' His voice was detached and thick with the cold. 'Not many, but enough to make up a category. People who are in a mess, and who are too scared to let someone else clear it up for them. It's an inability to delegate, I suppose. But you still want to pay us good money to come along and hold your hand.'

'I've had enough of this.'

'Extraordinary, isn't it?' Dougal stared at the ceiling. He seemed perfectly relaxed, which Graham registered as a further insult. 'You call in a specialist, and then you won't let him do his job.'

'I'm not going to listen to—'

'Actually, I think we serve a double function in cases like yours. First, clutching on to us is like a child clutching a teddy bear. And just about as useful.'

'Get out.'

Dougal looked at Graham. He stood up and began to gather his belongings. 'Secondly, you're hiring a scapegoat. You can blame us when it all goes wrong, as it almost certainly will.'

Graham sat down suddenly. He hated Dougal and linked to the hate was a faint feeling of uncertainty, the sort of preliminary queasiness that afflicts you at three o'clock in the morning when you have eaten and drunk too much the previous evening. In this life, he thought, you have to look after yourself and your own interests; that's self-evident – it's the first and only duty, and sometimes it means you have to tell lies. But if you tell lies habitually to other people, perhaps it is possible that you also tell them without knowing to yourself.

'You want me to go?' Dougal said.

'All right.' Graham stifled his anger and tried to make his voice conciliatory. 'Sit down. Perhaps I made a mistake. What do you advise?'

'The same as always: that you and Mrs Burwell go to the police.'

Graham shook his head.

'OK. Then we have to wait for the next time.'

'But how do we know—'

'Don't worry about that. Unless you're very lucky, one of

you will get another demand. So maybe we should make a start by recording all your incoming phone calls. We're probably dealing with someone local, an amateur, and amateurs make mistakes. Try and make him talk, get him away from the script. If you can study a tape, you may even be able to recognise the voice.'

'But if I can't, or if he phones Felicity—'

'You'll act as if you're going to pay up as before. Then there are several things we can do. For example, we could include a bug with the notes or try to monitor the scene of the drop. It depends on circumstances. We might need a major surveillance operation to do an effective job. All this may cost you a great deal of money. But in the end we should catch your blackmailer.'

'I'll have to think about it. Maybe even talk to Mrs Burwell.'

Dougal followed his train of thought. 'I thought she was broke.'

'She's got jewellery she could sell or pawn. This could cost thousands.'

'It would probably work out cheaper than the alternative.'

'I'll need help. Financially, I mean.'

'But Mrs Burwell may not want to help you. Quite the reverse.'

'There's no way you can find out?'

'If she's the blackmailer? You want me to ask her or something?'

Graham said stiffly, 'I just wondered if you had any constructive suggestions.'

Dougal blew his nose. 'You could let me come with you tonight. Then I could talk to her. She's got no idea who I am, has she?'

'Of course not.'

'Maybe I can poke around a bit. And it may help if I get to know some of the other people involved.'

'But what do I tell the Burwells?'

'No problem there. You've already told Kevin I'm an old

friend. We can just elaborate on that. Where were you a medical student?'

'At Guy's.'

'Right. I used to share a flat with a friend of yours, another medical student. A flat in Dulwich. That's how we met. I'm a freelance publisher's editor – that's what I told the policeman, by the way. I need somewhere quiet to do some work, and I may spend some time here in the next week or so. It was your idea – all these burglaries have made you worried about the house being empty.'

'How did you know about the burglaries?'

'I bought a local paper. Anyway, the policeman mentioned them.'

Graham looked at his watch. He loathed the idea of Dougal's having access to his private life: he would meet Felicity and Joanna, not to mention the Errowbys; he would ask questions, and live at White Cross House among Graham's possessions; he would make judgements. It was almost as bad as asking a psychoanalyst to take your mind apart. Yet, as before, Graham had no acceptable alternative. He looked at Dougal: a skinny, red-nosed, insignificant man: an unlikely teddy bear.

'Time's getting on,' Graham said. 'I suppose we'd better be off.'

'Oh my God,' Felicity said. 'You don't expect much, do you? First the Errowbys, then a completely unknown young man. What had you in mind? A last-minute miracle with the loaves and fishes?'

'You always cope so well,' Kevin said, sniffing to show his appreciation. 'It smells wonderful.'

'It's coq au vin.' She pushed Simba out of the way with her foot and opened the fridge to get the salad dressing: evasive action to prevent his kissing her. 'It's been in the freezer for nearly a year so it'll probably give everyone food poisoning.'

'I'm sure it'll be lovely.'

'You might have tried to get back a bit earlier. Have you sorted out the wine?'

'It's all under control.'

'I wish I could say the same. I have to do everything myself.'

'Come on, love. Joanna does her bit.'

'Maybe you know something I don't. When she got back from work she went upstairs to wash her hair, make herself sweet for lover-boy, and I haven't seen her since.'

Kevin took a step backwards as though she were attacking him, which she was. To her relief he changed the subject: 'Where's Leonie?'

'In her room. She doesn't want to eat with us. Can't say I blame her.'

'Do you think she's well enough to go back to school full-time? She always seems so tired in the evenings.'

'It's her decision. The doctor says it's up to her.'

'I'll get some wine from the garage.' Kevin hesitated in the doorway. 'All the same, I think I'll have a word with Graham about Leonie. Won't do any harm.'

Felicity went upstairs to get changed. She was badly behind schedule. Afterwards, as Joanna was still in her bedroom, she was forced to lay the table herself. Usually she took pride in her dinner parties, both in the food and how it was presented. Tonight, she told herself, they could eat off the carpet for all she cared. It had been one of those days; on top of everything else, she'd had another nasty letter from the bank. She tossed mats and plates and cutlery on to the table. Then habit reasserted itself. She arranged the table as carefully as ever, and the familiar routine soothed her. It was a question of her own self-respect. One had standards.

The same self-respect had prevented her from phoning Graham. Why hadn't he been in contact? He must have known she was worried sick.

The doorbell rang as she was polishing the glasses. She and Kevin converged on the front door. June and Bernie Errowby swept into the house in a draught of cold, damp air.

'Thought we'd never get here,' Errowby said. 'June was driving.'

Mrs Errowby was larger than her husband in all directions, and probably heavier than Kevin. Inside the ballooning white flesh were the mortal remains of a slim, intelligent woman smothered to death by her marriage.

'Still raining, is it?' Felicity said in a chilly voice.

'It's bloody pelting.' Errowby kissed Felicity; in the process he managed to transfer several raindrops from his mackintosh to her dress. 'You're looking lovelier than ever. Here, these are for you.'

He passed her a small bunch of pink carnations. Felicity murmured her thanks and backed away. She abhorred pink. The carnations would clash with the colour scheme wherever she put them; and the flowers themselves were best described as being in late middle age.

Kevin took the Errowbys' coats and hung them in the hall cupboard. June smiled at everyone, twisted her hands and said as little as possible. She was wearing a sack-like dress with a bold floral pattern. Kevin edged the Errowbys towards the drawing room.

'Come and get warm. What can I get you to drink?'

The doorbell rang once more.

'I'll get it,' Felicity said.

'For you, Felicity,' Graham said, thrusting a gift-wrapped box of handmade chocolates into her hand. 'My favourite mother-in-law-to-be.' He was lit up with excitement or perhaps nervousness; Felicity wondered if he had been drinking. 'And this is William Dougal.'

Her first impression of Dougal was unfavourable: he looked older than Graham; and his baggy jersey and unpressed corduroy trousers were scarcely suitable for the occasion. He smelled of cigarettes and eucalyptus oil. As Felicity was hanging up their coats, Kevin came out to shake hands with Dougal.

'Whoops, you've dropped something,' Graham said, so quietly that only Felicity heard.

He bent down. Felicity saw her driving gloves in his hand. She realised that they must have been at the flat all the time. Kevin might have noticed them when he went to see Graham at lunchtime.

'I – I thought I'd left those in the car.'

'Apparently not,' Graham said.

She snatched the gloves. Kevin had taken Dougal into the drawing room. She mouthed, 'What happened about the money?'

He shrugged. 'It's gone.'

'Graham, darling.'

Joanna swept down the stairs. Her eyes were huge and anxious. She had changed into a tight black dress with a hem above the knee. A prude in tart's clothing, Felicity thought; she suspected that the lovers had had a quarrel last week and that Joanna was now trying to make it up. She left them to it.

Time stretched; the evening threatened to become a desert of boredom without an oasis in sight. The chicken was tough, almost inedible, and the wine in the sauce had combined with time and sub-zero temperatures to produce a strong vinegary flavour. Despite Felicity's efforts, the conversation proceeded by fits and starts. Graham said hardly a word: he was obviously in a bad mood – no doubt because of the blackmail but also, Felicity hoped, because the lovers' quarrel was still in progress.

William Dougal, however, proved to be an unexpected ally. Unlike the Errowbys, he knew how to pull his weight as a guest. He talked especially to Felicity, and she could tell, as one always could, that he thought her attractive. She found herself thinking that he could really be quite attractive himself if someone took the trouble to smarten him up.

Errowby ate little but drank a lot. At first he talked mainly about his forthcoming promotion. Later he told funny stories. He was one of those unfortunate men who believe they have a talent as a raconteur.

'I hope you're not driving, Bernie,' Kevin said as he opened another bottle. 'People like you should set a good example to the rest of us.'

'It's June's turn.'

'These days it's always my turn,' June said. Her eyes widened, as if her boldness frightened her.

Errowby chuckled. 'Ah, I do it for your sake. You know what drinking does to your waistline.'

He looked up, expecting applause. June stared at her lap. The others sat in embarrassed silence.

'Isn't it St Valentine's Day this week?' Dougal said. 'Does anyone know when?'

Felicity smiled her thanks for the diversion.

'The fourteenth – Thursday.' Joanna's eyes slid towards Graham, then down to her lap. Her face was almost shy.

'I can never remember.' Dougal sneezed. 'Excuse me,' he said to Felicity. 'I'll just get a handkerchief from my coat.'

A moment later she left the room herself to fetch the apple tart, which was almost as old as the coq au vin. For a split second she saw Dougal before he was aware of her presence. He was standing by the open door of the hall cupboard, frowning at something in the palm of his hand. It looked like a small chemist's bottle.

He looked up. 'I must have got the wrong raincoat. This one and mine are identical.'

'There's a box of tissues in the lavatory.'

'I've got some here, thanks.' He dropped the bottle into the pocket of one coat and took a packet of paper handkerchiefs from the pocket of the other. 'Can I help carry?'

Felicity smiled at him. 'Why not?' In her mind she gave the same answer, albeit a provisional one, to quite another question.

The bleeper in the top pocket of Graham's jacket came to life at exactly the right moment – after the first cup of coffee and the third chocolate, just as Kevin Burwell was threatening to pin him down to another lengthy discussion about Leonie's state of health.

The call wasn't urgent – Graham could have handled it on the phone. But he wanted to escape and in any case nothing was too much trouble for the perfect GP. The patient lived on the Paulstock side of Abbotsfield so Graham could reasonably say that he would go straight home to the flat afterwards. Dougal said he would walk back to White Cross House, and refused offers of lifts from both the Errowbys and Felicity.

Even Graham's lonely bed was preferable to another hour with Joanna's parents and those awful Errowbys. Today had been a disaster, and the sooner it was over the better.

Joanna followed him into the hall. 'William's nice, isn't he?' she said brightly. 'He's not on your list of guests. Don't you want to invite him to the wedding?'

'I don't know him *that* well,' Graham said. 'We'll think about it. Are you sure you're feeling better?'

'The tummy-bug? It's as if it never happened.' She helped him on with his coat. 'You will drive carefully, won't you, darling? The roads are probably icy.'

She came out to the porch and flung her arms round him. It was no longer raining. The night was cold and clear. To his surprise he felt not only her lips but her tongue touch his.

'I'm sorry about last Wednesday,' she murmured. 'It was the time of the month and I was probably going down with that bug. But I didn't mean to be so horrible to you. I love you so much.'

'It's all right. I understand.' He didn't understand, but he knew a good line when it presented itself. 'I love you, too.'

'I don't know how you put up with me.' Her body writhed against his. 'You forgive me?'

'Of course I do.' He proved it with another, much longer kiss, during which she continued to writhe with an unpractised enthusiasm he found most erotic. 'Why don't you come over to the flat on Thursday evening?' he suggested when she drew herself away. 'On St Valentine's Day.'

'I'd love to.'

I've done it, Graham thought as he drove off, I've cracked

it. Unless Joanna had changed her mind, surely she wouldn't have humbled herself so much, wouldn't have kissed him like that or agreed to come to the flat?

'Who was that on the phone?' Suzette said, her eyes fixed on the screen.

'None of your bloody business.'

Jimmy slammed the living-room door and stood in front of the television, blocking her view and switching rapidly from channel to channel. They were by themselves; Tammy was presumably upstairs. Suzette had been enjoying the American romantic comedy on BBC1.

'Do you mind? I was watching that.'

'Well, you're watching something else now.'

He was looking for a video now, running his finger along the spines of his special tapes, the ones in plain black boxes that he bought from the barman at the Boar.

'I think I'll go to bed.'

Jimmy's finger paused. She hoped he would rise to the bait. But he didn't even turn round. 'Suit yourself.'

The bounce had gone out of him. Usually when he did those things to Tammy, he was full of energy for the rest of the evening. It was often quite exciting when they got to bed. Not tonight, though. Disappointment made her want to needle him.

'Jimmy? You know that kettle you gave me? It smells funny.'

'I told you – it was dangerous. I had to clean it and change the plug.'

'Why was the copper so interested in it?'

'How do I know?'

'Was it nicked?'

'Don't be stupid. Only a fool would bother to nick a kettle.'

It was almost half past eleven before Bernie Errowby succumbed to combined pressure from his wife and his hosts and tore himself away from the Burwells' increasingly lukewarm hospitality. Joanna had gone upstairs soon after Graham's departure;

to Felicity's annoyance, she was pink with happiness. William Dougal had left, still declining a lift, at the same time.

Kevin muttered something about a VAT inspection and went into his office beyond the garages. Felicity was used to his abandoning her to the domestic debris of an evening's entertainment. She saw nothing of him for thirty minutes. Then he burst into the kitchen like a bear on the warpath while she was washing the casserole dish.

'What's happened?' she said.

'Did you hear the phone?'

'It hasn't rung.'

'No, the office one. Can't you leave the washing up for a moment? Someone's trying to bloody blackmail me.'

He was so angry that the story came out in a shout: the whispering voice; the allegations of financial impropriety – credit for Errowby in return for special treatment over the hit-and-run investigation; and the demand for a thousand pounds. While he talked, Kevin paced up and down the kitchen, barging into chairs and hammering his hands on the work surfaces. Felicity leant against the draining board and watched him.

'I can see your problem,' she said.

'What do you mean?'

'Well, in a manner of speaking it's no more than the truth. You and Bernie *have* been doing a bit of back-scratching. I dare say neither of you wants the world to know.'

'That's not the point,' Kevin said; he was calmer now, his voice lowered to its usual rumble. 'Anyway they can't prove it. The point is, I'm not letting some little bastard take me to the cleaners.'

'Have you any idea—'

'Who it could be? Ten to one it's Nimp. I told you I got Harry Quarme to give him the elbow. He's probably guessed it was me.'

'What will you do?'

'I'm going to phone Bernie. He should be back by now. If he—'

He broke off. His face changed: it was as though someone had wiped away the anger with a sponge.

'Leonie,' he said gently. 'Do you know what time it is? What are you doing downstairs?'

She was standing in the doorway to the hall. She wore her old dressing gown. Her eyes were smudged with weariness.

'I couldn't sleep. I wanted a drink.'

'Hot milk, sweetheart,' Kevin decided. 'Mummy will bring it up. Come on, I'm taking you back to bed.'

15

Being on call at night was always a lottery: sometimes the patients had the sense to leave you alone; other nights were spent on the phone, in the car and appearing, a little god in a four-wheeled machine, in the middle of strangers' crises.

On Tuesday night, or rather early on Wednesday morning, Graham had no sooner got back to the flat when Felicity rang with the bad news. Ten minutes later, while he was still wondering what to do, he was called out to a farm east of Abbotsfield where an old man was taking a long time dying. So it went on through the empty hours before dawn; it was an unusually busy night. There were compensations: you had little time for your own problems, you were well-paid for your trouble, and the people you visited were always so vulnerable, so grateful.

'Thank God,' a woman said as her four-year-old son reverted to his usual colour and began to breathe easily. 'Oh, thank God.' And Graham had known that she was thanking not God nor even the bronchodilator that had done the work, but himself. It occurred to him that losing such gratitude would be almost as bad as losing the money and the security.

Just before seven, Graham drove into Abbotsfield. Not for the first time he regretted the fact that he had succumbed to Joanna's sales talk and leased the Copeland Court flat: the ten miles to Paulstock, even on a fast road, were simply ten too many. He was due at Abbotsfield Health Centre for the nine o'clock surgery, and it was hardly worth going back to the flat beforehand. The Boar started serving breakfast at eight. In the meantime he would go to White Cross House, where he could shave, change and give himself the minor pleasure of disturbing Dougal for a professional consultation.

On the way Graham stopped at the newsagent's near the Boar to buy two identical Valentine cards. He drove to the house. To his surprise, the kitchen light was on. A pot of freshly brewed tea was on the table. It was standing on one of his medical textbooks. Underneath the chipped saucer that served as Dougal's ashtray were back numbers of the *British National Formulary* and the *Monthly Index of Medical Specialities*. He went upstairs.

Dougal was having a bath. Graham gave him a shout and went back to the kitchen. He removed the ashtray from the table, poured himself some tea and sat down to write the cards. He was writing the addresses when Dougal came downstairs. He had washed his hair. It clung like a tight black cap to his skull.

'What are you doing with those books of mine?' Graham said.

'I hope you don't mind.' Dougal blew his nose. 'I was trying to find a way to cope with my cold.'

Most of Graham's books were in one of the front rooms, piled on the floor or packed in cardboard boxes. There wasn't room for them in the flat.

'There isn't a cure for the common cold. Except time.'

'Oh well. Worth a try.' Dougal sat down and picked up the teapot.

'If you really want to help yourself you should give up smoking.' Graham found some stamps in his wallet and put them on the envelopes. 'Felicity phoned me late last night. Someone's trying to blackmail Kevin Burwell.'

Dougal poured himself some tea. His face was impassive. Graham was disappointed by the lack of reaction. It annoyed him, too.

'You don't seem very surprised.'

Dougal shrugged. 'How was it done? Another phone call?'

'Yes. After everyone had gone home.'

'Was anyone else in the room?'

'How should I know?'

Dougal sipped his tea. 'So what's Kevin been up to?'

'Does it really matter?'

'Possibly.'

'You know this business about Leonie being knocked down? There's some suggestion that Errowby's been giving the investigation special treatment.'

'And why should he do that?'

'Because Kevin's building him that great big eyesore down the lane. And Errowby's having difficulties with his cashflow.'

'Difficult to prove there's anything criminal in the arrangement,' Dougal said. 'But you wouldn't need proof, would you?'

'That's their problem.'

'And what's yours?'

'Kevin's not taking this lying down. He's told Errowby.'

'Privately or officially?'

'Officially. Errowby tried to calm him down, but Kevin wasn't having any. Felicity says he wants a proper investigation. He's an obstinate sod. There's nothing Errowby can do to stop him. There's nothing anyone can do.'

'Have some more tea,' Dougal said.

'I don't want any more,' Graham shouted. He swallowed, and went on in his normal voice: 'What if they catch the blackmailer? What if he talks?'

The kitchen was very quiet. The radiator groaned like a distant foghorn. Dougal opened his tobacco tin, glanced at Graham and closed it.

'There's no doubt it's the same person?'

'The voice was the same. The whispering. But this time the price was a thousand.'

'What about the drop?'

'Kevin put the phone down before that was mentioned. But there can't be two blackmailers. What do we do?'

'The sensible thing would be for you and Felicity to go to the police.' Dougal held up his hand to prevent Graham from interrupting. 'But you're not very sensible so you'll have to hope that the police don't find him, which is perfectly possible. Even if they do find him, you might be OK if we track him down first and manage to do a deal. It's not what I'd advise.'

'Do you think it could be Felicity? Would she blackmail her own husband?'

Dougal's eyebrows rose. 'Wasn't she in the house? Would she have taken the risk of going outside to phone?'

'She wouldn't have had to go outside. They've got two lines.' Graham pushed the cards away from him. He stood up and rubbed his chin. 'Kevin thinks it's Nimp. I told you about him – the old man in the bungalow next door. He's got a grudge against the Burwells.'

'If you want I'll go and see him,' Dougal said. 'I'd like to meet the gnomes.'

'You can't just barge in.'

'Why not? I'm a temporary neighbour. I'll say I've run out of sugar.'

'Do what you like.' Graham scowled at Dougal. 'If you've quite finished in the bathroom, I'm going to have a shave.'

Sharon put two spoonfuls of sugar into her coffee to mask the flavour. 'The promotion board's on Monday. No wonder Errowby's in a state.'

Oliver forced himself to chew three more chips. They were pale in colour, a greener shade of white, and on the cooler side of tepid.

'He'll be even worse this afternoon,' Sharon went on. 'George is here. They're having lunch together.'

'Really?' he said with a careful lack of interest; he wondered what quirk of his upbringing made him discourage gossip, even gossip he wanted to hear. Detective Chief Superintendent James George was the head of the county's CID. It wasn't difficult to guess the reason for this unscheduled call on Errowby.

'Yes, really,' Sharon said. She wasn't beautiful but she had a vitality that made her almost attractive. She went on, 'And don't pretend you're not fascinated.'

Oliver pushed away his plate. The canteen's idea of a nourishing lunch involved chips and indigestion with everything. It was Wednesday 13 February; he needed to get rid of Sharon, if only for half an hour.

'Aren't you hungry?' she said.

He shook his head.

'It's going to be unbearable if Errowby doesn't get the job after all. Fintal lengthened the odds to four to one this morning.'

'It can't be that bad, can it?' Oliver said, surprised. Fintal was running a book on who would get the vacancy.

Sharon ticked off the arguments on her fingers. 'Divisional figures for unsolved crimes are up. The press are beginning to make murmurs. And now' – she licked her lips with unconcealed pleasure – 'and now there's even a hint of personal corruption.'

'The board won't take any notice of that. It's nothing substantial.'

'Not yet. But Errowby must be praying for a few arrests.'

Errowby was asleep. No doubt it had been a heavy lunch; George was reputed to be a good trencherman. Errowby opened his eyes when Oliver tapped on the open door.

'Sorry to disturb you, sir. Shall I come back later?'

'No, come in. I was thinking.'

Just a two-minute cat-nap, Oliver thought, a sign of greatness manifested by other great men, such as Winston Churchill and Napoleon, and probably Hitler and Stalin too.

'Anyway, what is it?'

'I've just had a call from Forensic,' Oliver said. 'Perran's car's clean. And his blood's not even the same group.'

Errowby gave one of his more disapproving grunts. 'Got any good news?'

'Mrs Fish can't remember the colour or make of the kettle. We haven't been able to trace its purchase. The old man could have got it in Bristol or at a market.'

'You've not got much to go on, have you?'

'Perran had recently cleaned the outside of that kettle with white spirit. Why should he do that? He's got form—'

'For GBH, not breaking and entering.'

'He's got transport, both a car and a van, and a lot of dodgy friends. And I swear he's been keeping something in that outhouse. You'd expect it to be full of junk but it wasn't. It was almost empty – just a few tools, a rotary mower, one or two cans of petrol. And the whole place was immaculate. You could eat your dinner off the floor.'

'You asked what he was doing at the material times?'

'And I got the obvious answer. He can't remember. But he thought that he was either up at the Boar or watching telly or asleep with his wife. Someone or something must have tipped him off.'

'If you're right. Could he have been driving the van when he knocked down Leonie?'

'He didn't have the van that Sunday. He took it into a garage for its MOT on Saturday and didn't get it back till Monday evening. I checked with the garage – Abbotsfield Motors on the main road.'

'Got any more bright ideas?'

'I mentioned Kevin Burwell to him and that touched a nerve. I'd like to talk to the neighbours. I think Nimp might know more than he's saying.' Oliver paused, aware that the questioning of minors was hedged about with safeguards and regulations; remembering Tammy's tearful face, he thought that she needed all the protection she could get. 'There's a daughter, you know. Friend of Leonie Burwell's.'

'I'd go easy in that direction,' Errowby said. 'Don't take any risks. By the way, I've got a job for you when you go back to Abbotsfield this afternoon. Go and see the Burwells. I said we'd send someone to check that their phone calls are being recorded.'

'We're providing the equipment?'

A nod. 'And I want to be sure that it's working.'

Of course he did, Oliver thought. Errowby couldn't afford

any mistakes on this investigation. Not that he was likely to retain control of it for much longer. Probably George would take over, if he hadn't done so already.

Errowby picked up a file and lowered his head, intimating in his usual fashion that the interview was at an end.

'One other thing, sir.' Oliver knew that he was trespassing in a delicate area where George had no doubt been before him.

'What is it now?'

'Nimp drew my attention to the fact that someone's staying at White Cross House.'

'I know.' Errowby continued to study the file.

'I met him last night—'

'Congratulations, Rickford. So did I. Had dinner with him, in fact – Graham brought him to the Burwells'.'

It was 'Graham' now, was it? 'Just on the off-chance I checked his car number with Swansea. And the result was interesting.'

Errowby looked up. 'You mean it was nicked?'

'Not as far as I know. It's registered in the name of a London-based company called Custodemus.'

'Never heard of them.'

'I have, sir. They do private security. They've got quite a sizeable private investigation division.'

On Wednesday afternoons they had a double art lesson immediately after lunch. The art room in the main building of Brush Hill Comprehensive had been out of service since the Christmas holidays, when Dale Perran, Tammy's second cousin, had broken into the school and, finding nothing he wanted to steal, had set fire to it instead. Only the art room had been seriously damaged. In consequence Mr Ingrams had been exiled to a former scout hut, which was separated from the rest of the school by a pair of playing fields.

Mr Ingrams never appeared to notice who turned up to his lessons and never remembered his pupils' names. He was known to be on terms of active hostility with the rest of the staff. Tammy and Leonie were not alone in habitually playing truant on Wednesday afternoons. You could slip away at lunchtime and catch the bus to Paulstock; as long as you got back in time for the end of school, no one was going to bat an eyelid.

On Wednesday 13 February they were in Paulstock by 1.15. They had lunch in a Wimpy bar before going shopping. As always they were careful. The main danger was from stray teachers and, to a lesser extent, other truants. Today they spent most of their time in Dorothy Perkins' and Burton's. They planned to leave their purchases in a disused garage belonging to Dale Perran's mother, an incurious woman who lived conveniently close to the railway station.

There was only one bad moment, and that was towards the end when they came out of Burton's and went into the newsagent's across the road. The policeman was there, the detective called Rickford. Until they got inside he was invisible behind a display stand. He looked up and saw them, laden with carrier bags, as they approached the counter.

At the same moment Tammy saw him. In fact she noticed the cards before the face – he was studying two Valentines, both huge and pink, and obviously trying to make up his mind which to buy. She nudged Leonie's arm. For an instant the three of them were locked together in a silent triangle. Then Rickford blinked; he put the cards back on the rack and turned aside to examine a rack of magazines.

Leonie pulled Tammy out of the shop. Once outside they walked quickly, without speaking, along the pavement. They dived into Woolworth's. The store was crowded at this time of day.

'Separate,' Leonie said. 'Meet at the station.'

Tammy blundered down the aisles. She was too full of panic to be able to think. She left the store by the side entrance. Fear made her cunning: she walked through the park, which was considerably out of her way, because in that green, uncluttered place a follower would be obvious. No one was behind her.

To her relief, Leonie was waiting outside the railway station.

'He must have recognised us,' Tammy said. 'Do you think he'll tell?'

'I don't think so. He was trying to pretend he hadn't seen us.'

'I think he's nice.'

'Yes,' Leonie said. 'He's not like a policeman at all.'

Oliver delayed going to the Burwells' house for as long as he could. He got there just before six. Joanna's car was not in the drive. He had hoped that she might be home early from work.

Leonie opened the door. She had changed into jeans and a baggy t-shirt. Alarm flickered in her eyes when she saw him.

'Is your mother in?'

The girl nodded. 'I'll get her.'

'Just a moment.'

Her face was unreadable but he guessed what was going through her mind. She and Tammy must have recognised him in the newsagent's. Strictly speaking he should have said something to them, or notified their truancy to the school or their parents. But at the time he had been absurdly embarrassed. He had imagined Joanna showing her Valentine cards to her sister, and Leonie saying with a giggle, 'Oh, but I've seen that one before.' Now he was glad he had held his peace for another reason: he thought that the girls had enough to worry about without another helping of trouble on their plate. He would have liked to put her mind at rest but his dignity as a policeman, as a responsible member of society, prevented him.

Instead he asked, 'Are you better now?'

'I'm fine.'

'You know why I'm here?'

'They told me, of course.' Suddenly Leonie was very much an adolescent standing on her almost-adult dignity. 'As a matter of fact I heard the phone call.'

Oliver frowned. 'You were with your father? He didn't mention that.'

'No, I mean I heard the phone ringing. It was just after midnight. I was with Joanna in her room, you see – it's on the same side of the house as the office. Joanna heard it too.'

'Heard what, darling?' Felicity Burwell had suddenly appeared in a doorway on the left of the hall.

'The blackmailer ringing Daddy.'

'Oh, *that*.' Felicity switched her tone from the maternal to the commanding. 'And what can we do for you, Sergeant? My husband's not back yet.'

'Sorry to disturb you. Mr Errowby wanted me to check that the equipment is working properly.'

She dismissed Leonie and showed him the two main phones, the one in the hall and the other in Burwell's office. Felicity watched him the whole time – as though she suspected him of having designs on the silver. He played back a few seconds of tape from each line: Felicity agreeing to have coffee with someone called Margaret; Kevin chasing up an unpaid bill.

'Satisfied?' Felicity asked.

'Yes, thanks. It all seems to be working perfectly.'

On Burwell's desk there was a photograph of Joanna and Leonie beside a swimming pool. Joanna in a black one-piece swimming costume smiled demurely at the camera.

'Well, if there's nothing else?' Felicity said.

A moment later Oliver was back in his car. He drove, rather faster than usual, down to White Cross Lane. The sleeping policeman at the end of Meadow Way took him by surprise. He had one more call to make. Hanslope's house was in darkness. Oliver roared up the drive and parked in the yard at the back.

The Sierra wasn't there – but Dougal might have left it at the Boar or garaged it in one of the outbuildings. Oliver switched off his engine, turned off the lights and got out of the car. The kitchen was dark. However, there was a strip of light between the partly drawn curtains of one of the upstairs windows.

He was not looking forward to this interview. Even a policeman has feelings. At their first meeting he had rather liked William Dougal. Now Oliver knew that the man was a liar, and he needed to find out why.

The yard was full of shadows. The back door was a pale

glimmer in the corner. Oliver walked towards it. He raised his hand to knock. Then his right foot landed awkwardly at an angle, and he stumbled. Automatically he bent down. Something sharp and cold pricked the tip of a finger. He swore under his breath. He swept his hand across the gravel and made out the outlines of a rectangle of wood with small nails projecting upwards from it.

What a bloody dangerous thing to leave lying around. He knew exactly what it was: the plywood that had been tacked to the back door to cover the broken pane of glass. He was aware of the hairs shifting on the back of his neck, of the spatter of gravel behind him, of the need to stand up and turn round.

Instead he was falling forward and his head was full of pain. The pain shaped itself into a scream: the scream made a word, *Joanna*: nothing else existed.

16

Neither of her parents was at home when Tammy got back from school. She knew that Suzette was working late at the Cattery this evening – not waiting at tables but cleaning with extra thoroughness for twice her usual hourly rate. Margaret Telford had heard a rumour from a friendly Paulstock councillor that the Environmental Health Department was planning to mount a raid on Abbotsfield, which in practice meant on the Boar and the Cattery.

Tammy made herself beans on toast and took her plate upstairs. Her father came home just after five o'clock. The police still had the Cortina so he was in the van today. He backed it down the garden to the shed. She waited for the bang of the kitchen door. But the minutes passed and he did not come up to the house. That was a relief: no need to cook him a meal, no need to share a room and breathe the same air.

When she had finished her own meal she tried to concentrate on biology for the test tomorrow. She was meant to be revising the human sensory system. One of the diagrams in another chapter of the textbook started her thinking about butterflies. The way they changed fascinated her – from drab, earthbound caterpillars to glorious winged beauties. She had always loved the idea of transformation: the beast who, when kissed, became a prince; the girl in rags among the cinders who, at the wave of a magic wand, was equipped to win a royal heart.

'We don't have to stay as we are,' Leonie had said this afternoon. 'We can be whoever we want to be.'

Tammy lay on her bed and slid into a reverie about how she would change herself. Not totally, of course, because otherwise you would not know that you had changed. Some part of you, probably the memory, would have to stay the same so that you could revel in the difference between then and now. She thought about Thomas and Lara, the butterflies, and imagined *them* thinking of Tammy and Leonie.

A car came down Meadow Way. It broke her concentration. She could tell by the changes in the engine note that the car was going up the drive next door. A little later, Tammy heard the whirr of the van's starter motor. Her father drove slowly down the garden and turned left into the lane. She glanced at the clock by her bed. It was already twenty past six. But there was still time. Her mother wouldn't be back for at least an hour.

She went into her parents' room at the back of the house. She heard another car outside but ignored it – the engine was quieter than the van's; it wasn't a danger. Her father would have padlocked the shed – he was meticulous about that – but she knew where he kept the spare key, fixed to the base of the dressing table with a blob of Blu-Tack. She took the key downstairs, pulled on her duffel coat and went outside.

God, it was cold. She walked slowly down the garden, wondering what she would find this time. Or not find. The night was full of noises. Once she thought she heard footsteps on the path that ran parallel to the lane behind the shed. Leaves rustled to the left of the shed. A cat or perhaps a fox was moving in the scrubby hedge that divided the bottom of their garden from Dr Hanslope's.

Her hand touched the cold metal of the padlock. A door slammed in White Cross House or the bungalow beyond. Someone was running down Dr Hanslope's drive, his feet sliding on the gravel. The sound was too close for comfort. If you could hear, you could be heard. Tammy waited. Her fingers squeezed the padlock key into the flesh of her hand. The footsteps came nearer and now they made a different, crisper sound. She realised with a shock that the person was running up the concrete path that led to the Perrans' front door. She heard banging and, more faintly, the chimes of the doorbell.

Tammy was used to waiting, just as she was used to feeling afraid. Everything eventually comes to an end – she had learned that, if nothing else, from living with Jimmy Perran. There was another burst of knocking. At last the footsteps retreated, still at a run. She heard them on the lane. She listened so hard that she thought she heard in the still night air the click of the latch on Mr Nimp's front gate.

Swathed in his overcoat, Bert Nimp was sitting at his typewriter in the bay window of the sitting room. At lunchtime he had visited the public bar of the Boar and invested in half a pint of bitter. The investment had been richly rewarded. He had overheard what the local sergeant was saying to the barman, and some of what the barman later said to Jimmy Perran. The gossip dovetailed with what he already knew.

Nimp typed slowly, drawing out the pleasure. As a child he had loved jigsaws. Now he did jigsaws with human pieces.

Prominent Abbotsfield developer Kevin Burwell is again facing serious problems. We understand that the police are investigating allegations of impropriety concerning the house he is building in White Cross Lane for Detective Chief Inspector Errowby, head of Paulstock CID. Readers will recall that Mr Burwell is no stranger to such allegations.

Quarme wouldn't print it, of course. He didn't have the guts. But in a way it hardly mattered. Nimp had the satisfaction of writing it and – until the end of March – of knowing that someone on the *Guardian*, almost certainly Quarme himself, would have to read it. In any case there were other methods of making sure that the news was circulated, methods that avoided the risk of libel prosecutions.

Councillor Robbins, for example, suggested recently that Mr Burwell had been using undue influence on other members of the Planning

Committee of the District Council with regard to an application for developing—

The doorbell rang. Nimp sighed. Gripping the edge of the table he levered himself out of the chair. The caller began to hammer on the door.

'I'm coming,' Nimp said. 'I'm coming.'

He shuffled into the hall and opened the door. A man was waiting outside – Dougal, that was the name, Dr Hanslope's friend.

'May I use your phone?' he said. Before Nimp could stop him he had edged into the hall. 'It's an emergency.'

'Well, of course. But—'

Dougal wasn't even listening. He had found the phone and was dialling a number from a piece of paper in his hand. It was most irregular. Why wasn't he using the phone in White Cross House? A most peculiar young man, he'd come round this morning and asked to borrow sugar; but Nimp was sure that, like Jimmy Perran before him, Dougal had an ulterior motive, which in this case Nimp had failed to discover.

'What emergency?' Nimp said, his voice squeaky and pettish. 'I really think you owe me an explanation.'

Dougal said, 'Just shut up for a moment, will you?'

Kevin Burwell met Errowby at 6.30 in the golf club bar. The location was Errowby's suggestion, as was the meeting itself. It suited Burwell well enough – he had a late-afternoon meeting with the Chief Planning Officer so he was already in Paulstock; and if Errowby didn't mind returning to the place where he had made that ridiculous scene, that was his affair. There was a lot to be said for meeting in public. It showed that one had nothing to hide.

The bar wasn't crowded but it was busy. The Chief Inspector, however, sat alone at a table with a large whisky in front of him, marooned among empty chairs. Burwell collected a Perrier water from the bar and made a point of greeting several members he knew. None of them shied away from him, though one or two might have liked to do so. But he had no intention of letting anyone treat him as a pariah by default, and no one had the courage blatantly to ignore him. Honour satisfied, he went to join Errowby.

'How's it going, Bernie?'

'I don't know about you, but I've had a piss-awful day.'

'Come on. It can't be as bad as all that.' Burwell registered the blotches on Errowby's face and the dab of spittle on his chin. The policeman had always been a steady drinker but lately he had taken to knocking the stuff back as though there were no tomorrow. Last night he had drunk more than the rest of them combined.

'Had my Chief Superintendent over today.' Errowby's voice wavered in volume as though he were having difficulty in breathing. 'Man called George. You know him?'

'No.' Burwell nodded at the whisky. 'How many of those have you had?'

'A couple, maybe. Are you counting or something? Has June asked you to spy on me?'

'Hey – what is this? Calm down.'

Errowby dropped his eyes to his glass. 'Sorry. Forget I said it. Look, I just wanted to make sure we say the same thing.'

'About what, exactly?'

'I did you a favour, you know. I'm allowed a certain amount of discretion over how I allocate resources. George has gone over the last month with a fine-tooth comb. You can imagine it, can't you? "What was your precise thinking about the manpower allocated to the Burwell hit-and-run case?" He's all waffle and velvet gloves, that man – softly, softly when you're face to face. And then he comes up behind you with a memo like a blunt instrument.'

'You've done nothing wrong, surely?'

'In theory I've got nothing to worry about.' Errowby looked up. 'At worst, it's a small error of professional judgement. It's not a hanging offence. Just a rap over the knuckles from George or the ACC, not even an official caution. As long as that's all it is, Kevin.'

'No one's going to take this blackmailer seriously.'

'It's out of my hands now. I warned you. They'll probably come and talk to you – about you and me, I mean. They may even want to see your books. It's unlikely but possible.'

'They're welcome.'

'For God's sake, listen. George goes by the rules. If this goes wrong, I'll end up suspended from duty pending an inquiry. And if that goes against me they'll throw the bloody book at me.'

Burwell smiled and channelled all the force of his personality into soothing Errowby. 'Bernie, we're friends and fellow Masons. No one's denying it. We've got a gentlemen's agreement about that house of yours, and they can't prove otherwise because there's nothing to prove. The hit-and-run investigation is something quite separate. I didn't ask you for any favours. You didn't ask me for any. As far as I'm concerned, you were just doing your job.'

'You'll say that if they ask you? You promise?'

'Of course I'll say that, Bernie. It's the truth.'

Errowby swallowed the rest of his whisky. 'Christ, I wish this had never happened. However you slice it, it'll affect my chances. Do you want another drink?'

'No, I don't think so. I must get home.' Burwell stood up, leaving his untouched Perrier water on the table. 'You worry too much. Tell you what I'll do. I'll lay you five to one that you get promotion. In tenners.'

'You're on.' Errowby grinned, and the grin turned into a chuckle. His mood had swung without warning to the opposite extreme. 'You'd better watch out, Kev. I'll hold you to that.'

Oliver was lying on a stone pavement. Beige and yellow slabs stretched away for miles until they reached the base of a white cliff. Probably chalk, as at Dover. The clifftop was out of sight and there weren't any bluebirds. The slabs were cold beneath his cheek. He felt a light breeze on his skin.

Time passed. His head hurt. He analysed the situation to make time pass more quickly and to distract him from the headache. He was lying on his stomach with his head tilted back so that he could see the white cliff. He could also see one arm; the other was somewhere behind him. His legs were out of sight but he knew they were there. The right leg was more or less straight. The left knee was bent. He had covered himself up with a brown blanket. How very sensible. The light was too bright so he closed his eyes.

He often slept in this position. But why had he wanted to go to sleep on a stone pavement? Was it stone or something smoother, like plastic? A plastic pavement seemed improbable. He tried to recall the events that had brought him here.

He'd been to the Burwells' to check the phones. Joanna wasn't there. Just a photograph of her looking coolly desirable in a swimming costume. *Joanna*. He had started to drive to White Cross House. He'd gone too fast over the sleeping policeman. Now *he* was a sleeping policeman. Was that a joke? Would other people find it funny? He had always harboured a secret suspicion that his sense of humour was in some way defective, or at least different from other people's. He often laughed at jokes because everyone else was laughing, not because he found them funny. On the whole he thought that the sleeping policeman joke *was* quite funny: the sophisticated sort of joke that earns a wry twist of the mouth, not a belly-laugh.

The belt buckle was digging into his groin. He moved his left hand down to investigate the problem. To his surprise he found that the belt was undone; so were his trousers and the top of his flies. This worried him. Suppose someone came along and saw him half-undressed?

He ran the hand up to his neck, discovering on the way that his jacket was unzipped, his tie loosened and his collar button undone. The observations he had made about himself since waking up suddenly re-formed into a familiar pattern. It took him back to a first-aid course – at Hendon, was it? – and a perfectly bald instructor saying, 'And this, ladies and gentlemen, is the recovery position for unconscious casualties.'

Metal clicked and scraped behind him. The breeze increased. A door closed. He heard footsteps.

'Are you awake?'

Oliver opened his eyes. William Dougal was crouching beside him. 'I was coming to see you,' Oliver said. It was surprisingly hard to articulate the words. 'I wanted to ask you something. I can't remember what it was.'

'Later. It can wait.'

Oliver tried to sit up but it wasn't worth the effort. Dougal went away and came back with a cushion. He lifted Oliver's head and slid the cushion underneath.

'This is White Cross House, isn't it?' Oliver said triumphantly. 'We're in the kitchen.'

'That's right. Can you remember anything?'

'I was driving here . . . I went over the sleeping policeman at the bottom of Meadow Way, a bit of a bump . . .' He hesitated. 'That's all.'

'I found you just outside the back door. Someone had knocked you over the head. It looks like the blow was from behind and above.'

Oliver licked his lips. 'Call the police.'

'I have.'

'I *am* the police.' He giggled weakly, and Dougal smiled. A nice man, Oliver thought with a rush of affection, and capable of appreciating a joke. They must share a sense of humour.

'I had to go next door to phone,' Dougal said. 'Someone's pulled the plug off the phone in the hall.'

He sat cross-legged on the floor where Oliver could see him. For a moment neither of them said anything. Oliver thought that it was a companionable silence. He was the first to break it. He wanted to be helpful.

'If the phone isn't working you can use the batphone in the car.'

'I don't think anyone will be using that for a while, either.'

Oliver considered this. He struggled to formulate a question. It was too complicated. In the end he simply said, 'Why?'

'Why have the radio and the phone been sabotaged? To delay pursuit, I suppose. Or do you mean, why did you get hit over the head?'

'That too.'

'At first I thought you'd been mistaken for me or even Graham Hanslope. But my camera's gone – it was on the hall table by the phone. Maybe other things too. I haven't had time to check. It looks as if you may have walked into a burglary.'

'Damn. Wrong time, wrong place.'

'What?'

'It doesn't matter.'

'You've had a spate of burglaries, haven't you? This doesn't fit the pattern?'

Suddenly wary, Oliver tried to shrug. The pain made him wince. Dougal was too confident for comfort, too quick and too well-informed. In the middle of an emergency he had taken the time to note the angle of a blow. He knew the textbook treatment for an unconscious casualty and what a batphone was. Oliver remembered why he was here.

'Are you a private investigator employed by Custodemus?'

'Who told you that?' Dougal waited, then answered the question himself. 'You checked the car.'

'You lied. You said you were an editor or something.'

'I didn't lie. I do that too.'

Oliver wondered why people had to make themselves so complicated. At the time it did not occur to him to doubt Dougal's explanation. He was relieved that Dougal hadn't lied. No time to think about that now. There was work to do.

'But you're not a friend of Hanslope's, are you?' he said with an effort. 'He's employing you. Why? Is he being blackmailed too?'

Dougal smiled. 'Listen,' he said.

Oliver listened. In the distance but coming nearer was the panic-stricken wail of a siren. His headache worsened.

'And where were you when I got knocked on the head?'

'Me? I just went out to post a Valentine card.'

17

Felicity was the first downstairs. She had not been sleeping well in the last few weeks. Receiving a display of early-morning affection from a starving Simba was marginally preferable to lying wakeful beside Kevin.

Sleep did not improve her husband. He snored. His body would inch towards the centre of the big bed, squeezing hers closer and closer to the edge. His arms had a habit of reaching out for her. She hated the restrictions his sleeping body imposed: sharing a bed with him was like sharing it with a ball and chain.

The great advantage of Simba was that you could always lock her and her breakfast in the garage. The post arrived as Felicity was drinking her second cup of coffee and watching the news. She sorted it out on the kitchen table. For Kevin there were bills and a long brown envelope from the Inland Revenue. For her there was a catalogue of clothes she couldn't afford, which she didn't bother to open, and a letter informing her that she could no longer use her Barclaycard.

No Valentines for her. Kevin no longer bothered, and nor apparently did anyone else. She didn't want a Valentine from Kevin but she was perversely irritated by the fact that he hadn't sent one. Joanna had four. Even Leonie had one, enclosed in an enormous white envelope addressed in block capitals. Felicity turned the envelope over. The triangular flap at the back was only partly gummed down.

Children, she told herself, need their space, their privacy, if they are to become mature human beings capable of existing apart from their parents. That, at least, was the theory. On the other hand, one had to be practical. A mother has her responsibilities. She must exercise a discreet surveillance if only for the ultimate good of the child. In any case no one would ever know.

Partly convinced by her own arguments, Felicity turned down the sound of the television and opened the kitchen door so that she would hear if someone came downstairs. Hastily – if she lingered she might change her mind – she slid the flat, rounded blade of a dinner knife under the flap of the envelope. The gum gave way without tearing the paper.

On the front of the card was a rampant pink kitten with a purple bow round its neck. It carried between its front paws a terrestrial globe garlanded with red roses. Above it was the legend TO MY VALENTINE. Felicity opened the card and read the rhyme inside.

> *If I owned the world*
> *I know what I'd do*
> *I'd wreathe it with roses*
> *And give it to you!*

Beneath the rhyme were three crosses, kisses, in pink felt-tip.

Ten to one Tammy Burwell had sent the card. There might be a boyfriend at school but Felicity had seen no evidence of one. The Valentine was a direct contravention of parental authority. Its size and vulgarity added to the defiance. Felicity used the card as one uses a magnifying glass: her anger was the sun, and she concentrated it to burning point.

She fetched the kitchen scissors and cut up both card and envelope into very small pieces. Pulling on her rubber gloves she opened the rubbish bin. The bin liner needed changing. She pushed aside potato peelings and empty tins and worked the fragments of card and paper into the lower levels of the rubbish. She washed the gloves and hung them to dry. Finally she gathered up the rest of the post: the opened letter from Barclaycard went in her bureau; she replaced the remainder in an untidy heap on the mat by the front door.

When Leonie came down, Felicity was laying the table for breakfast.

'Hello, darling,' she said. 'Sleep well?'

'All right.' Leonie slouched across the kitchen and opened the refrigerator.

'Has the post come yet?'

'I didn't notice,' Leonie said.

Graham had two Valentine cards. He saw them on the mat as he passed through the hall on the way back from the bathroom. He left them lying there.

In the living room he picked up the phone and punched in a number. 'Come on, come on,' he muttered as the rings went on and on. At last there was a click. A woman answered.

'Sue? Can I speak to the birthday boy?'

'For God's sake, Graham, he's in the middle of his breakfast and he's still not dressed.'

Too busy opening presents, Graham thought. 'Did the Lego come?'

'Yes. And the leather jacket. You spend too much on him.'

'Let me have a word. Just this once. He'll be at school all day and I've got a busy evening. I may not have another chance.'

'All right. Not for long, though. I'll see you Saturday.'

'I'll come to the house if you want.'

'No, I'll meet you at the station at nine forty-three. I'm going shopping in Queensway.'

A moment later Michael came to the phone. Graham sang him 'Happy Birthday'. Michael thanked him for the presents in the wooden voice children use on the telephone.

'I'm looking forward to Madame Tussaud's,' Graham said.

'Yeah. I wish we were going today.'

Soon afterwards Graham said goodbye. He didn't want to upset Sue by keeping Michael talking. It had been a good phone call, and Graham relished the memory of it as he shaved, dressed and made his breakfast. Michael could only have meant that he preferred being with Graham to being with his parents.

He opened the Valentine cards while he munched a slice of toast. Joanna's – it wasn't signed but it could only be from her – was an insipid affair involving pink hearts and cuddling teddy bears. The other was from Rachel. It was determinedly lewd. The joke concerned a vicar, a mini-skirted parishioner and a large church organ. Inside the card Rachel had scribbled, 'When will you get tired of shagging sheep?'

Soon he would have to make a decision about Rachel. It depended to some extent on what happened this evening when Joanna came to supper. Would she or wouldn't she? It also depended, more importantly, on what the blackmailer did. If the worst came to the worst, if they chucked him out of the Abbotsfield practice and struck him off the Register, he would go to Rachel. If he had a chance to explain to her, she would take him in; she'd look after him until he found his feet again. Like Michael, she was a person you could depend on.

Oliver had a Valentine card. He had sent one and expected none. It was postmarked Paulstock and addressed to him at the flat. The card was unsigned and, in comparison with others he had seen in the newsagent's, almost lukewarm in its sentiments: 'Thinking of you on this special day . . .'

Would Sharon be so stupid? It was the most likely explanation; he hardly knew any women in Paulstock. He threw the card away. Then the remote possibility that the card might be from Joanna made him retrieve it from the bin and tuck it safely out of sight in a pile of newspapers.

Despite his headache, he decided to go into work at the usual time. Last night the doctor had offered him sick leave, almost demanded that he take it, but Oliver had refused. This was not from a sense of duty – he knew that he would get no thanks from Errowby, and that most of his colleagues would treat his being knocked out at best as an excuse for mockery and at worst as further evidence of his professional inadequacy. He swallowed two painkillers and wished that there were some way short of a Ku Klux Klan mask to conceal the dressing on his head.

In the lobby of Copeland Court he met Graham Hanslope, who for once was almost amiable.

'How are you feeling?'

Oliver said he was fine.

'I wanted to find a chance to thank you. If you hadn't turned up I should have probably lost a lot more. The most valuable thing they got was my friend's camera, and that—'

'Your friend, Dr Hanslope? Is that what you call him?'

For a couple of seconds Oliver allowed himself to relish the shock on Hanslope's face. He walked quickly away, floating on an unwelcome sense of triumph, a feeling that he had at last managed to return evil for evil; it was unwelcome because he knew that he would later regret it.

Taking his time, he walked to work; he would be without a car for a day or two. At the station he made a detour to avoid the main entrance because the unbearably facetious Sergeant Wilson would be manning the desk. He went upstairs, braced himself and pushed open the door of the CID room.

'Look who's here,' Fintal said. 'It's the walking wounded.'

Everyone seemed in a good mood. Oliver answered enquiries about his health and sat down. Sharon brought him some coffee he didn't want.

'Are you really all right?' she said.

'I'm fine.'

'Tell you one thing: when they find whoever attacked you, Errowby's going to get him crucified. Can't let people get away with mugging police officers, can we?'

'That's a great consolation. Why's everyone so cheerful this morning?'

'The cat's away,' she said. 'The mice are having a ball.'

'I'm not up to riddles.'

'The AC has summoned Errowby.'

'A carpeting?'

'He didn't confide in me. Your guess is as good as mine.'

'Have we got any leads?'

She shook her head. Their eyes met. Sharon's eyes were brown, rather small and lightly made-up. Suddenly Oliver was tired of the uncertainty. There was too much of it in life, and a lot of it was unnecessary.

'Someone in Paulstock sent me a Valentine this morning.'

'Lucky old you.'

'I don't feel lucky.'

'They're a funny lot down here,' Sharon said, moving away from his desk. 'Warped sense of humour. It was probably Fintal.'

'The little minx,' Nimp said to himself.

The afternoon light was already beginning to fade from the sky. He walked back along the footpath, past the rear fences of his own garden and Errowby's, across the field and into the lane. The encounter had made him tremble. He was so wrapped up in his thoughts that he failed to hear the car approaching behind him until the driver hooted at him.

He scuttled to the side of the lane. A silver-grey Rover slid past him and turned into the track up to the half-built house. No one had done any real work on it for weeks.

Errowby was alone in the car; he hadn't bothered to wave. He usually waved, surely? The Rover's door slammed. Nimp walked slowly towards his garden gate. He wondered if the Chief Inspector had joined the conspiracy against him, the conspiracy that had cost him his job. Harry Quarme didn't like Errowby but both men had professional reasons for staying on good terms with each other. The more Nimp thought about it, the more likely it seemed that Burwell had not only put pressure on Quarme himself but also persuaded Errowby to do the same.

'Mr Nimp.' Treading softly, Errowby had come into the lane. He reached the gate of the bungalow just as Nimp was closing it. Errowby's raincoat was unbuttoned, and the skirts flapped around his legs. His tie was loose. There were bags under his eyes. He leaned on the gate and looked not at Nimp but at the garden.

'What can I do for you, Mr Errowby?'

'How many bloody gnomes have you got?'

Nimp thought he must have misheard. 'I – I beg your pardon?'

'Gnomes.' Errowby raised his voice. 'Those funny little objects with pointy hats. How many?'

'Seventy-eight, I think.'

'Coping all right, are you?'

With the gnomes? 'Yes. Of course I am.'

'Seeing all this' – Errowby's wave embraced the gnomes, the garden, the dilapidated bungalow – 'some people might not agree. They might think you needed a bit of help.'

'I'm quite capable of looking after myself, thank you. Now if you'll excuse me, I—'

'They had a case like that in Paulstock last winter. A widow – living alone. Neighbours got worried about the old dear. Ah, she was harmless by all accounts. But a little bit off her rocker. She used to spend her days walking. She'd go to the shops maybe five or six times a day. Each time she'd buy one thing – a packet of tea, a tin of beans. Thing is, it was a mile walk each time – a mile there, a mile back. So naturally the neighbours were concerned. I mean, it's not very nice living next door to a loony, is it? Lowers the tone of the neighbourhood. Not that they were being selfish. I don't mean to imply that. They contacted the social services for the best of reasons, I'm sure.'

Nimp backed away from the gate.

'Don't rush off.'

'I've just remembered something.'

A blue Sierra turned into the lane from Meadow Way. Both men glanced at it. The car swung into the drive of White Cross House.

'Dr Hanslope's friend,' Errowby said. 'I suppose Hanslope must be your GP. Nice chap – had dinner with him the other day. What did you forget?'

Nimp blinked, unsettled by the rapid changes of subject. 'It doesn't matter.'

'Do you find that happens a lot these days? Forgetting to turn off the chip pan – that sort of thing? It could be dangerous. Could lead to a nasty accident.'

'No.' Nimp squirmed. 'I never do things like that.'

'Where was I? The social services. They tried to call but the old lady wasn't in, so they passed the buck to the old dear's GP. He tracked her down and had a look at her. Bit eccentric, he said, even senile, but still fending for herself. So he passed the buck back to the social services. They tried home helps and meals on wheels, but that didn't work because the old lady was never in. So the social services forgot about it until the neighbours complained again. This time they got a councillor to help. You can't ignore a councillor, can you? It was old Robbins, and you know what he's like on his hind legs. Everyone thought something should be done and everyone thought someone else should do it. The old dear was making everyone uncomfortable, you see. So in the end everyone – the GP, the social services – signed on the dotted line and the old girl ended up in The Firs. She's dead now.'

Nimp knew all about The Firs, a Victorian mansion in the middle of a conifer plantation outside Paulstock. Technically a convalescent home, it was where old people were sent to die at the expense of the local health authority; the place was notorious as a sort of dustbin for the elderly – for those who were alone, who lacked the money for a private nursing home, whose relatives couldn't or wouldn't help.

'Well, I can't stand here chatting all day,' Errowby let go of the gate and rubbed his hands together. 'Mind you take care of yourself. Don't want you ending up in The Firs, do we?'

As Nimp was about to let himself into the bungalow, he heard the Rover's engine firing. Errowby had come here solely to talk to him, to make threats. Could he really carry them out? Possibly. Something very similar had happened to Jimmy Perran's mother when she took to soliciting strangers in her nightdress.

Nimp took the key from the door and waited for the Rover

to leave. As its engine dwindled, his anger grew. It was directed not so much at Errowby as at Kevin Burwell. It was obvious that he was behind this; he had Errowby in his pocket.

The little minx. Like father, like daughter. Bad blood.

Nimp hurried back to the lane and up the drive of White Cross House. Dougal was in the yard. He was checking the Sierra's tyres. By now it was twilight, and he was using a torch to read the pressure gauge.

'Is Dr Hanslope around?'

'No.' Dougal edged round the car to the next tyre. 'He's up at the Health Centre, I imagine.'

'Oh dear. I rather wanted a word.'

'Then you could phone him. Or I'll take a message.'

'Well, as you're staying here, perhaps you—'

'The thing is, Mr Nimp, I'm in a bit of a hurry.'

'This could be urgent. I caught a trespasser in your garden this afternoon.'

Dougal looked up. 'Who?'

'The Burwell child – Leonie. She was with that dog of theirs. I was walking along the footpath – you know it? at the bottom of our gardens? – and I saw her quite distinctly slipping through the fence. First the dog, then her. Naturally I thought I should investigate. She had actually pulled a plank out of the fence.'

'You saw her doing that?'

'Well, no. Not exactly. But she must have done. Technically I imagine that counts as criminal damage or something like that. The plank's hanging loose – a sheep or something could easily wriggle through.'

'There aren't any sheep in that field.'

'There will be. In any case, I thought I'd better do something.'

'Why?' By now Dougal was concentrating most of his attention on the footpump. 'I'm sure Graham wouldn't mind. Leonie's practically his sister-in-law.'

'I saw her going into that shed.' Nimp pointed at the

outbuilding furthest from the house; its door was on the garden side. 'Poking and prying around.'

'She was probably chasing the dog or something.'

'Not that dog. It's too old to run anywhere. Anyway, when she came out, I said something to her – well, shouted, actually – I had to, to make myself heard. And she just turned and ran, dragging the dog after her. Ran up the drive and vanished. If that's not a sign of a guilty conscience, I don't know what is.'

'She was probably just frightened.' Air hissed out of one of the tyres. Dougal closed the pump and stood up. 'Look, I think you may be making too much of this. Don't let it worry you. I'll mention it to Graham.'

'Don't you think you should have a look at the fence, the shed?'

'I will,' Dougal said. He got into the car. 'I promise. But I'll do it tomorrow, all right?'

18

'Let me freshen your drink, darling,' Graham said. 'And then I'll do something about the meal.'

'Just a little one. I really shouldn't have any. I'm driving.'

He turned his back to pour Joanna another substantial glass of wine, and to top up his own glass to create the illusion that they were drinking at the same pace. He put their glasses on the coffee table, where Joanna's Valentine card was prominently displayed beside a bowl of salted nuts, and rejoined her on the sofa.

'*Was* it you who sent the roses?' she asked for the third time.

'I'll tell you if you give me a kiss.'

She gave it to him without hesitation, and she allowed him to take his time receiving it. The twelve red roses had not been cheap – out of season; delivered by Interflora to Joanna at Lees and Bright during the afternoon – but the money had been well spent.

'Well, was it?'

He smiled at her. 'Of course it was.'

Joanna kicked off her shoes and snuggled up to him. She was looking very fetching in a cream silk shirt and a full black skirt. They sipped their drinks. Joanna nibbled a nut.

'Must you go up to London on Saturday?'

'A promise is a promise.'

'We get so little time together. I was hoping we could go to Hampton Hall – have some lunch and finalise the arrangements for the reception. We can't leave it much longer.'

'You know I'd love to. But you wouldn't want me to break my word, would you? Especially not to a child.'

'No, of course not.' Joanna sounded unconvinced. 'Where are you going?'

'Madame Tussaud's. He wants to look at the murderers. His idea of a birthday treat.'

'How ghoulish. You're very kind to him, aren't you? You'll make a wonderful father.'

'And you'll be a wonderful mother.' Graham spoke automatically; he was wondering how to move the conversation from the consequences of procreation to its method. 'I—'

'Have you and Michael always been close?'

'I suppose so.'

'Because of the way you grew up?'

Graham nodded. Just before their engagement he had given her an edited version of his fatherless childhood; he had stressed the poverty as a way of showing her what he had already achieved, and he had also hinted at emotional deprivation to arouse her maternal instincts.

'But surely Michael's got a father?'

'Between ourselves, some fathers are worse than none.' He added with a sincerity that took him by surprise: 'I don't want Michael to go through what I did. Not if I can help it.'

'I think that's lovely.' Joanna snuggled closer; Graham realised that by chance he was getting closer to his objective, not further from it. 'I tell you what,' she went on. 'Why don't I come too? I'd love to meet him.'

'That's a wonderful idea,' Graham said, making a virtue out of necessity. He couldn't keep Michael and Joanna apart for ever; it just wouldn't be practical, unfortunately. He would have to remember to warn Michael not to mention Rachel. 'Are you sure it wouldn't bore you? The Chamber of Horrors followed by beefburgers?'

'I'd enjoy it. And it'll be nice to meet your sister. What time would we be back?'

'Not late. Around seven, probably.'

'Well, in that case there's no reason why we shouldn't go to Hampton Hall for dinner.'

Graham agreed with simulated enthusiasm.

'I was wondering if we could do some work on the house this weekend,' she went on. 'We haven't much time.'

'Good idea.'

'Will your friend still be there?'

'Probably not. He had to go up to London today. He'll be coming back tomorrow but I don't think he'll be staying much longer. Then we can really get going. And talking of getting going – I must do something about supper.'

'Can I help?'

'You can help me make the salad in a moment.'

'What are we having? Or shouldn't I ask?'

'Cheese soufflé and champagne.'

'Oh, you are clever.'

Graham smiled modestly. His repertoire of recipes was eclectic and limited but chosen with care. All of them came from former girlfriends. The recipes had one thing in common: they were designed to impress women with his skill in the kitchen.

'You put your feet up for a bit.' He put the remote control on the arm of the sofa. 'See what's on television or put some music on. I'll go and potter in the kitchen.'

At the door he glanced back at her. She had stretched her legs along the sofa; she smiled with her eyes at him over the brim of her glass. She was more beautiful than any other woman he had known. He was almost tempted to leave the soufflé and make the direct assault straightaway. Caution prevailed: Joanna was not the sort of woman you could rush. This time he would make no mistakes.

The oven was already at the right temperature. He grated cheese into the white sauce he had made earlier. He set up the electric mixer and broke egg whites into the bowl.

'I'm going to shut the door on you,' he called to Joanna. 'Because of the noise.'

The mixer whirred for a couple of minutes. Graham greased the soufflé dish and washed up. His mind ran ahead: say forty minutes until the meal; should he open the champagne now or wait? He switched off the mixer, folded the cheese mixture into the egg whites and transferred this to the soufflé dish. He thought he heard talking next door. Joanna must have turned on the television.

She opened the kitchen door just as he was about to put the dish in the oven.

He began to speak: 'I won't be a—'

'That was your girlfriend.' Joanna's voice wasn't loud: it was high and distorted. 'Rachel.'

Graham swung round, conscious that the soufflé dish between his hands put him at a disadvantage. Joanna was carrying her coat and handbag. Her face was twisted out of shape: she looked like an ugly stranger.

'Darling, you've got the wrong idea,' he said.

'Oh, really? You expect me to believe that?'

'A *former* girlfriend. I haven't seen her for—'

'Shut up,' Joanna screamed. 'Don't make it worse. She was phoning to say thank you for her Valentine card. You've seen her lots of times since we got engaged.'

'I can explain that.'

'You were staying with her when you went up to London.' Joanna tugged at her finger. 'When you said you were staying with your friend Dave.'

'Joanna, listen—'

'Helping with his research, wasn't it? Research? That's a joke.'

At last she worked the ring free. She threw it with all her force into the soufflé mixture. It sank slowly out of sight.

Joanna backed into the hall. She lifted her hands, palms outward, towards him, as though she feared he might spring at her.

'Keep away from me. You're dirty. You're filthy.'

She turned, and ran out of the flat.

Oliver came into the foyer of Copeland Court. He had collected a Chinese takeaway on his way home and now wished he hadn't. He was dog-tired.

The lift beckoned him. Too easy, like the monosodium gluta-mate they put in Chinese food. He started to climb the stairs. If he pampered himself he would never get better.

As he rounded the first half-landing he heard the rapid clack of high heels above him. Someone was in a hurry. The lift whirred up its shaft. The footsteps came closer as he mounted the next flight. Suddenly Joanna appeared at the next half-landing. One hand on the rail, she swung round the corner. She saw him below her. Her left foot turned as it landed. She toppled sideways, gasping with pain. Her hand slipped from the rail. She cannoned into the wall and pitched down the short flight of stairs.

Oliver dropped the carrier bag. Joanna crashed into his outstretched arms. Her weight threw him backwards. He over-balanced. He fell down the last two stairs and landed flat on his back in the first-floor hallway. A second later, she landed on top of him. Her body, firm and unexpectedly heavy, drove the air from his lungs. Pain lanced through his head. He put his arms around her.

She was trembling violently. Something warm and wet trickled down his cheek.

'Are you hurt?' he said, and strands of scented hair brushed his lips as he spoke. Not blood, he realised, but tears. He smelled sweet-and-sour pork.

She rolled away from him. 'Oh God, I'm sorry,' she said. She stood up and pulled down her skirt. She must have seen the dressing. 'And your head – is it all right?'

'It's fine,' Oliver lied. He sat up, got a grip on the banister rail and pulled himself to his feet. 'It's you I'm worried about.'

She shook her head, disclaiming injury, and all the while the tears ran down her face. She stooped to pick up her coat and handbag. In the confusion of the fall the carrier bag had spilled its contents. Some of the aluminium containers had broken open. A rectangular mound of rice lay steaming on the landing carpet. Oliver's right elbow had landed in the sweet-and-sour pork.

'What's wrong?' he said. 'You're—'

'*Joanna!*'

Hanslope's voice reverberated around the stairwell. He'd taken the lift down to the foyer.

'What is it?' Oliver hissed.

'*Joanna!*'

'He mustn't find me,' she whispered.

They heard the main door opening.

'My car's outside. He'll know I'm still here.'

'Then come upstairs,' Oliver said. 'You can wait in my flat.'

'*Joanna!*'

She darted away from Hanslope's voice. Oliver followed, abandoning the Chinese meal. She took the stairs at the double. When they reached the third floor, she hung back. She was panting and flushed.

'I'm being silly.' She avoided Oliver's eyes. 'I'm imposing on you.'

'You're not.'

'If I could just wait up here on the landing—'

'You might as well be comfortable while you wait. Besides, he might come up to look for you.'

She swayed and steadied herself on the wall.

'You're in no condition to drive,' Oliver said with a policeman's impersonal authority. 'Come on. It's the second door on the left.'

He saw his home through Joanna's eyes, and for the first time he was ashamed of it. The air inside was chilly and a little damp. The overhead light shed a harsh glare on the square room with its two north-facing windows; he hadn't even bothered to draw the curtains before going out. The unwashed breakfast crockery was piled on the draining board in the kitchen alcove. The door to the glorified cupboard that served as a bathroom stood open, revealing his washing drying over the bath; he had left a towel in an untidy heap on the floor. From the clues the flat offered she could piece together his character. The evidence was everywhere: the lack of pictures, the dust, the pile of newpapers, largely unread, on the floor by the solitary armchair.

'Sorry about the mess. I've just been camping here.' He turned on the electric fire and drew the curtains. 'Do sit down. I'll put the kettle on. Coffee?'

'If you want.' She lowered herself into the chair; she sat well forward on the seat with her feet firmly on the ground and her knees together. 'I'm in your way.'

'No. It's – it's nice to have a visitor.'

'But your meal. All the mess on the stairs.'

'Don't worry. I'll sort it out later. I'd already decided I couldn't face eating it.'

'You're very kind.' She spoke in a mumble, like a child under adult direction expressing gratitude. He noticed that she was looking at her hands and frowning with disbelief. She was no longer wearing an engagement ring.

He busied himself making instant coffee and sponging the stains from his leather jacket. All the time he was aware of the strained silence behind him. He had fantasised about having Joanna in the flat but it had never been like this. She reminded him of a passenger in a railway waiting room: a passenger who feared that if her attention lapsed for a moment the train might come and go without her.

She took the coffee, holding the mug with both her hands. 'I owe you an explanation, I suppose.'

'You don't have to explain anything.'

'I answered the phone,' she went on as if he had not spoken. 'Her name's Rachel. Another girlfriend. All those visits to London and I never dreamed . . . And the funny thing was, she blamed me as much as him. As if I'd stolen him from her.'

Oliver sat down on the sofa. He recognised her condition; he had been trained to take professional advantage of the urge to confide that so often succeeds a wave of shock.

'She called me names – filthy, unfair names – she thought I'd let him . . . you know. Said she'd known for weeks he had someone else. One Sunday he told her a lie – said he'd been waiting hours for her at her flat, but a neighbour said he'd only just arrived. That's how she knew, she said, that and the fact he couldn't *do* anything that night. She thought he'd been with me. But he wasn't, so he must have had someone else too, mustn't he?'

'When was that?' Oliver said. 'Which Sunday?'

'I don't know. Three weeks ago? He said he had to help a friend with some research . . . Anyway, what does it matter?'

'What will you do?'

'What can I do? It's over. You know, if I hadn't answered the phone tonight, I'd be marrying him. I can't believe it.'

'At least you found out now rather than later.'

'It would have hurt whenever it happened.'

'If you're going to get hurt, you may as well get it out of the way as soon as possible.'

'Maybe.' She put down her untouched coffee and said in a strained, brittle voice: 'I must go home.'

'Take your time. You've had a shock.'

'I'm perfectly all right now.'

'Are you sure you're fit to drive?'

She nodded. Her mouth tightened. Oliver guessed that she was beginning to regret having said so much to someone who was almost a total stranger. She picked up her coat, which she had draped over the back of the chair, and started to put it on. Her hands were shaking. All her movements were clumsy and inefficient, as though she couldn't see what she was doing. He tried to help her.

'Don't touch me,' she said shrilly.

In Oliver's mind something snapped. 'I'm sorry. I was only—'

'It's all right.' She edged away from him. The hysteria had drained from her voice. 'I can manage by myself.'

'I'll see you down to your car. Just in case.'

Joanna considered the offer, her hands twisting the strap of her bag. Oliver watched her. For the first time, he thought, he was seeing her directly, rather than reflected in the distorting mirror he had made for her. And simultaneously he saw himself as an uninvolved outsider would see him; someone like Dougal, say. Fool, he thought, fool.

She glanced at him and nodded. He guessed that she had weighed the protection of his company against the possibility that he might make a pass at her, and that her fear of Graham Hanslope had won.

They took the lift to the ground floor. She kept as far away from Oliver as possible. The foyer was empty. Outside, the evening was cold and clear, with enough of a wind to make him wish he had brought a coat.

'His car's gone,' he said.

They both glanced up at the second-floor windows. Graham Hanslope's were dark.

'He must have gone out.'

She shivered. 'Probably looking for me.'

She ran across the tarmac and got into her car. Oliver followed.

'Thank you for your help,' she said. 'Goodbye.'

'Don't mope,' he said suddenly; he no longer needed to worry about making a good impression. 'Whatever you do, don't just sit around thinking. It won't help. Keep active. Do something different.'

The engine fired. She slammed the door. In the dim light he thought he saw her lips moving. The car reversed jerkily out of the slot and drove on to the road. Joanna belatedly remembered to turn her lights on. He watched the tail-lights until they disappeared.

Oliver went back inside. He collected the more obvious remains of his supper from the stairs. In the flat he went through the newspapers until he found the Valentine. He stuffed the card in the takeaway's carrier bag and dropped the whole lot in the bin.

Unhappiness he was used to coping with. But this evening it mated with despair, and their offspring was the desire to hurt someone very badly, preferably Graham Hanslope. Ignoring the twinges of his conscience, he thought about the scrap of information that Joanna had given him. According to her, according to Rachel and her neighbour, Hanslope had lied about his whereabouts one Sunday evening – almost certainly Sunday 27 January, the evening of Leonie's accident. It was a third-hand rumour, barely worth thinking about. Oliver dwelled on it; he added the possibility that Hanslope was being blackmailed.

He crossed the room, picked up the phone and dialled the CID office on the direct line. Sharon answered.

'It's me, Oliver. Can you spare a moment?'

'Depends what for.'

'It's just an idea, but would you check out Graham Hanslope for me?'

'Why?'

'Something I heard tonight. I wondered if he's quite as squeaky clean as he should be.'

On Thursday night Nimp awoke suddenly from yet another dream about counting the gnomes.

Nowadays he slept fitfully. Anything could wake him – an unsettling emotion generated by a dream, the yowling of a cat in the garden, or the irritation of too thin a layer of flesh squeezed between bone and mattress. His difficulties with sleeping had become so acute that in the end he had mentioned the problem to Dr Hanslope. The result was another bottle of pills to join the row in the bathroom cabinet.

He lay on the verge of sleep and looked at the illuminated figures of the clock: not Thursday night but nearly two o'clock on Friday morning. He'd had this dream so often before that it bored him.

'Lawrence and Malcolm and Nigel . . .'

In the dream he was counting the gnomes, and Muriel was

lying in this very bed and watching him through the bay window.

'Olive and Philip, Quentin and Russell . . .'

One of the gnomes was missing; and this was worrying – less for the loss itself than for the effect it would have on Muriel. Sometimes the missing gnome was Simon, but more usually Xanthippe or Imogen. Who had it been tonight? He attributed his uncertainty to the sleeping pill. The pills put him to sleep but they failed to keep him there. And when he woke up, his mind was full of a mist through which thoughts moved sluggishly, indistinct like ghosts.

He turned over. The movement brought his nose into contact with an unexpected smell – something tangy, almost alcoholic. Petrol, he thought, definitely petrol. Could one dream smells?

A floorboard creaked. Nimp lifted his head an inch above the pillow. The dream dropped away from him. He knew the sounds of the bungalow. That was the board by the sitting-room doorway in the hall: when you trod there, it emitted a two-tone creak resembling a donkey's bray.

'Is anyone there?'

His voice was barely audible even to himself. The bungalow was silent. He wondered if he had dreamed the creak. Slowly, the familiar fear crept over him. Lie doggo; that would be best; pretend to sleep like the dead. If there were burglars, let them take whatever they wanted and go.

He listened; the sounds of the night and the warmth of the bed gradually reassured him. The urge to sleep was an antidote to fear. In any case he found it hard to concentrate even on being afraid. 'I was dreaming,' he murmured. You could dream of anything – of fear and gnomes, creaks and smells. He had often dreamed of burglars.

The room filled with a flash of light. He opened his eyes but everything was dark again. Footsteps stumbled across the floor towards the bed. He felt the pillow being jerked away. He began to scream. The pillow came down on top of his face.

The pressure made it impossible to breathe. But someone was breathing in great, ragged gasps.

Nimp struggled beneath the heavy bedclothes. He kicked. He writhed like a dying fish.

19

On Friday morning Leonie was late for breakfast. Kevin Burwell, who was sheltering behind the newspaper from his wife's hot, accusing eyes, examined his daughter's face. Leonie had the sort of pale, almost transparent skin that marks easily. When she was tired, her face showed it with bruises under the eyes.

'You look as if you haven't slept a wink,' he said.

'The sirens woke me. What's been happening?'

Felicity slammed the refrigerator door. 'Why aren't you dressed? You'll be late for school.'

Leonie ignored her. She stared at her father, who was spooning marmalade on to the side of his plate.

'There's been a fire,' he said. 'It was on the local news just now.'

'Where?'

'Bert Nimp's bungalow.'

'Oh, God. Is he all right?'

'No.'

Leonie sat down and put her head in her hands. Her appearance of grief confused Kevin Burwell. Why should she bother to grieve for Bert Nimp? If she grieved for him she would grieve for anyone. It made her vulnerable.

'A nasty way to go,' he said. 'I won't pretend I liked him, but I'm sorry it happened like that.'

'Are you?' Felicity said.

He pretended that he hadn't heard. Last night they had quarrelled. During the day, the bank manager had had a word with him, off the record of course, about the extent of her overdraft.

Felicity had no idea how to manage money. He suspected that she was concealing other debts. The timing of her extravagance couldn't have been worse. For the first time in their married life she had stormed off to sleep in the spare bedroom. Even the news of the fire had failed to effect a truce.

He finished his toast and poured a second cup of coffee. 'Where's Joanna? She'll be late for work if she's not careful.'

Leonie lifted her head. 'She's not going in today. She broke up with Graham last night.'

'She did *what*?'

'He's got a girlfriend in London.'

'Well I'm damned. When did she tell you this?'

'Just now. She told me to tell you.'

Last night Joanna had come back home while Kevin and Felicity were arguing. She had gone straight to bed without saying goodnight.

'Good riddance to bad rubbish,' Felicity said. 'I never liked him much.'

'How did the fire happen?' Leonie asked. 'Did they say?'

Kevin shook his head. 'Well I'm damned,' he repeated.

'Aren't you pleased?' Felicity said. 'You won't have to pay for the reception now, will you? Or the dresses and presents.'

Leonie gripped her father's arm. 'Dad? Was anyone else hurt?'

As far as we know, Tammy Perran's alive and well,' Felicity said. 'Are you going to have any breakfast?'

'I feel sick.'

'I think you should stay at home today,' Kevin said.

Felicity clicked her tongue against the roof of her mouth. 'You pamper her.'

Kevin Burwell looked at his wife. She held his gaze for a few seconds. Then she shrugged and dropped her eyes.

After breakfast, Tammy Perran spent most of the morning in her bedroom. She should have tried to rest but lying down was out of the question. Too much was happening. The Perrans had all been up since three o'clock, when a distraught house-holder from Meadow Way had hammered on their front door.

The Perrans had joined the little crowd of oddly dressed and eager-faced sightseers in the lane. By then, the bungalow was well alight. The atmosphere was almost like that of a bonfire party. You could feel the warmth of the flickering orange flames on your skin, hear the wood cracking like pistol shots, and smell the smoke.

'He must be still inside,' Suzette said, her voice shaking with excitement. 'Shouldn't we do something?'

'Don't be stupid.' Jimmy was staring intently at the bungalow. 'It's too late. Much too late.'

Soon afterwards, the first fire engine had arrived and the crowd, grumbling, was forced to disperse. The Perrans sat in the living room, drank tea and watched what they could from the window.

'Jesus, if only we had a video camera,' Jimmy said. 'Wouldn't that be something?'

At half-past five a uniformed constable rang their doorbell. He had asked her father a few questions – Tammy heard their voices in the hall – and then requested that everyone stay at home until the police had time to interview them properly. Tammy didn't mind not going to school. There was still plenty to watch.

After most of the fire engines left, the police blocked the lane with two sets of crash barriers, one in front of White Cross House, the other in front of the building site. Between the barriers they parked a large caravan bristling with aerials. Everyone who went into the bungalow's garden had to wear white paper zipper overalls and overshoes. They looked like spacemen.

Men and a few women swarmed everywhere, some in uniform, some in plain clothes, each with his allotted task. Their cars lined the lane. With a thrill of pride, Tammy recognised Chief Inspector Errowby, Sergeant Rickford and the woman detective constable. The most exciting moment was when they brought out the body – it could only have been the body – in a sort of plain coffin. They loaded it into an unmarked van, which had been backed up to Mr Nimp's front gate.

There were other watchers. People from the town gathered as near to the barriers as the police would let them. They waited in little knots, hardly talking. A television crew arrived. They argued with one of the policemen, who refused to let them through the barrier. Tammy felt comfortably superior to them all.

It was clear that the police were searching Mr Nimp's garden very thoroughly. They lifted up the gnomes and examined the lawn as if each blade of grass were a potential clue.

Occasionally she heard her parents talking in the living room. She guessed that they were watching the proceedings from the window downstairs. She wondered if they were worried about the interview. She was. She would have liked to get it over with as soon as possible.

As time went by, her worry increased.

The police came midway through the morning. There were eight of them. One constable remained by the front gate. A guard, Tammy thought – but to keep others out or to keep the Perrans in? Chief Inspector Errowby, the woman detective constable and two others went inside the house. Sergeant Rickford and two men in uniform began to search the garden. The sergeant had a dressing on his head, which made him look incongruously comical, like a clergyman wearing a false nose.

Tammy slipped on to the landing. No one was in the hall but there were voices in the living room. She took off her slippers and tiptoed down the stairs. The living-room door was closed. She walked through the kitchen and out into the garden.

'And what do you think you're doing?'

The head and shoulders of a uniformed constable appeared like a jack-in-the-box beside her. His head was on a level with her waist; he was standing in the little room next to the kitchen, the former coal hole where the central-heating boiler was, with his top half poking through the hatch.

'Please, I want to speak to Mr Rickford.'

'Your turn will come.' He was a stringy young man with worried eyes. 'You wait inside and an officer will talk to you in due course.'

Rickford himself came round the corner from the path along the side of the house. Tammy turned to him with relief.

'This young lady wants a word with us,' the constable said. 'I told her to wait inside.'

'I want to talk to *you*,' Tammy said to Oliver Rickford. 'Please, it's important.'

For lunch the police ate ham sandwiches made from stale white bread and drank grey coffee from an urn. Detective Chief Superintendent George had arrived with the sandwiches and the urn. While they ate, he held an impromptu conference in the caravan.

Just the three of them were there – George, Errowby and Oliver. George, Oliver guessed, would be monitoring this investigation more closely than usual because of Errowby's personal involvement; he might even take over full control and bypass Errowby altogether. That was one reason why Oliver had been asked to join them. Errowby didn't like his being there. He kept glancing at Oliver as if the latter were the source of an offensive smell.

'The preliminary report indicates arson,' George said. He was a big man, and his presence dominated the little room. He scratched the wart on the tip of his large and shapeless nose. 'Petrol. Not much doubt about it. An efficient job, but not necessarily a professional one: it was windy last night and there was a lot of dry old timber in that bungalow. Went up like a torch for at least half an hour before anyone noticed. So the fire had plenty of time to get going. And to make matters worse, the Fire Service took their time responding – they were having a busy night in Paulstock.' With his forefinger he pried open one of the sandwiches and examined its contents. 'So, gentlemen – this may well be a murder investigation. What have we got so far?'

Errowby cleared his throat. 'We've recovered what looks like the top of a petrol can from the hall. In the garden we made an interesting discovery in one of the gnomes.'

'Those gnomes give me the creeps,' George said. 'Wait till the press get hold of them.'

'A lot of them are hollow. We found a package concealed in one of them, or rather in the plastic wheelbarrow it was attached to. It contained a hundred pounds in tenners and an audio cassette.' Errowby coughed. 'The tape records what appears to be a couple engaged in lovemaking and conversation. A man and a woman.'

George reached for a second sandwich while still chewing the first. 'You've identified them?'

'Dr Graham Hanslope and Mrs Felicity Burwell. Dr Hanslope has confirmed. We haven't spoken to Mrs Burwell yet.'

George stared in silence at Errowby for a few seconds – just long enough, Oliver thought, to make everyone else uncomfortable. 'Felicity – she's Kevin Burwell's wife?'

'Yes, sir. And the doctor owns the house next to the bungalow. Mrs Burwell used to meet him there. He's a young man – just joined the Abbotsfield practice. He's engaged to the Burwells' elder daughter.'

'So you know them all? Socially, I mean?'

'Yes, sir.'

'Rickford?'

Oliver hastily swallowed a mouthful of sandwich. 'We've got a certain amount of evidence against Jimmy Perran. The Perrans live on the other side of the doctor's house. He's definitely in the frame for the housebreaking. He was storing petrol in cans in his shed. The tins are still there. They were full when I saw them on Tuesday but they aren't any more. One of them has lost its cap. We also found a scarf smelling of petrol in the hall cupboard. His daughter told me that she'd heard someone moving in the garden last night. Perran himself won't answer questions, and nor will his wife. We removed his working boots when we searched the house. They smell strongly of petrol too, and they match a couple of footprints in the deceased's garden.'

'Any other contact traces?'

'Nothing so far,' Errowby said. 'We're still trying.'

'What about the house next door? Hanslope's?'

'It was empty, sir. Hanslope's got a flat in Paulstock. A man called Dougal had been staying there for the last couple of nights, Tuesday and Wednesday, but he went up to London yesterday afternoon. He should be back today and we've arranged to talk to him. As a matter of fact, I've already met him.' Errowby smiled. 'Hanslope claimed he was a friend.'

'But?'

'Well, we had occasion to run a check on his car.' Errowby's use of the royal 'we' avoided the need to share the credit with Oliver. 'It turns out he's a private investigator employed by Custodemus. The company's confirmed that, by the way, though they wouldn't say what he was doing down here. Not that they needed to. It's as plain as the nose on your face. Dr Hanslope admitted that he and Mrs Burwell were being blackmailed about their affair. Interestingly enough, Hanslope says he left two payments, each of five hundred pounds, in an empty cement tin at the back of my garden.'

'Are you planning to eat those sandwiches, Bernie, or just look at them?'

'Do you want them, sir? I'm not very hungry.'

George pulled the plate towards him. 'So what's the story? Nimp was also blackmailing Perran and Perran lost his temper?'

'It looks like it,' Errowby said. 'Leonie Burwell gave us a statement. She was walking their dog down here early yesterday evening. She says she saw Nimp in the footpath that runs parallel with the lane. He was most upset to see her – she got the impression he was fiddling with something in the hedge at the back of my property. It dovetails with what Hanslope told us about the tin.'

The Chief Superintendent munched with deliberation and

efficiency. A minute passed. Errowby squeezed his plastic cup until it cracked; a dribble of coffee ran down the side.

'Right,' George said at last. 'You're working on the assumption that Nimp was blackmailing not only Kevin Burwell but Hanslope and Perran. And Perran, you think, is the man behind the burglaries, and that was the handle Nimp had on him?'

Errowby leaned forward, his face eager. 'There's another possible handle, sir. Perran might also have been the hit-and-run driver who hit Leonie Burwell. He certainly changed the front wings of his car just after the accident. His blood doesn't match the stain we've got, but the blood might easily have come from another source – a nosebleed in the school playground, for example.'

The Chief Inspector dangled the theory like a carrot in front of George. Oliver had to applaud Errowby's ingenuity. If he were right, he would have wrapped up four cases – Nimp's murder, the blackmail, the burglaries and the hit and run. And if Perran was the burglar—

'And of course if we're right,' Errowby said, 'there's a strong presumption that Perran was also responsible for the attack on Sergeant Rickford.'

George attacked the last of the sandwiches. The others waited in respectful silence. The Chief Superintendent's tongue worried a shred of ham which was stuck between two teeth. Suddenly he snapped his jaws shut with an audible click.

'Right,' he said. 'I want to talk to Perran.'

Perran talked for most of the afternoon. It was hard to stop him talking. George and Errowby asked the questions; Oliver took notes. It was a curious business, watching a man's defences being chipped away one by one. George and Errowby were like sculptors attacking a block of marble with their chisels. Slowly a shape emerged. But it wasn't quite the shape they'd wanted to see.

It didn't take much to make Perran admit to the burglaries. Sweating in his stuffy little living room, he gave them chapter and verse on each one. He gave them the name and address of the man in Bristol who bought most of what he stole. Yes, he'd nicked the kettle from the house in Paulstock; Suzette had kept badgering him to buy a new kettle.

'That's right,' Errowby said. 'Blame the missus.'

With a little more pressure, Perran admitted that he was being blackmailed. But he swore he had no idea that Nimp was behind it. When pressed a little harder, he admitted to a slight suspicion. He swore on his mother's grave that he hadn't talked to Nimp about it. He had been too scared.

The blackmailer, he said, knew about the burglaries and had demanded £200 in return for his silence. Perran didn't have £200. In desperation he had ignored his rule of avoiding nearby houses and broken into Hanslope's. Yes, he had hit Sergeant Rickford over the head.

'Jimmy,' Chief Superintendent George said softly. 'We take attacks on police officers very seriously. Very seriously indeed.'

Perran gnawed the knuckle of his right thumb. He was very sorry, honestly he was. He hoped the sergeant was feeling better. He was not a violent man but on that occasion he had panicked. The sergeant had taken him by surprise while he was investigating an outhouse.

Errowby grunted. 'Crap. You were after his wallet. You hadn't found much worth nicking in the house. And when you realised who you'd hit, you panicked.'

All Perran had stolen that evening was a camera, a portable television and an electric drill. They hadn't raised much. After a quick trip to Bristol on Wednesday evening, he had managed to scrape together £100, which he had left, as instructed, in the empty cement tin in Errowby's hedge.

'Bloody cheek,' Errowby said.

The room smelled of cigarettes, fatty meals and fear. The outside world barely impinged on them. Occasionally a car went up or down the lane. Once or twice Oliver heard the murmur of voices elsewhere in the house and footsteps in the room above; the place was being searched again. Suzette and

Tammy Perran were in the kitchen with Sharon and Fintal to keep them company.

Errowby pressed Perran hard on the hit and run. At first he denied all knowledge of it. Later, after his first bout of tears, he admitted that he had driven up Meadow Way on the evening of Sunday 27 January and seen Leonie's body. He had not known who it was or even that a car had hit her. Just a body. Perran had been late for a rendezvous with the man from Bristol, and his car was full of stolen goods. Later that evening he planned to visit Willow Lodge. All in all it had seemed better to allow someone else to play the Good Samaritan. Afterwards he had wondered if perhaps there had been blood on the road. Some of it might have splashed on to the Cortina. You heard so much about the forensic miracles of modern technology. So he decided to change the wings – they had needed replacing in any case. Once again he was very sorry. We all make mistakes, he said. He was very glad that Leonie was all right. To think that it might have been his own dear Tammy. Yet again he sought temporary refuge in tears.

'And what about last night, Jimmy?' George said softly.

'What about it?' Perran sniffed. 'We were in bed by eleven. I was out like a light. Next thing I knew, it was three o'clock, and this bloke was banging on the door and shouting.'

Errowby took him through the evidence, stage by stage. True, there were some tins of petrol in the shed, but Perran couldn't remember whether they were empty or full. Yes, he always kept the shed locked; there were only two keys – one was always in his pocket and the other he had hidden in the bedroom. He was surprised to hear that his scarf and boots smelled of petrol but he might have spilled a few drops on them when he last filled the car or the van.

'When was the last time you filled up?' Errowby said.

'I don't know. Last week, some time.'

'Petrol evaporates, Jimmy. So does its smell. And how do you explain your footprints in Nimp's garden?'

'Suzette and me, we were always popping over.' Perran

blinked rapidly. 'You know, giving him a helping hand? Natural enough, isn't it? That's what neighbours are for.'

George beckoned Errowby out of the room. Oliver sat by the door, alone with Jimmy Perran.

'Mr Rickford? What will they do to me?'

'That depends.'

'Ask anyone. I wouldn't hurt a fly.'

'That wasn't the impression I got.'

Perran squirmed. 'Look, I've been trying to help, haven't I? Doesn't that count for something? I've been answering all your questions. I've not even made a fuss about seeing my solicitor.'

The voice died away. Oliver watched Perran take another cigarette. This time he did not light it. He rolled it to and fro between the thumb and fingers of his right hand. They were big hands, strong and capable. Shreds of golden tobacco fell to the carpet.

The door opened. 'Come along, lad,' Errowby said. Fintal loomed behind him.

The cigarette snapped. 'Where are you taking me?'

'Paulstock station. Your wife's packing a bag.'

'You're charging me?'

'My, you're quick. Rickford, nip out and tell them to bring a car down to the gate.'

'What are you charging me with?' Perran screamed.

Oliver escaped into the hall. Once outside, he took great gulps of fresh air. He passed on Errowby's message to the constable at the gate. George was already in the lane, talking to the uniformed sergeant in charge of the Abbotsfield section station. Oliver lingered by the gate. Sharon came out of the Perrans' house and joined him.

'I've not had a chance to talk to you all day,' she said.

'We've all been busy.'

'You got lucky.'

'What do you mean?'

'Hanslope.' There was a hint of conspiracy in her voice, as

if she had guessed that his enquiry last night had a personal element to it.

'He's got form?'

'He was done for drinking and driving eight years ago. He was still a student then. He lost his licence for a year.'

Oliver glanced involuntarily at the sleeping policeman across the entrance to Meadow Way.

'Well?' Sharon said. 'Aren't you pleased?'

Behind them, Errowby shouted. Oliver swung round. Perran ran down the hall. Errowby pursued him. Fintal was on the floor, shouting.

Perran shot through the open door. He swerved away from the gate towards the van, which was parked on the hardstanding at the side of the garden. Sharon and Oliver broke into a run. Errowby launched himself into a perfect running dive. His arms snapped round Perran's knees. Perran hit the ground.

In a couple of seconds his prostrate body was surrounded by police officers. Errowby stood up and dusted his hands. Oliver and Sharon rolled Perran over on to his side. He was short of breath. His nose was bleeding. He was crying again.

George opened the gate and moved unhurriedly towards them. The crowd parted to let him through.

'Well done, Bernie,' the Chief Superintendent said. 'Most impressive. You're a fitter man than I am.'

20

'There's a Mr Dougal in the waiting room,' Miss Jevons whispered. 'He says it's personal.'

Graham looked at his watch. 'I'd better see him. Send him in before the next patient.'

There was a sharp intake of breath at the other end of the line. 'We're already running rather late, Doctor.'

'I can't help that.'

He put down the phone with a sensation of well-earned satisfaction. As part of his campaign to be the perfect family doctor, it had been necessary to handle the practice's senior receptionist with a degree of tact that verged on flattery. Now he could treat that domineering and sexually frustrated anachronism with the firmness she deserved.

Dougal tapped on the door and came in.

'Where have you been?' Graham said without looking up from his notes. 'I expected you much earlier.'

'I took my daughter to the zoo.'

Graham frowned. 'So you haven't been in touch with your office?'

'I dropped in early this morning to pick up the equipment we discussed. That's why I—'

'We won't be needing that now. You've missed all the excitement.'

Dougal sat down uninvited. 'Suppose you tell me all about it?'

'I can only spare you a moment.'

Graham rapidly explained how Nimp and his bungalow had gone up in flames during the night; how the police had found evidence to prove he had been the blackmailer, including the tape he had played back to Graham and Felicity; how the police had arrested Jimmy Perran, another of Nimp's victims, and charged him with the burglaries and the assault on Sergeant Rickford; how it was only a question of time before Perran was charged with Nimp's murder and the hit-and-run accident as well; and how the police had told Graham – tactfully, man to man – that they did not think they would need to use the tape as evidence.

As he talked, Graham filled in his notes on the last patient. 'The police want to interview you, of course. I got the impression that they're feeling rather impatient.'

'Oh dear,' Dougal said.

'They've been trying to reach you through Custodemus. They asked me to pass on the message if I saw you.'

'Who do I contact?'

'Sergeant Rickford. If he's not still in White Cross Lane he'll be at Paulstock police station.'

Dougal got up. 'So – all's well that ends well?'

'Yes. I no longer need your services.' Graham smiled. 'In a word, you're fired. No doubt you'll be sending me an absurdly inflated bill. I wish I could say that I'll be recommending Custodemus to all my friends. But that wouldn't be accurate, would it? The door's behind you.'

Dougal nodded and turned to go.

'One moment. I'd like my key back.'

'I need to collect my bag from your house,' Dougal said. 'When I leave, I'll put the Yale down and leave the key on the kitchen table. OK?'

Left to himself, Graham sat back and stretched. Had he been a cat, he would have purred as well. Miss Jevons buzzed him on the phone; he ignored it. He had handled the interview really rather well.

His life stretched invitingly in front of him. For the first time in what seemed like years he had nothing whatsoever to worry him. True, a single unlucky phone call had lost him both Joanna and Rachel. But had it been so unlucky? Both of them, considered as long-term prospects, had serious drawbacks. There would be other women; there always were. Meanwhile, tomorrow was Saturday. Tomorrow he would see Michael.

Graham picked up the phone and buzzed Miss Jevons. 'Send in the next patient.'

'I reckon he was trying to break into the doctor's house,' Fintal said. 'I caught him sneaking through the fence at the bottom of the garden.'

'I do have a key, actually,' Dougal said. He was staring at the blackened ruins of the bungalow. 'So I wouldn't have had to break into the house. And I've just come from seeing Dr Hanslope.'

'It's all right,' Oliver said to Fintal. 'He's harmless.'

Fintal sniffed and sucked in his wrinkled brown cheeks; the tips of his ears were pink. 'How was I to know?'

'You weren't. Just one of those things.'

'I was coming to see you,' Dougal said. 'I just wanted to fetch my bag first.'

Oliver invited Dougal into the caravan. Errowby and George had gone back to Paulstock, leaving Oliver and the Abbotsfield sergeant to co-ordinate the house-to-house enquiries on the Meadow Way estate. Oliver was in need of light relief. The memory of this afternoon's interrogation lay raw and undigested in his mind. It was never pleasant to see someone stripped one by one of all his pretensions to dignity, to see on display before strangers the whimpering child that lives within us all. To this discomfort was added the sour taste of doubt. Perran had cracked. Why hadn't he admitted everything?

When Fintal arrived with his prisoner, Oliver had been making a mental list: *Kevin Burwell, Felicity Burwell, Graham Hanslope, Bernie Errowby(?)*: all the other people who might have had reason to kill Albert Nimp.

As soon as the door was shut, he rounded on Dougal. 'Now let's have the truth, eh? What did you do with your car?'

'I left it in the lay-by on the main road. I came along the footpath. I fancied stretching my legs, you see.'

'I imagine Hanslope told you what's happened?'

'Yes.'

'So you must have known there'd be some sort of police presence in the lane. So you decided to come in the back way. Why?'

'I saw Nimp yesterday – just before I left. It was about five o'clock. He was talking to Errowby in the lane.'

Oliver nodded. At least Errowby would be pleased to have the confirmation: he had explained how he had visited his new house yesterday afternoon and passed the time of day with Nimp; and he had noticed Dougal's arrival at White Cross House.

'Then Errowby left,' Dougal went on. 'That is, I assume he did – I heard a car leaving. I was checking my tyres in the yard behind the house. Nimp came round to talk to me. He had some story about seeing Leonie Burwell trespassing in Hanslope's garden.'

'In the garden?'

'According to Nimp she broke through the fence by the footpath and went into one of the outbuildings. He shouted at her, and she and the dog ran off up the drive.'

Oliver was silent. He wished he had an excuse for not hearing this. He wished that someone else had to deal with Dougal.

'He wanted me to make a fuss about it. Tell Hanslope and so on. I'm surprised he didn't mention it to Errowby. I was in a hurry so I didn't take much notice of him. Anyway I thought he was just being malicious, trying to get even with Burwell.'

'That's probably all it was. Maybe Nimp made it up. What's this got to do with you sneaking in the back way?'

'So Leonie *didn't* mention it to you?'

Oliver sat down on the edge of the table. *If Leonie had been lying* . . . 'Could be she felt embarrassed,' he said. 'We'll check it out. How about answering my question?'

'Nimp said she was poking around in a shed. I thought I'd take a look while I was passing.'

'Are you still working for Hanslope?'

'He's just sacked me. No further need for our services. Do not apply to him for a reference. You know the sort of thing.'

Despite himself, Oliver grinned.

There was an answering gleam of amusement in Dougal's eyes. 'It is Custodemus's policy to co-operate fully with the police whenever possible,' he continued in a prim voice. 'Of course, in practice that becomes much easier when there isn't a potential conflict with the principle of client confidentiality. Do you think I might collect my bag?'

'I'll come with you.'

Oliver found a torch. The two men walked in silence down the drive of White Cross House.

'Nimp saw Leonie going in there.' Dougal pointed at a small stone building with a pitched roof of corrugated iron; it was the only one of the outhouses that did not front on to the yard at the back of the house. 'I'm sure you've already searched it.'

The grounds of White Cross House had been Fintal's responsibility.

'I might have another look,' Oliver said.

He followed the path into the garden, which sloped down for at least fifty yards in a widening wedge to the fence. The single window of the outhouse had been boarded up. The low door was made of worm-eaten planks coated with creosote. There was neither lock nor handle. He heard Dougal's footsteps on the path behind him. In the unlikely event of there being something to find, an independent witness might be no bad thing. Oliver pushed the door, gently at first and then with increasing force. It scraped slowly backwards across an earth floor. He switched on the torch.

The place was empty apart from a rusting tin bath, an untidy pile of books and a stepladder leaning against the wall just inside the door. It had certainly been searched – there was a jumble of scuffed footprints in the powdery dirt of the floor. Oliver turned over the bath and found a large, surprised spider. The books were old and ruined by damp and stone dust from the crumbling walls. He glanced at a couple of titles: a volume of eighteenth-century sermons and a copy of the New Testament. Perhaps one of Hanslope's predecessors had suffered a religious crisis.

Dougal had produced a small torch from his pocket. 'There's no dust on the ladder.'

'Perhaps Hanslope's only just put it in here,' Oliver said. Like any sensible policeman he disliked it when a member of the public tried to play detective.

Nevertheless he climbed a few rungs and shone the torch along the tops of each of the beams; in section the beams were roughly six inches square. Within comfortable reach of Oliver's hand was a rectangular mark in the dust measuring perhaps nine inches by five. It was overlaid by other, similar rectangles. The marks might have been made by a box or a tin removed and replaced several times, and now removed for ever. Oliver shone the torch in the opposite direction, towards the point where the beam met the wall plate. Silver glinted in the angle between them. He was looking at a Yale key.

Using a pencil, Oliver edged the key along the beam and on to an envelope. He passed the torch down to Dougal and descended the ladder. Dougal fumbled in his pocket. Oliver rested the envelope on the broad rung of the ladder and examined his discovery. The key looked like a recently made copy, machine-cut in an ironmonger's or shoemender's.

'Look,' Dougal said softly.

He had another key in his hand. He laid it on the rung a couple of inches to the left of the first key. As far as Oliver could tell, the two were identical.

Dougal cleared his throat. 'It's the key of the back door.'

'Maybe Hanslope left it here. In case he locked himself out.'

'You can check. Felicity Burwell used to have a key. Hanslope made her give it back to him when they broke up. But someone might have copied it first.'

Before Oliver could stop him, Dougal had climbed the ladder and was shining his torch along the beam.

'Could I try an idea on you?' Dougal said.

'It depends what you want me to do with it.'

'I think you've got a similar idea yourself. Otherwise you wouldn't have let me come with you.'

'I'm in a bit of a hurry.'

'All right. Perran's admitted the burglaries and being black-mailed. But what evidence have you got that Nimp was the blackmailer and that Perran murdered him?'

'You know I can't discuss that.'

'Maybe your evidence is just circumstantial. Oh yes, and Leonie or maybe Tammy must have told you something too: something that doesn't fit with Nimp's story to me, something that puts the finger on Nimp or Perran. But, if anything, that key and the mark in the dust supports Nimp's version of events.'

'Look, what are you getting at? You can trust us to draw the obvious conclusions from the evidence. It's what we're trained to do.'

'I'm sure you are,' Dougal said hastily. 'I'm not trying to do your job for you. It's just that – if anyone had wanted to frame Nimp as the blackmailer and Perran as his killer, Leonie would have been in a very good position to do it. She and Tammy Perran, I mean.'

'That's ridiculous,' Oliver said, breathless with surprise. 'They're scarcely more than children.'

'They're teenage girls. Emotionally very close. Hanslope told me that their parents are trying to break up the relationship. It's almost a rerun of the Parker case.'

Oliver leaned against the jamb of the doorway. He remembered seeing the girls playing truant in Paulstock the day before yesterday; he remembered how they had fled from him as if from a monster. A memory – something incongruous he'd seen on that occasion – bobbed towards the surface of his mind but vanished before he could retrieve it.

'New Zealand,' Dougal said, joining him in the doorway. 'Nineteen fifty-four or five.'

Yes, Oliver thought, of course: the Parker case. Another

memory slid into place. '*Folie à deux,* you mean? Is that what you're getting at?'

Dougal nodded. Oliver felt curiously pleased: it was as though in a strange land he had unexpectedly met a fellow-countryman – someone who spoke his language and shared his assumptions. He wondered whether Errowby or Fintal or Sharon had heard of *folie à deux.*

'As you know,' Dougal went on, 'it's a rare but well-documented condition. A shared delusion, powerful enough to override all other considerations like common sense and conventional morality.'

A sort of madness, Oliver thought, born of love.

'It's usually between husband and wife or between sisters,' Dougal was saying. 'But in the Parker case it was between two friends, teenage girls. One of their mothers was threatening to separate them. So they hit her with a brick in a stocking until she was dead.'

'It's pure speculation. You must realise that.'

'You could see the blackmail as revenge as well. Who were the victims? Hanslope, the Burwell parents, Perran. All members of their families, more or less. And then perhaps the blackmail got too dangerous or it gave them an appetite for something more thrilling. Or maybe Nimp saw something yesterday afternoon and Leonie was scared of what he might say. Or maybe they had a particular reason for wanting Perran out of circulation.'

Oliver stared down the rapidly darkening garden. You could understand the motives of a man like Perran – a mixture of greed and fear; both commonplace emotions, and differing from other people's only in degree.

'Rather clever of them, really,' Dougal said. 'Either that or they've been lucky. Assuming I'm right, of course.'

But if Dougal were right, how could you hope to understand the motives of Leonie and Tammy? They must have chosen to maroon themselves on an island in the middle of the human race, an island with its own incomprehensible codes and customs. The question would not have troubled Oliver's parents. They read the answer in their Bibles and they heard it from the pulpit. Satan was everywhere, and all his works were evil.

'After all,' Dougal went on, 'it's only an idea. I don't know what evidence you've got.'

Oliver knew that the very fact of his listening to Dougal meant that the idea was not just an idea. Potentially it was a seed that might flourish because the ground was already fertilised with doubts and ambiguities. He was jealous of Dougal's licence to speculate. Dougal didn't have to do the dirty work; he was free of the rigid framework of a police investigation. Above all, Dougal didn't have to deal with Errowby.

'We shall want a statement from you.' Oliver was grimly determined to bring the conversation back to its proper level. 'A purely factual account of your movements yesterday afternoon and evening – your meeting with Mr Nimp and how you saw Mr Errowby.'

'I imagine he's over the moon at present,' Dougal said. 'One arrest – four, even five cases wrapped up.'

'Five? Yes – if you include the hit and run.'

'It's come at just the right time for Errowby.'

'And what do you mean by that?'

'I had dinner with him at the Burwells' on Tuesday. He's after promotion, isn't he?'

'That's got nothing to do with it,' Oliver said, not because he believed Errowby was above such considerations but because loyalty to the job prevented him from admitting the possibility to an outsider. 'I hope you're not—'

'Perran's ideal. Everyone *wants* him to be guilty.'

'The odds are, he is.'

'But will anyone trouble to go through the motions of looking at the other possibilities? Will anyone bother to talk to those two girls? Will you search their houses for a box that fits the mark on the beam? Will you ask Hanslope why he told me he'd been here on the evening of Sunday the twenty-seventh and told Burwell quite the opposite? Will you bother to—'

Oliver lost his temper. 'Why the hell are you bothering yourself?'

'Because if I'd listened to Nimp, if I'd searched this shed, he might be still alive.'

Dougal began to roll a cigarette. They stood there in silence looking out over the garden and the deserted countryside beyond. A match flared, a brief light in the gathering darkness.

'And because,' Dougal continued in a voice not much louder than a whisper, 'I think it's important to get these things right. And I think you believe that too.'

'You mentioned Hanslope,' Oliver said. 'What did you mean exactly?'

21

On Friday evening, Kevin Burwell went to the golf club on his way home. Harry Quarme was at the bar. He was perched on a stool and his thin body was all head, knees and elbows.

'What are you having, Kevin?' he said.

'Scotch, please.'

Quarme nodded at the barman.

'Needn't have bothered, need we?' Kevin said.

'Nimp?'

'Yes.'

'A tragedy.'

'Nothing to blame yourself for,' Kevin said. 'You said it yourself: he was over the hill.'

'We'll give him a good write-up,' Quarme said. 'Luckily it's not public knowledge that we just sacked him.'

He swayed as he spoke. That and his unusual loquacity made Kevin Burwell wonder if Quarme had had too much to drink.

The barman brought their drinks.

'A sad loss for the *Paulstock Guardian*,' Quarme said with careful dignity. 'A journalist of the old school.'

'Of course.'

'Cheers.' Quarme waited until the barman was out of hearing. 'And, as it happens, the victim of a particularly vicious murder.'

'Murder? Are you sure?'

'Hush. Not official yet.'

'Oh, bloody hell.'

'Yes.' Quarme's fishlike eyes were as intelligent as ever; he was no more drunk than Kevin himself. 'The police may want to talk to us.'

Kevin nodded: Quarme's staff must know about the sacking so it couldn't be concealed entirely. 'I've nothing to hide.'

'Quite so. All this fuss . . . Still, at least it'll be good for circulation. I'm sure Bert would have liked that. A professional to his fingertips.'

'Any details?'

'I'm expecting a phone call this evening.'

Kevin grunted. No doubt Quarme had a friend in Paulstock CID, someone like Josh Fintal.

'Too close to home for my liking,' he said. 'In more ways than one.'

Quarme shrugged. 'It's nothing for you to worry about. Anyway, what's this I hear about Joanna?'

Kevin sipped his whisky: the change of subject made him wary. 'She's having second thoughts about Graham Hanslope. How did you hear?'

'I'm told that she phoned us up with an announcement for next week's *Guardian*.'

'Breaking off the engagement? In black and white?'

'I thought you knew.'

'I didn't know she was planning to put it in the paper. Not like her. It only happened yesterday evening.'

'That's children for you,' Quarme said with sudden venom. 'Full of bloody surprises.'

They had another drink. Kevin drove home to Abbotsfield. He left the car in the drive and went in by the front door. 'I'm back,' he shouted. No one answered. He prowled through the house until he found Felicity and Leonie in the kitchen.

'You're feeling better?' he asked Leonie.

She nodded and slid out of the room. He heard her running upstairs to her room. He felt unwanted.

'Have you seen Joanna?'

Felicity said, 'Not since lunchtime. She came down, made herself a cup of coffee and a sandwich and said she was going out.'

'Was she all right?'

'How do I know? She didn't confide in me.'

'Harry Quarme said she phoned the *Guardian* today. She put in an announcement about the engagement being off.'

'I'm surprised she had the guts.'

'Me too,' Kevin said. 'Though I wouldn't have put it quite like that.'

'And what's she going to do now? Spend the rest of her life moping round here?'

'Harry says Nimp was murdered.'

He watched the panic sweep across his wife's face. Then her face was blank once more.

'Oh really?' she said. 'A tramp or something?'

'Or something. I'm going to get myself a drink—'

'I thought you'd got yourself several already.'

'And then we're going to have a talk.'

'About what?'

'Among other things, about money.'

'I hoped we'd exhausted that subject last night.'

'I wish we had. You're going to—'

The front door slammed. A moment later Joanna came into the kitchen. For once her face was scrubbed of make-up. Her cheeks glowed with cold. She wore jeans and a heavy army-surplus jacket. Kevin thought she looked astonishingly like her dead mother.

'Where've you been?' he demanded. 'We've been worried.'

She stood on tiptoe and kissed his cheek. 'I'm sorry.'

'We haven't had a chance to talk about you and Graham.'

'There's nothing to say. I nearly made a mistake. End of story.'

'Are you sure you won't regret this?'

Behind him, Felicity snorted in derision.

Joanna shook her head. 'There's something else I should tell you. I'm moving out tomorrow.'

'But why?'

'I should have done it ages ago . . . I need a change. I'm in your way.'

'But where will you go?'

'A friend at work has just bought a house between here and Paulstock. She's looking for a lodger to help with the mortgage. I went to see her this afternoon, and the house. It's all fixed up.'

'And when are you moving?' Felicity asked in a hard, clear voice.

'Tomorrow morning.'

'Joanna—'

'It's her decision, Kevin,' Felicity said.

'You can always come back here if you want and when you want,' he said. 'This is your home.'

'Oh *God*,' Felicity said softly. 'Bring on the violins.'

Kevin pretended he hadn't heard.

'Thank you.' Joanna smiled at her father. 'I'd better go and start packing.'

After she had gone, Kevin went to fetch himself a whisky. When he came back Felicity was hunched over the kitchen sink. She was scrubbing carrots. The light glinted on a tear rolling down her cheek.

'What's wrong?' Kevin said.

'At least Joanna can get out of this house. At least she can make a fresh start. It's so bloody unfair.'

According to Sharon, Chief Inspector Errowby was over the moon and still rising.

When Oliver got back to Paulstock at eight o'clock, he left Dougal to Fintal and went upstairs to the CID office. Sharon brought him up to date. Perran hadn't confessed to the murder yet, but the general feeling was that it was only a matter of time before he did. Detective Chief Superintendent George, who had now returned to headquarters, was said to believe that a confession, though desirable, might not be essential. Errowby's spectacular flying tackle – not the sort of thing you expected from a middle-aged senior officer – had already won an approving phone call from the Assistant Chief Constable.

The mood of elation crash-landed when Oliver gave Errowby Dougal's account of yesterday afternoon and described what they had found in the outhouse. The Chief Inspector paced up and down his little room and made a number of derogatory and indeed blasphemous remarks about private investigators and policemen from London. Goaded, Oliver outlined Dougal's theory that Leonie Burwell and Tammy Perran might have been responsible for both the blackmail and the murder.

'For Christ's sake,' Errowby roared, his face engorging. 'You can't be serious.'

'Dougal is, I'm afraid.'

This time the outburst was much worse. Oliver almost sympathised. Perran was an easy target to hit: a rustic half-wit with a criminal record, a partial confession and a pile of evidence against him; so poor that he would have to depend on Legal Aid for his defence. Leonie Burwell, on the other hand, was not only a minor, with all the problems that entailed, but also the cherished daughter of Kevin Burwell, who would make a formidable opponent; and the evidence against her was so insubstantial it was practically invisible. Errowby modulated gradually from a tantrum to a fit of sarcasm.

'No doubt you think those girls masterminded the burglaries? No doubt you think that Leonie knocked herself down?'

'No, sir. But it's just possible that Hanslope was responsible for the hit and run.'

'Oh dear God. How many more crackpot ideas have you got?'

Oliver, suppressing the feeling that he was breaking a confidence, explained what Joanna had told him: that Hanslope had lied about the time of his arrival in London on the night of 27 January.

'Fourth-hand hearsay,' Errowby snarled. 'Anyway, it doesn't prove anything. He might have been visiting another girl.'

Oliver mentioned Hanslope's previous conviction.

'You have been busy,' Errowby said. 'Fancy her yourself, do you?'

This time the malice was automatic, barely conscious, and Oliver tried to pretend that he hadn't heard. They both knew what a driver stood to lose if he re-offended within ten years of the original offence: disqualification from driving for at least three years, up to six months in prison and/or a fine of up to £2000. And in this case the offence would have been compounded by the injury to Leonie and the fact that Hanslope had driven away from her battered body.

'He was using White Cross House for his assignations with Mrs Burwell. According to Dougal—'

'You've been talking about this with him? Are you off your rocker?'

Quite possibly, Oliver thought miserably. 'He raised the subject himself, sir. It seems that during their interview at Custodemus, Hanslope referred in passing to him being at White Cross House on the Sunday evening in question. Custodemus tape their initial interviews with clients, as a matter of course. Later, Dougal was present when Hanslope went out of his way to tell Burwell that he hadn't been near the place that evening. Which is what Hanslope told me as well.'

Errowby was looking sullen again. 'Depends on the precise wording, doesn't it? A good lawyer makes mincemeat of that sort of evidence. You've got no way of finding out who this floozy is, have you? The one Joanna talked to. Discreetly, I mean.'

'Her first name's probably Rachel. If so, she lives in Frangbourne Terrace, London W-twelve.'

'Is this fact or psychic detection?'

'Dougal saw the name and address on an envelope Hanslope was writing.' The envelope of a Valentine card; and there had been another card to Joanna Burwell.

Errowby grunted. 'Nosy bugger. Where's this Dougal now?'

'Downstairs. Fintal's taking his statement.'

'I'd better see him. Not that I think there's much point. We're in the middle of a murder investigation, Rickford. You're missing the obvious. And the obvious has got a name: Perran. That's who we're going to concentrate on. Hanslope will keep, and the other stuff smells like a bunch of shit. Understood?'

'Shouldn't we at least—'

'I take the decisions in this division. Right or wrong?'

'Right, sir.'

'I thought you'd see it my way. Come on. I haven't got all night.'

Dougal was downstairs in one of the basement interview rooms. Oddly enough, Fintal was the one with sweat on his face, generated perhaps by unaccustomed mental exertion; Dougal, Oliver suspected, might be a difficult person to interview. A young constable on temporary secondment from Uniformed was taking down the statement.

'Hello, Chief Inspector,' Dougal said when Errowby and Oliver appeared. 'Keeping up with the medication?'

Errowby took a step backwards as though he had been stung.

'Leave us alone for a moment,' he said.

Fintal and his colleague stood up and edged out of the room.

'You too, Rickford. And shut the door behind you.'

Oliver and the others waited in the corridor. They heard voices inside the room.

'He's a funny bugger, that Dougal,' Fintal said. 'Swallowed the bloody dictionary.'

Oliver said nothing. Fintal shrugged. The minutes passed. The young constable stared at his feet. Oliver leaned against the wall. Fintal stubbed out one cigarette and lit another. His face was puzzled.

After ten minutes the door opened. Errowby came out. He jerked his head at Fintal. 'Pull your finger out and get that statement finished.' He set off for the stairs, calling 'Rickford!' over his shoulder as though he were summoning a straying dog.

Oliver trailed after him. Errowby said nothing until they were back in his room.

'On reflection,' he said, 'I think I'll mention your idea to Mr George. No harm in covering all the bases.'

Oliver realised that his mouth was open. He closed it.

'You're going to London tomorrow,' Errowby went on. 'Catch the through-train, the seven forty-five. Dougal will meet you at Paddington and give you that tape. After that you'd better go and see this Rachel person. I'll clear it with the Met, and get her surname and full address.'

Oliver swayed on his feet. His head was throbbing.

'You look like death warmed up,' Errowby said. 'Don't just stand there. Go home and get some sleep.'

The phone rang just before midnight.

It was the phone in the office, not the hall. Kevin Burwell was in the drawing room going through the drawers of his wife's desk with the assistance of a chisel. All the interconnecting doors were open so the ringing was audible throughout the house. Felicity and the girls were already upstairs.

Whoever it was could talk to the answering machine. He let the phone ring. But the caller didn't give up and the answering machine didn't cut in. Maybe it wasn't plugged in. With a pile of unpaid bills in his hand, Kevin padded quickly through the house and into the office.

'Burwell.'

'Kevin. It's Bernie.'

'For God's sake, do you know the time? What is it?'

'Before I forget: did they have time to collect the monitoring equipment this afternoon?'

'I presume so. It's certainly not here now. Did you ring me just to ask if your bloody—' He broke off as the penny dropped: no tape recorder – no record of the conversation. In a much quieter voice he said, 'Well, what is it?'

'I've just been talking to George,' Errowby said. 'We're coming to see you tomorrow. We'll have a WPC in tow.'

'To see me? What about?'

'Not you specifically. There's a small discrepancy in the statement that Leonie volunteered. Or rather a discrepancy between her statement and someone else's . . . Don't worry, I'm sure it's nothing serious.'

'Then why—' Kevin stopped. Then why had Errowby phoned? Then why was he coming to the house with a Detective Chief Superintendent under one wing and a WPC under the other?

'I thought I'd better give you a bell beforehand,' Errowby said hurriedly. 'Just in case you were all planning to go out.'

'OK, Bernie. Do you know what time you'll come?'

'Probably morning. Earlyish. In fact, George may decide to come without me. Seeing as how I know you all.'

There was a short, awkward pause.

'I'll make sure the coffee's fresh and hot. Thanks for letting us know.'

'See you tomorrow then, Kev. Or not as the case may be.'

'Goodnight.'

Kevin put down the phone. He looked at the unpaid bills. He threw them in the waste-paper basket and left the office.

In the hall he hesitated for a moment. Then he went upstairs.

Leonie's door was ajar. He peeped inside. She was lying on her stomach and breathing heavily. He watched and listened for a long moment. He returned to the landing and tapped on the door of the spare bedroom. Felicity didn't answer. He opened the door and went in.

22

Leonie waited in the darkness.

She heard her father tapping on the door of the spare bedroom; she heard the door closing behind him. The voices began, an irregular flow of murmurs punctuated by silences. Leonie slipped out of bed and tiptoed on to the landing. On the ground floor, the interior doors were made of hardwood but upstairs they were much flimsier. She listened for several minutes. Her feet grew colder and colder. She went back to bed and warmed them on her hot-water bottle.

Gradually the trembling subsided. She lay there thinking. Lists unscrolled in her mind, lists that had been ready for weeks. If you wanted to, you could change anything as long as you went about it in the correct, properly organised way.

Next door, the voices gave way to other sounds. The bed creaked; her mother moaned; a rhythm developed and gradually acquired an urgency, a sort of desperation. Leonie recognised the noises for what they were. For once her disgust was mixed with relief: afterwards her parents would sleep. People lived their lives according to patterns.

Her mother got up briefly to go to the lavatory in the en-suite bathroom. Silence descended on the house. Leonie waited. Her mother said something and was quiet again. The minutes stretched to ten, then twenty. Her father began to snore. They were asleep. It showed how much they cared.

Leonie stared at the illuminated face of her watch. Her eyelids were growing heavy. She dug her nails into the palms of her hands. One trick never failed to keep her awake: pushing the duvet away from her, she sat up in bed and stared through the darkness at the future.

'May I have this dance?' Thomas says, his voice hoarse with passion.

Lara places her champagne glass on the table. Diamonds flash on her fingers. With the languid grace that characterises all her movements, she lays her hand on the sleeve of Thomas's dinner jacket.

'Your hand is like a butterfly,' he says.

As Lara rises to her feet, the band strikes up a waltz. The dance floor of the nightclub is crowded with young and elegant people; but as Lara and Thomas approach, the other dancers move aside to make room for them. The men stare at Lara with open admiration, but she has eyes only for Thomas.

A celebrated gossip columnist is sitting at an adjacent table. Ignoring his titled companion, he summons the wine waiter with an imperious finger.

'Who are they?' he demands. 'I must know.'

The wine waiter shrugs his shoulders with Gallic expressiveness. 'Tonight everyone asks the same question, Monsieur. No one knows the answer. Me, I think they must be royalty incognito.'

Thomas and Lara swirl around the dance floor. The other patrons are watching, not dancing. When the waltz comes to an end, they burst into spontaneous applause . . .

At three o'clock Leonie judged it was time to start moving. She put on jeans, thick socks, a shirt and two jerseys. Her father continued to snore. Carrying her shoes and a small leather shoulder bag, she tiptoed out of the bedroom.

For a few seconds she waited on the landing. The central heating was off and the house was bitterly cold. Closed doors separated her from her parents and from Joanna. The knowledge that she was the only person awake in the house gave her a comforting sense of her own superiority. She smiled to herself and glided to the head of the stairs.

Once downstairs, she collected her coat, scarf, gloves and hat from the hall cupboard. In the kitchen, Simba threatened to become hysterical with joy; Leonie had to feed the dog to keep her quiet. She made herself a mug of instant coffee and forced herself to eat a few spoonfuls of muesli. While she ate, she consulted the train timetable, which was in her bag. She dressed herself for the outside world. The last thing she did was pull on her gloves.

Turning out the kitchen light, Leonie let herself into the garage block. She tried the door of her father's office, but it was locked. She would have to do without the petty cash.

Joanna's car was at the far end of the garage. Beside it was a small, freestanding cupboard, a relic of a previous kitchen. Its shelves were filled with the sort of rubbish that her father was too mean to throw away; paint tins with half an inch of paint in the bottom, a broken footpump, a bicycle bell for a vanished bicycle. On the bottom shelf was a paint tray with a paint-encrusted roller inside. Leonie removed the tray and then lifted out the entire shelf. The hollow space beneath, enclosed by the base of the cupboard, had served as a temporary hiding place.

Method and organisation: they were the keys. Consider the details. The rectangular biscuit tin with kittens frolicking on the lid had once belonged to Joanna. There were no fingerprints on the tin, only glovemarks. But there were definitely Joanna's fingerprints on the Top Shop carrier bag inside, and even a till receipt for a t-shirt Joanna had bought. As it happened, no one had found the tin, but such details were still a source of pride. Leonie opened the tin, took the money from the bag and zipped the bundle of notes into the inside pocket of her coat. She knew to a pound what was there: £1000 from Graham Hanslope and her mother; plus the £840 which, after necessary expenditure, was the balance left over from the programme of small, steady withdrawals from her building society account.

A separate door led from the garage block to the garden. It was now almost half past three. Leonie walked down the lawn on a course parallel to the drive. Once she reached the road, one of the more dangerous parts of the enterprise began. The possibility of a passing car could not be discounted. There was also a chance that the police were still keeping watch over Nimp's bungalow. Leonie was obliged to take a roundabout route – three sides of a square – which allowed her to approach the Perrans' cottage along the footpath at the back and climb over the wall into their garden. Luckily she met no one. Two cars passed her, but each time she was able to hide, once in someone's driveway and once in a ditch.

When she reached Tammy's garden, Leonie relaxed a little. Jimmy Perran was where he belonged, which was in prison; and Suzette always slept like the dead, like the unfeeling zombie she was. Tammy had shown Leonie how to manipulate from the outside the catch on the door of what had once been a coal hole next to the kitchen; now it housed the central-heating boiler and Suzette's and Tammy's bicycles.

Leonie knew the Perrans' house almost as well as she knew her own. It was familiar even at night. She went upstairs, wrinkling her nose at the smell of stale cigarette smoke. Suzette was snoring behind a closed door; Tammy said she had pills to help her sleep. Leonie pushed open the door of Tammy's room and went inside. Tammy was breathing slowly and evenly.

Leonie closed the door behind her. Here the darkness seemed thicker. She crossed the room to the window; it could be seen from the lane, so it would be silly to risk turning on the light. Leonie parted the curtains and looked out. The windows of the police caravan were alight. What were they doing in there? She frowned, partly worried by the implications for her plan and partly pleased that her earlier precautions had paid off. If the police were about, she would have to improvise.

She crossed the room and sat down gently on the bed. She stroked Tammy's shoulder until she found the bare, warm skin of the neck. For an instant she was blindingly happy.

'Darling,' she whispered. 'Darling . . .'

Tammy stirred, began to speak.

'Hush, it's me. It's all right.'

Tammy sat up with a jerk, knocking away Leonie's arm and breaking the spell.

'What's happened?'

'I heard my parents talking. I'll explain later. We're going now.'

'Going—?'

'We're *leaving*. Today. As soon as you're dressed. We should be able to catch the six twenty-three.'

Tammy swung her legs out of bed and groped for her glasses.

'Warm clothes,' Leonie said. 'Jeans and jersey.'

While Tammy was dressing, Leonie peered out of the window. 'And there's another change of plan,' she said. 'We can't use the bikes. It would be too dangerous. The police are still around.'

In her anxiety, Tammy raised her voice: 'But how shall we get to Paulstock? The buses don't start till eight.'

'Hush. We'll cut across the fields to the main road. Then we'll have to hitch.'

'But hitching's dangerous . . .'

'Not now, remember?' Leonie let the curtain drop and came close to Tammy. 'Everything's changed. You'll look after me.'

Graham slept through the alarm. He was going to miss the train. It was most unlike him to oversleep. Perhaps the sudden release from tension was responsible. He had slept for ten hours, and so deeply that he did not remember dreaming.

No time to wash or shave. He scrambled into yesterday's clothes. No time for breakfast, either, or even a hot drink. He slipped a battery razor and a bar of Dairy Milk into his pocket and hoped there would be a buffet on the train.

Graham had planned to walk to the station. Instead he had to drive. He abandoned the Golf in the rank opposite the ticket office, where parking was limited to thirty minutes. The train was already standing at the platform. He ran through the ticket office. The train shuddered. He pushed between an elderly couple and gripped a door handle on one of the carriages.

Behind him someone shouted. The door swung open. The train was moving. Graham hauled himself on board.

'Bloody fool,' a man on the platform said. 'Could have killed himself.'

It didn't matter. Graham was on the train and the door was closed. He wouldn't have to postpone taking Michael to Madame Tussaud's, he wouldn't have to risk upsetting Sue.

The train was nearly full. The 7.45 was a popular choice: it was the only train of the morning that went direct to London; otherwise you had to change at Bristol and the journey took twenty minutes longer. Graham shaved in a swaying lavatory and bought a ticket from a ticket inspector. He walked along to the buffet car for sandwiches and coffee. He decided to go forward to the front in the hope of finding a seat.

On his way through the train he had to pause to allow a woman to pass in the opposite direction. As he waited he glanced idly at the seated passengers around him. The shape of a man's dark head seemed familiar; a patient, perhaps. Beside him was an empty seat. The man was looking out of the window. He was wearing a brown leather jacket. Graham glimpsed the pale rectangle of a dressing on the back of his skull, and realised who it was.

He felt faint with shock. Then he remembered that Rickford could not possibly have followed him on the train, and in any case he had no reason to do so. That the two of them were travelling on the same train was no more than a coincidence – a minor coincidence, given the popularity of the 7.45 to London.

Sergeant Rickford was apparently engrossed in the *Paulstock Guardian*. Graham took a step towards him, intending to say hello, even to sit beside him. At present he was feeling almost amiable towards the police, who had handled the Nimp business with remarkable discretion and efficiency.

Your friend, Dr Hanslope? Is that what you call him?

Graham changed his mind about being sociable. The policeman's problem was simple jealousy: the poor fool was clearly infatuated with Joanna.

And the best of British luck to you, Graham thought as he hurried up the train; you're welcome to her.

'What's wrong?' Leonie said.

As she sat down, Tammy glanced at the clock. It was only 9.30. Could the clock have stopped? She could scarcely believe that they had been at Paddington for less than an hour.

'What is it? You're shivering.'

'It was horrible. It smelled. All these men kept looking at me. I had to go into one of the cubicles and the lock didn't work properly and it was filthy.'

She blinked back tears, safe from observation behind the dark glasses. It was all very well her wearing sunglasses, and Leonie said they made her look suave and sophisticated; but without her real glasses anything more than six inches away was blurred.

'I'm sure you managed perfectly,' Leonie said.

'Someone laughed.'

'You're imagining things.'

'And on the way back there was a beggar. A little boy.'

'Well, I hope you didn't give him anything.'

The boy had sidled up to Tammy as she came up the steps from the men's lavatory. 'Spare change,' he'd said in a lifeless voice. 'Spare change.' He couldn't have been more than nine or ten. And when she tried to blunder past him, he had stood directly in her path and pirouetted with one arm outstretched; his grimy fingers had missed her face by a hair's breadth. He whirled away towards fresh victims. It was as if he were not just begging but playing an unpleasant secret game.

Tammy had hurried back to the buffet. 'Spare change,' she heard behind her; and the childish voice was dull but full of menace. 'Spare change.'

'It shouldn't be allowed. He was so young.'

'It doesn't matter.'

But it did matter. It was as though she and Leonie had died and gone to heaven and found the pearly gates locked and St Peter slaughtering the angels.

'I never thought it would be like this.'

'Stop being stupid,' Leonie said. 'Don't you understand? London's whatever we make it.'

Tammy subsided into silence. Leonie studied the *A to Z* map. She had bought it along with newspapers and magazines at the big John Menzies on the station concourse. Strangers ebbed and flowed around them. At the next table an unshaven man was talking to himself; he waved his arms to emphasise the points he made to his invisible audience.

Leonie too was worried; Tammy could tell. Once, twenty minutes earlier, they had got as far as the entrance to the Underground. Two policemen were standing at the head of the flight of steps, near a statue of a seated man. Leonie had suddenly changed her mind. She said they should make another list before they went to the West End, a list of employment agencies for Monday morning. They had trailed back to the buffet, to the same cigarette-scarred plastic table and another unwanted cup of coffee.

In Abbotsfield, this part of the plan had seemed so simple and so wonderful. This was the goal they had aimed for, the reward for everything they had endured. Tammy had assumed that once they arrived in London their new lives would begin instantly without the need for any further effort; Leonie had everything planned – a hotel for a couple of nights while they found a flat and jobs. Tammy had not foreseen the difficulty with her glasses, the problem of finding somewhere to stay or the worry about how her clothes looked. She had not anticipated the nightmare of a men's public lavatory, the presence of beggars or the effect that policemen would have on her.

She peered across the table at Leonie. The silly little hat, the smudges of eye make-up and the red smear of lipstick had transformed her into someone else. She walked differently because of the three-inch heels on her shoes. She even talked like another person.

According to the original plan their new life had been due to start during the Easter holidays. 'It'll be like being reborn,'

Leonie had said. But things had gone wrong. First they had had to do something about Mr Nimp because he was threatening to tell tales and because Mr Burwell had told the police about the blackmail. Then they had to leave today, with less money than planned, because of the police being stupid. And now London had let them down. It wasn't exciting. It was frightening. Paddington Station was a terrifying place. But Tammy didn't want to leave. The rest of London might be even worse.

'Thomas?' Leonie said. 'I'll be a while longer. How about getting us some more coffee?'

Tammy licked her lips. 'All right.' She knew that Leonie was waiting expectantly. 'All right, Lara.'

The train drew into Paddington at 9.43; it was almost exactly on time.

Graham was the first in the queue for the door. He pulled down the window and leaned out. A knot of people had gathered by the barrier at the end of platform five. Among them he glimpsed Michael in the new leather jacket. Sue was standing behind him with a cigarette in her mouth and her arms folded across her chest.

Graham jumped down before the train stopped. He walked quickly to the barrier. His sister nodded to him. They had given up kissing when he left home.

'You shouldn't have jumped out like that,' she said. 'You know it's a bad example.'

Michael's face looked thinner than ever and pinched with cold. He stared at Graham, who winked at him.

'Back home by four,' Sue said. 'All right? And you be good, young man. See you later.'

She strode away, her back straight, her shoulders squared.

'There's no time to waste,' Graham said. 'Madame Tussaud's is waiting. We'll take the tube to Baker Street.'

The area in front of the departures board was unusually crowded for a Saturday morning. Graham put a proprietary hand on Michael's shoulder and steered him through the swarm of people. Passers-by, he thought, would assume that he and Michael were father and son. He glimpsed the back of a hurrying man in a beige raincoat like Bernie Errowby's or William Dougal's. All that was over and done with. They ran down the stairs to the ticket hall of the Underground. They wanted the southbound platform of the Bakerloo Line.

'It won't take long,' Graham said. 'It's only three stops.'

'Do they look just like they looked in real life?' Michael said while Graham was counting change for the ticket machine.

'Who?'

'The murderers.'

'Oh yes,' Graham said. 'Absolutely identical.'

Oliver walked slowly up platform five. Coming to London should have been a refreshing break from the monotony of Paulstock. But he would rather have been back in the office. This assignment was a typical Errowby ploy: the Chief Inspector had pushed him on to the sidelines. If the Abbotsfield investigation prospered, Errowby would effortlessly take the credit for the change of direction; if it didn't, he would pass the blame to Oliver, who wouldn't be there to defend himself.

Dougal was waiting by the barrier.

'Kind of you to come all this way,' Oliver said stiffly.

'I've got the tape.' Dougal took an envelope from the pocket of his raincoat and passed it to Oliver. 'It's a copy of the whole interview with Hanslope. You're going to see Rachel?'

'Yes.' Oliver hesitated, aware of curiosity working like yeast inside him. 'Have you got time for a cup of coffee?'

Dougal nodded. They crossed the concourse and went into the buffet. There was a queue along the L-shaped self-service counter.

'How's the head?' Dougal said as they were waiting to pay.

'As well as can be expected.' The heart, Oliver thought, was in much the same condition.

They reached the head of the queue, and he paid for their

coffee. The seating area of the buffet was crowded but an ungainly young couple were abandoning their table near the door.

'I'll grab their seats,' Dougal said.

Oliver registered a boy in a black hat, dark glasses and a pinstripe suit that didn't fit him; he was with a small girl dressed to kill, or at least to impress, in a short dress, patterned tights and high-heeled shoes; both of them were laden with coats and bags. The girl grabbed the boy's hand and dragged him through the door. Judging by their haste, they were on the verge of missing their train.

Dougal moved swiftly to claim the vacant table. By the time Oliver joined him, he was rolling a cigarette. They sipped their coffee. Dougal blew his nose. Neither of them spoke. One of the things Oliver disliked about Dougal was his patience.

'I'd like to ask you a question,' Oliver said. 'I don't suppose you'll answer.'

'If you don't ask, you'll never know.'

'How did you get Errowby to change his mind last night? And what was all that about medication?'

Dougal ran his fingers through his hair. 'It's none of my business. I'm not sure it's any of yours, either.'

'Errowby doesn't like me,' Oliver said. 'He doesn't like you. I don't believe in miracles. So what have you got on him?'

'Why do you want to know? Just curious?'

Oliver nodded.

'A good enough reason.' Unexpectedly Dougal smiled. 'Errowby's raincoat is very similar to mine. When we were at the Burwells on Tuesday night, I was looking for a handkerchief. I went through his pockets by mistake. I found some pills.'

'The medication, I suppose. What were they?'

'Dexedrine.'

'You're joking.' Oliver boggled at the unlikelihood of Errowby's being a speed-freak; and in the same instant he recalled some of the symptoms of regular amphetamine use – irritability verging on paranoia, violent swings of mood, lack of appetite.

'Don't get me wrong. These were all above board and properly dispensed – by a chemist in Marylebone High Street. I imagine he went privately to a specialist in Wimpole Street or Harley Street. It's not the sort of thing he'd take to his GP.'

'But what was the dexedrine for?' Oliver asked. 'I thought it wasn't prescribed nowadays.'

'I rummaged through Hanslope's textbooks and drug catalogues. It's recommended for one thing: to counteract narcolepsy.'

'And what's that?'

'It's a painless condition, and very rare. You just keep falling asleep, especially in quiet surroundings or when you're doing something monotonous like driving. You can't stop yourself – it happens very suddenly. It's chronic and there's no known cure. Gets worse as you grow older.'

No known cure . . . Gets worse . . . An Assistant Chief Constable who was a keep-fit maniac. A healthy mind in a healthy body. The difference between a chief inspector's pension and a superintendent's.

'So you used the dexedrine to blackmail him?' Oliver said.

'Whatever gave you that idea?' Dougal finished his coffee, stubbed out his cigarette and pushed back his chair. 'I was just asking how he was.'

Oliver grinned. They both stood up.

Dougal glanced at his watch. 'Ten o'clock. What do you think is happening to them?'

'Those kids? Probably George and Errowby are talking to them at this very moment.'

They looked at each other. Oliver wanted to say that he felt sorry for the two girls and even more sorry for their families: that when you were infatuated with someone you did damn silly things, and that when the infatuation was mutual, as with *folie à deux*, it must be ten times worse. He said nothing because he didn't know Dougal well enough. They moved towards the door.

'Ever come up to London?' Dougal said. 'Apart from work, I mean.'

'Sometimes.'

'If you'd like to meet for a drink or something, you could always give me a ring. Or you could come over and have a meal with us. We're in Kew.'

'Thanks,' Oliver said, surprising himself. 'I'd like that.'

23

'It's all right,' Leonie muttered. 'It's all right.'

As she was speaking she fumbled at the zip of her purse, which had stuck. Suddenly the zip gave way. Coins rolled across the floor, among the hurrying feet of uncaring strangers.

'Why didn't they come after us?' Tammy said. 'They must have seen us.'

'Help me pick these up. Of course they saw us, but they didn't recognise us. It's all right.'

'The policeman saw me with a Burton's bag on Wednesday. He must have wondered why I was buying men's clothes.'

'He probably didn't notice.' Leonie squatted inelegantly on the floor and scooped up coins. 'Or he thought you were using an old carrier bag of your dad's.'

'But what's he doing here? And why's Graham's friend with him?'

'Give us a hand.'

'I can't. I've got all this stuff.'

Tammy was carrying the coats and the bags. Besides, she felt that bending down would make her even more vulnerable. She couldn't see anything clearly but she thought she would recognise Dougal's beige raincoat and the policeman's brown leather jacket.

She was still short of breath – they had spent quarter of an hour walking – sometimes half-running – through the streets around Paddington Station. Tammy had wanted to take a taxi to the West End; but Leonie had said a taxi would make them too conspicuous and in any case they couldn't afford one.

'Maybe it would have been safer to take a bus,' Tammy said.

'I haven't worked out the bus system yet. Just stop worrying, will you?'

Leonie had collected the fallen coins and restored them to her purse. She rejoined the little queue in front of one of the self-service machines in the Underground ticket hall. Tammy stood very close to her.

'What are they doing?' she said.

'How do I know?'

'They're following us. They must be.'

'Don't be stupid. They probably came up to London on the seven-forty-five, like everyone else.' Leonie fed two pound coins into the machine. 'By that time no one would have even known we'd left, let alone where we'd gone. In any case, they'd be looking for two girls, not sitting down for a cup of coffee. Use your head.'

Tammy was so miserable that she found herself snapping back: 'You were scared too. You panicked when you saw them.'

'No, I didn't. Anyway, we were just about to leave.'

Tammy couldn't face quarrelling with Leonie, who would never admit to being in the wrong. 'Where are we going?'

'Piccadilly Circus. We need the Bakerloo Line. Damn, I think I've paid too much for these tickets.'

Tammy hopped from one foot to the other. 'Shouldn't we be off? They might come down here.'

'Don't panic, Thomas. I want to check the map.'

Leonie took her time; she was showing off, proving how calm and mature she was. Tammy almost hated her.

'Yes,' Leonie said. 'The Bakerloo Line going south. It's the sixth station.'

As they walked towards the electronic turnstiles, Tammy looked back at the steps leading up to the concourse of the mainline station. Perhaps Leonie was right and there really was nothing to worry about.

Leonie went through the turnstile first. She waited for Tammy, who was still burdened with their luggage.

'You'll have to do better than this, now we're in London,' Leonie said. 'I'm a bit disappointed in you.'

Tammy put down the heavier of the two bags. She wanted simultaneously to weep, to scream, to stalk off, to say something both cutting and irrefutable and to make Leonie cry. Instead she fumbled in her pocket. People eddied around her.

'What are you doing?' Leonie pointed to the long corridor on their left. 'Come on. The Bakerloo Line's down there.'

'I want my glasses.' Tammy found their case. She put them on and stuffed the dark glasses into the top pocket of her jacket. The world came into focus.

'You look stupid in those,' Leonie said. 'Anyway, I thought we agreed—'

She broke off. For a second she stared at the turnstiles. Her mouth was open. Tammy glanced over her shoulder.

Rickford and Dougal were walking through the ticket hall towards the turnstiles. Tammy's eyes met Rickford's. She saw with painful clarity the recognition springing into his face.

Leonie was running down the corridor. Tammy dropped the coats and the other bag and ran after her.

A barely audible voice crackled above the heads of the waiting passengers: '. . . due to a points' failure at Queen's Park, we apologise for a restricted service on the southbound Bakerloo Line . . .'

Graham looked at his watch. They had been waiting down here for over fifteen minutes. The announcement ended in a crackle of static. There were shouts in the distance – from the escalators? – and in the hallway between the two Bakerloo Line platforms a solitary busker was still playing 'When You're Smiling' on her saxophone.

'Can I have another bit of chocolate?' Michael said.

Graham gave him the rest of the bar; he had eaten none himself. They were standing at the end of the platform, where the crowds were thinnest. Graham despised the herd instinct that made people cluster together while waiting for a train.

227

'I'm sorry about this wait,' he said.

'Doesn't matter,' Michael said. 'Not your fault.'

No, it didn't matter: they were together. Graham stared at the top of Michael's head and thought how pleasant it would be to watch him sleeping.

Michael munched on. 'Hey, look at those two,' he said with his mouth full. 'Real weirdos.'

Two teenagers, a boy and a girl, were elbowing their way along the platform. It wasn't so much their clothes that made them stand out as their air of urgency. The girl teetered on high heels and the boy, his face obscured by a black, broad-brimmed hat, lumbered along behind her. Deep in the crowd a man was yelling, but his words were distorted beyond recognition by the acoustics of the tube station.

The teenagers were no more than five yards away. Graham's attention was distracted by two men behind them: they were running along the edge of the platform. The girl looked back.

A rumble like a deep whisper ran along the rails. With it came fear. The fear flooded into Graham's mind.

Sergeant Rickford? William Dougal? What are they doing here? They've come to get me . . .

The boy in the hat screamed. He grabbed the girl's arm and pointed at Graham. It wasn't possible. The boy had Tammy Perran's face.

'Bloody hell,' said Michael; he sounded interested but detached, like a spectator who knows that the play is only a made-up story and the people only actors.

Graham realised with a shock of relief that Dougal and Rickford did not even know that he and Michael were here. They were after the teenagers. He glanced down at Michael's eager, amused face. Behind the boy, a single light hung in the black mouth of the tunnel. The light was swaying. A current of air swept along the platform. Graham wondered if he should do something. Beyond Rickford and Dougal was a mass of intent faces: the rest of the audience.

Leave it to Rickford. After all, that's what coppers are paid for.

'You bastards.' The girl's mouth was a bright red gash in a white, familiar face. *Leonie?* She looked from Graham to Rickford. 'It's a trap.'

'Gently,' Rickford said. His eyes flicked towards Graham, then back to Leonie. He and Dougal had stopped. They were at least ten yards away from the girls. Rickford edged forward, holding out his hand as though trying to propitiate a nervous dog. 'Leonie, it's OK. It's not a trap.'

'Then what's Graham doing here?'

'How should I know? It's just—'

'I don't believe you. You're all liars.'

Leonie swooped. She was a blur of colour and movement, like a butterfly on the wing. She seized Michael's ear. The boy screamed. She jerked him away from Graham to the very edge of the platform. Michael shouted and kicked at her legs.

Tammy grabbed Michael's other arm and shook him violently. 'Stop it,' she yelled. 'Stop hurting her.'

'Go away,' Leonie said. 'All of you. If you don't go right now—'

'Look,' Rickford said. 'We can sort something out.'

The breeze had become a small hurricane, the faint rumble a roar; the rails vibrated. Rickford had halved the gap between himself and Leonie. Michael's face twisted with terror. He stared at Graham.

'We just want to be left alone,' Leonie said, and now she had to shout to make herself heard. 'That's all we ever wanted.'

Graham plunged towards Michael. Tammy raised both fists, clenched as though they held hammers, and flung herself at him. They collided. Graham's weight drove Tammy back against Leonie. For an instant the four of them clung together, an unwieldy organism at war with itself, on the very edge of the platform. Graham saw the gleaming rails below him.

Oliver ran. Dougal ran. The tunnel filled with the glowing

windows and headlights of the train. Graham jerked himself back from the edge of the platform.

Leonie smiled. Michael's mouth gaped in a silent scream. His arms flailed, and at last he was free. The boy fell backwards under the train.

If you enjoyed the novels in the William Dougal series, why not read Andrew Taylor's acclaimed Lydmouth crime series.

ANDREW TAYLOR

AN AIR THAT KILLS

The first book in the Lydmouth series

Workmen in the small market town of Lydmouth are demolishing an old cottage. A sledgehammer smashes into what looks like a solid wall. Instead, layers of wallpaper conceal the door of a locked cupboard which holds a box – and in the box is the skeleton of a young baby.

Items within the box suggest that the baby was entombed early in the nineteenth century, but when a man is also found dead, the evidence suggests that the baby's death is more recent than it seems and that a killer is on the loose . . .

Journalist Jill Francis, newly arrived from London, has her first assignment.

'Taylor is top of the crime writing tree, his linked series of Lydmouth novels one of the most interesting developments in the crime writing genre in recent years.' *Publishing News*

Out now

HODDER

ANDREW TAYLOR

THE MORTAL SICKNESS

The second book in the Lydmouth series

When a spinster of the parish is found bludgeoned to death in St John's and the Lydmouth chalice is missing, the finger of suspicion points at the new vicar, who is already beset with problems.

The glare of the police investigation reveals shabby secrets and private griefs. Jill Francis, struggling to find her feet in her new life, stumbles into the case. But even a journalist cannot always watch from the sidelines and she is soon inextricably involved in the Suttons' affairs. Despite the electric antagonism between her and Inspector Richard Thornhill, she has instincts that she can't ignore . . .

'A notably uncosy novel . . . a fine, atmospheric thriller.'

Mail on Sunday

Out now

HODDER

ANDREW TAYLOR

THE LOVER OF THE GRAVE

The third book in the Lydmouth series

After the coldest night of the year, they find the man's body. He's dangling from the Hanging Tree on the outskirts of a village near Lydmouth, with his trousers round his ankles. Is it suicide, murder, or accidental death resulting from some bizarre sexual practice?

Journalist Jill Francis and Detective Inspector Thornhill become involved in the case in separate ways. Jill is also drawn unwillingly into the affairs of the small public school where the dead man taught. And there are more distractions, on a personal level, for policeman and reporter . . .

'Taylor keeps up the suspense until the very end . . . And in the process, the chill heart of a society that got it all wrong is equally well exposed.' *The Sunday Times*

Out now

HODDER

In the best books, the ending often comes as a shock.
Not just because of that one last twist in the tale,
but because you have been so absorbed in their world,
that coming back to the harsh light of reality is a jolt.

If that describes you now, then perhaps you should track down
some new leads, and find new suspense in other worlds.

Join us at www.hodder.co.uk, or follow us on
Twitter @hodderbooks, and you can tap in to a
community of fellow thrill-seekers.

Whether you want to find out more about this book,
or a particular author, watch trailers and interviews, have
the chance to win early limited editions, or simply browse
our expert readers' selection of the very best books,
we think you'll find what you're looking for.

And if you don't, that's the place to tell us what's missing.

We love what we do, and we'd love you to be part of it.

www.hodder.co.uk

 @hodderbooks

HodderBooks

 HodderBooks